A GOOD LOOKING MAN

A GOOD LOOKING MAN

Andrew Moncur

HEADLINE
REVIEW

Copyright © 1996 Andrew Moncur

The right of Andrew Moncur to be identified as the Author of the Work has been asserted by him in accordance with the Copyright, Designs and Patents Act 1988.

First published in 1996
by HEADLINE BOOK PUBLISHING

A HEADLINE REVIEW Hardback

10 9 8 7 6 5 4 3 2 1

All rights reserved. No part of this publication may be reproduced, stored in a retrieval system, or transmitted in any form or by any means without the prior written permission of the publisher, nor be otherwise circulated in any form of binding or cover other than that in which it is published and without a similar condition being imposed on the subsequent purchaser.

All characters in this publication are fictitious and any resemblance to real persons, living or dead, is purely coincidental.

British Library Cataloguing in Publication Data

Moncur, Andrew
  A good looking man
  1. English fiction – 20th century
  I. Title
  823.9'14 [F]

ISBN 0 7472 1736 X

Typeset by Palimpsest Book Production Limited,
Polmont, Stirlingshire
Printed in England by
Clays Ltd, St Ives plc

HEADLINE BOOK PUBLISHING
A division of Hodder Headline PLC
338 Euston Road
London NW1 3BH

For C. G. W. Benbow, 1930–1995

Chapter One

The wasps in the apple orchard were growing drunk on windfalls. It was cool inside the house where the air prickled with the smell of sawdust, resin and sharp, wet lime. Roger Cole lay on the elm-board floor of his new parlour, looking at the sheep on the ceiling.

He kicked his little legs in the air. His chin, brimming over his collar, bristled with life. He had on buff-coloured breeches and thread stockings, worn into holes where two toes poked through; his iron-shod shoes had been left at the doorway. The door itself had yet to be hung on its brass hinges. A butterfly hammered softly at a window pane and a snail, laying its own tiny silver carpet across the floor, seemed to turn its stalky gaze on Mr Cole before creeping on its way.

The plasterers had almost, but not quite, finished their work. Their tower remained in place, a tottering maze of scaffolding poles which had been cut from the alder trees in the water meadow below the bend in the river. Sheets, splashed with liquid plaster, were still spread on that side of the room.

The craftsmen were absent. They had departed on Shy Bacon's brick cart saying they would be gone for two days, celebrating the feast of St Barbara the virgin martyr. So far as Mr Cole could tell – their English was fragmented – the men reckoned she had lived as a hermit in a bath-house. It followed, they seemed to imply, that she should be the patron saint of lead formers and plasterworkers.

That was as maybe. His keen mind knew one thing for sure: that the making of the ceilings in his new house was costing five shillings and sixpence the square yard. It was a considerable sum; one that assured the county, the household, his wife and Mr Cole himself that here was a man of standing. He was not to be taken lightly. His plasterers, the rogues, had now been missing for a week.

It was Mr Cole's gift to hold figures in his head: one horse might move a load of six hundred bricks, provided the weather and the road held up, they cost four shillings and fourpence per thousand to buy and another shilling a cartload to deliver.

He had ordered the sheep patterns for this ceiling, a horned ram and a thickset ewe, from a book of emblems found by his master builder. He had done so with great content. It was fitting, he told his wife, to mark in such a way the first source of his family's fortune.

By now the plasterwork was all but finished. It was, at this stage, pure white. The parlour's elaborate pattern of strapwork, with the fat animal devices, entwined initials and deep finials, resembled a vast, inverted wedding cake.

He looked into the far distance. This work would, with God's grace, stand for a hundred years. It would remain when the present Scotch king was long dead; and the next. It would survive when all England had forgotten even so great a villain as Guy Fawkes, whose head was impaled on a spike at Westminster where it had parted company, in stages, with his body. The house would be here when the Cole family had, like mustard seed . . .

At that instant the slight form of Zebulon Cole, his only son, plunged past the westernmost of the parlour's four great windows.

The boy's astonished face was framed there for what seemed a long moment. Mr Cole would always remember the curious shape of his petticoat breeches, ballooning in the mad rush of his fall. Those breeches had cost one shilling and eightpence the pair.

* * *

The llama, its lips pursed, fixed a pale, glassy stare on the roofline of the post office extension. A flight of starlings wheeled across the square and, banking sharply above a row of buses, scattered to settle along the parapet. In seconds they burst into the air again. A clock chimed the quarter hour. The llama looked on, unblinking.

Albert Tongue tapped his ash into the coal scuttle. He pinched out the still hot cigarette end and then, slowly, he smiled.

'How do you come to be in the middle of this lot?' he said softly. He stroked the llama's ragged ear. From the stairwell came thunderous hammering then a brief, surprising silence.

'Of course, it's all hush-hush,' said a man's voice, climbing the stairs, 'but, take it from me, the ministry boys have been working on it for years – donkey's years.'

'What, a death ray?'

The hammering started again. A locomotive, down the hill at the station, released a great cough of steam.

Bert Tongue laid one hand on the llama's threadbare flank and looked out, beyond its ears and haughty nostrils, through the tall sash window. There was something, a movement, on the stepped roof on the far side of the square. For a moment he could not quite grasp what he had seen. Then the light altered a fraction and this time he caught and held it.

The front of the Victorian terracotta building was stained the colour of old flower pots. The line of the roof was broken by a shape already becoming familiar: a platform bearing an electric motor or, perhaps, a small winch.

It was an air raid warning siren. To the left was a glazed skylight, and now he saw that those panes of glass were being painted out, one by one, from the inside.

'That's the blackout, old son. We're getting ready for Mr Hitler,' said Bert. 'You should have stopped in Peru.'

Then, very deliberately, he lodged his cold cigarette end between the stuffed llama's hairless lips.

* * *

It was a glad-to-be-alive sort of a day, flooded with brilliant light from an unblemished sky. A bright gift of a day; a picture of gold and marine blue, enough to make strangers in city streets greet one another and the shining morning.

'Oh, bugger,' said George Benbow, looking at his feet. A strange expression spread across his face, making him crease up his eyes and bare his teeth. Bending, he started to pummel his right knee.

Soon he stopped thumping and seemed to swivel his lower leg on its axis. He was, quite unmistakably, realigning an artificial limb. Finally he swung into a stiff-legged stride and bobbed off along the pavement, head up, like a particularly game invalid.

Benbow was prepared to go to practically any length to avoid being stopped in the street by a market researcher. Anything, that is, short of looking another adult in the face and saying no. He seemed to think that a limp conferred immunity.

This odd, hopping charade had almost taken him past the woman with the clipboard. She was, in fact, briefed to interview a sample of women aged from twenty-four to thirty, which meant that the young man was of no practical interest to her whatsoever. But now she adjusted her red-framed spectacles and stared at George with frank curiosity as he stomped by, swinging his leg like a metronome.

He met her eyes and smiled into them with full force. The woman hesitated, frowning slightly. Then she smiled in return. Her hand involuntarily checked the top button of her blouse.

George lifted his face. He looked high up, above the lines of slow-moving traffic, the plane trees and the dark bulk of the war memorial, allowing his eye to follow the city skyline, lit now with wonderful clarity. On the roof of the large Victorian building on the far side of the square he could make out a television satellite dish.

He felt an unreasonable hostility towards television aerials. At the same time he knew that for most people they had all but ceased to exist. They simply no longer registered; they had become invisible.

He also had strong views about street lighting, domestic drainage downpipes, mobile phones and lottery scratchcards. George tried never to talk about these feelings any more. He had seen too many people hurting themselves in the rush to get away.

He was always looking up. A girlfriend had told him so once, adding, with a harder edge, that it would make life easier for all concerned if from time to time he watched instead where he was putting his feet.

He had reached the foot of a flight of stone steps and now took them at the run, two at a time. He moved in a surprisingly easy, lightly-balanced way.

'Benbow,' he said, staring at the top of the receptionist's head. He examined her parting. 'That's me,' he said, pushing the blue card forward another inch.

He cleared his throat. 'I think you'll find that's a valid pass, allowing access to most reference collections. It's recognized by the keepers of the national public records and by the Royal Commission on Historical Manuscripts. Oh, yes – and by all county archivists and many antiquarian societies in England and Wales. But not necessarily in Scotland. For some reason. No.' His words trailed away.

'The Vincent Museum and Art Gallery. How may I help you?'

A Good Looking Man

said the receptionist, suddenly coming to life. She appeared to be looking into vacant space somewhere beyond his left shoulder.

'Benbow. To see Dorothy Parker.' George felt a stab of compassion; obviously the young woman on the reception desk was blind. Her whole expression was blank, her unblinking attention fixed some miles away.

'Who was it you wanted?'

'Miss Parker.'

'And what name was it?'

'Benbow.'

'Could you speak up, please,' she said, her eyes still unfocused.

'Benbow. To see Miss Parker,' said George, raising his voice and enunciating each syllable. Dear god, the poor woman was patently bloody well deaf, too. 'I have come. To see. Miss Parker.'

'Hold on. I'll see if he's in,' said the young woman.

'No, no. Not he. She. Dorothy. Dorothy Parker,' boomed George.

'I'm sorry, madam. He is engaged at present,' she said, giving an oddly impatient little wave in George's direction.

'No. Please. Wait! I'm Benbow,' he practically bellowed, stabbing a finger at his chest. 'To see Dorothy Parker. She's a woman. For God's sake, can't you see . . . Oh, lord. No, of course you can't. I'm sorry. I am most terribly sorry . . .' He ran a hand distractedly through his dark flop of hair.

'Could you hold on one minute, caller,' said the receptionist. Then, covering the tiny wand microphone at her throat, she turned and snapped at Benbow: 'Would you please stop shouting. Can't you see I'm busy?'

'Ah,' he murmured. 'So sorry.' It's at times like this, George thought to himself, you want to go out and kill yourself with a grapefruit knife.

'Yes?' she asked in a cool way when a little time had elapsed, 'And how may I help you? Basically?'

It was quiet in the cavernous, marble-pillared entrance hall. He glanced around, taking in the patterned and polished floor, the empty stairway with its beautifully turned handrails and the wall panels of heavy, dark wood. Light was pouring into the stairwell from some high window.

'Yes?' she was sounding dangerously testy. The iron has entered the receptionist's soul, George thought. And possibly the ironing board as well.

'Yes? What is it?'

'Oh, I see,' said George. 'You're talking to me?'

Her fingers remained at rest on the keyboard. She rocked forward slowly until her forehead arrived with the faintest thud against her computer screen.

'Benbow,' he announced finally. 'George Benbow. To see . . . I've come to see Miss Parker. Local history.'

'Keeper of Local History,' said the young woman, staring determinedly into her screen. 'By appointment?'

For heaven's sake. Did he need a royal warrant?

'I'm a bit, well, late.' George fought with his cuff and discovered that he was exactly fourteen minutes overdue. At that moment, far overhead, a clock began to strike the half hour.

* * *

On Tuesday, 28 March 1939, a consignment of twenty stirrup pumps and a similar number of buckets arrived at the Vincent Museum and Art Gallery. The delivery docket described them as 'ARP sundries'.

The government had increased spending on air raid precautions five times over since the Munich crisis which had threatened to shatter the uneasy peace of Europe the previous year.

'Fifty one million quid to fight off the hun and his airborne legions – and what's our share? A crate of bloody stirrup pumps,' Bert Tongue had remarked. 'Oh, yes. And some galvanized pails.'

Now he bent his knees and caught his reflection in the glass of a display cabinet. He smoothed his hair, then felt the knot of his tie. He brushed his large hands down the sides of his brown cotton overall coat and, finally and unconsciously, checked with two fingers that his fly was buttoned.

The preserved swordfish inside the case continued, unswervingly, on its perpetual course, the great blade jutting forward from its upper jaw.

Bert appeared for a moment to be adjusting the typewritten card which fitted into a brass holder on the side of the display case.

'NH/2904: Britain's smallest native rodent,' it read. 'The harvest mouse (*Micromys minutus*), a shy and diminutive creature, typically makes its breeding nest among the stalks of growing crops in the farmer's field. Presented to the Vincent Museum by Mr Frederick Storey Matthews, 1929.'

Bert gave the brass a little rub with his sleeve. Then he picked

A Good Looking Man

up the scuttle and, glancing down at the coal, stepped to the door. He rapped twice, just above the black-lettered plate. He did not wait for permission to enter.

* * *

Dorothy Parker's parents had never heard of the Algonquin. They knew nothing of its round table or its vicious circle and not one word of any wisecrack. If they ever thought for a single second about the *New Yorker* or *Vanity Fair* then they didn't bother to mention it at home.

They named their first daughter for an elderly and supposedly wealthy relative. The old lady had proved disappointingly indestructible; she had lived on and on, oblivious of her namesake. When they last met, some time in 1978, the wispy, long-legged child had made no impression whatever on her Aunt Dorothy (a distant cousin, in reality).

Despite this early experience of the frailty of blood ties, Miss Parker had gone on to become a historian devoted to the family as a vehicle for research. In her own time she was a genealogist, reasonably widely known – at least, widely known among members of the D'Arcy family of Swinton, now part of Greater Manchester. They had been a special interest of hers since university.

'You were – let me understand this correctly, Mr Benbow – inquiring about a ceiling?' said Miss Parker, leaning back slightly in her office chair. She pulled aside a strand of fine, yellow hair and tucked it behind her ear. Across the desk, George was obscured by the lid of his briefcase which he had opened while he searched for his notebook. One corner was resting on the saucer, tipping her spider plant to a dangerous angle.

She could only see the top of his head, which looked as though it had been left out in a strong wind. Or, perhaps, he had not found time to brush his hair that morning. He was, she guessed, about thirty; a couple of years younger than herself.

'A Jacobean plaster ceiling,' said George, snapping shut the lid. With a single confident movement he slid the briefcase forward towards his chest and then allowed it to make a sort of controlled dive to his feet.

His chin smacked into the desk top with shocking force. The pot plant seemed to fling itself sideways, scattering soil in an arc across the carpet. George's eyes, when they focused, were trained on the electric fire beyond Miss Parker's chair. He found that he was counting the dark green tiles, probably Coalbrookdale, and noting the clumsy way in which the original fireplace had been blocked with a panel of plywood.

It was only then that he started to ask himself why he had been attacked. Why this unprovoked assault?

'Hinngg,' he whimpered. He could taste blood; he had bitten the inside of his own lip.

Miss Parker was on her feet. A look of utter bewilderment was stretched across her face. Her mouth was open in a perfect circle, a caricature of astonishment. Worse, she knew it – and there was nothing to be done about it.

George noticed, for the second time, that she was unusually tall; possibly six feet one or two. She had very long legs in very black tights. Her hair was held in a loose, thick plait. Her eyes were a serious, deep, dark brown. She had strong features which could fairly be described as striking.

'Shut my tie in the briefcase,' he murmured. 'Sorry. Terribly. So stupid . . .'

Dorothy Parker, sinking back in her chair, looked up at the greying plaster. A crack ran from the elaborate central rose towards the window. It resembled, she now saw, a map of the Rhône. And she asked herself again, as she had not yet tired of doing, how a museum and art gallery of some repute could possibly have lost an entire seventeenth-century ceiling.

Chapter Two

B ert Tongue came through the door with a muted clatter of fire irons. He stamped his feet just a little too loudly.

'. . . deferred, until the 1940 estimates, work in one of the mammal bays, whereby more space would have been gained for the exhibition of about six important . . . Tongue.' Dr Mackie raised a thin hand and then allowed it to drop to the desk. 'Tongue,' he hummed again, running the word over his own.

Miss Hopkins looked up from her notebook, momentarily puzzled. She shifted slightly in her chair as Tongue came – no, that wasn't quite the word; he jigged – to attention. The assistant foreman did everything, she thought, with a trace of insolence. It was often, as in this case, so faint as to be almost imperceptible. Dr Mackie seemed to notice nothing, which did not surprise her.

'Carry on, Tongue. Just, please . . . as you . . .' The director was already looking down into his lap where he had bunched his handkerchief. His jacket was thrown open, half slipping off one shoulder, but his waistcoat remained neatly buttoned. Its tight little cylinder emphasized the narrowness of his chest; his stiff collar, perversely, seemed too loose, like a ring on a bird's leg. His teeth were unnaturally prominent. He was old and he was not well.

'Sir!' snapped Tongue, just too loudly. Then, turning to Miss Hopkins, he drew the long poker from the scuttle and holding it like a sabre sketched a salute in the air, finally bringing the hilt end to his lips.

She looked down immediately, angry that she had somehow allowed this to happen. She touched the brooch on her blouse and the notepad slipped across her stretched skirt. Bending to retrieve her pencil, she went as though to smooth a stocking – but, instead, sat up and straightened her back. Her nail varnish was like ruby port. Bert's iron poker rattled against the fender. There was dust on the dark green ceramic tiles.

Andrew Moncur

The director, dropping his handkerchief into his lap, raised his eyes to Miss Hopkins's face and nodded. Her pencil glided smoothly across the page in pace with his dictation, given in what she thought of as his committee voice. 'Your director is pleased to report that a very important group of gifts and bequests has been added to the permanent collection.

'Item one: an oil painting, *Motes in the Crosswind* – that's motes as in beams, if you follow – by J.A. Hunt, R.W.S., of whose work there are already several examples in the Vincent collection. That which now has been added is one of outstanding – no, exceptional – quality and your director has been informed that the executors will undertake the cost of the restoration – make that the small amount of restoration – which will be . . .'

Tongue, on his haunches, glanced sideways at Miss Hopkins and wondered how heavy her hair would feel laid across his forearm. Her blouse was open just one button too far for safety. He thought he saw a faint flush rising on her neck but could not be sure. It was pale there, beneath the line of her hair which was strong and red-brown. His own was darker but with traces of grey now.

Christ, he was nearly old enough to be her father. He was old enough. He reached forward and arranged new coal in the cold hearth.

'Item two: a most important and interesting allegorical subject, *Dancing at Dawn*, by the great French painter Henri Fantin-Latour . . .' Dr Mackie looked across at his secretary, who nodded without lifting her eyes from her notepad. 'This painting, which is of a most exceptional character, is a brilliant example of Fantin-Latour's peculiarly delicate technique . . .'

God, but she was a smart one, thought Tongue. He could show her an interesting allegorical thing or two of a peculiarly delicate nature. He started to sweep up the ashes.

* * *

'Miss Parker told you to wait out here. Right?' The secretary was peering short-sightedly at George Benbow. 'And she thought you should have a plaster for your chin. Right?'

'Yes, I think . . .'

'You banged your chin. Right?' God, she seemed to be squinting up his nose.

'Yes. Only a little . . .'

A Good Looking Man

'In her office. Yes?'
'Yes. Just now . . .'
'It's a nasty bang. Yes?'
'Not too . . .'
'You're going to have a bruise. Right?'
'Well . . .'
'I'm a secretary. Right? I'm not a casualty nurse. Right?'

So help me, thought George. I'm going to swing for this woman. The authentic voice of the age. Why did every sentence she uttered have to become a question – or, at least, a request for confirmation? Did she talk like this in bed?

Take me. Yes? Now. Right? Oh, God. Right? Oh, yes. Yes? Yes. Right? Right. Yes? Oh, oh, oh. Right?

The secretary handed him another paper tissue. 'Just sit there and I'll bring you a cup of tea. Right?'

'Right,' said George. 'Thank you very much.'

* * *

Dr Mackie leaned forward. 'A bequest of the highest importance is that of the late Mr A.N. – that's as in Norman – Butler of his entire collection of British, Dominion and Colonial stamps, together with a sum of £1,700 upon which the primary charge is – just one minute . . .'

He ran a finger through the topmost pile of papers on the left-hand side of his desk. 'Oh, yes. The proper classification, arrangement and exhibition of the collection. The surplus, if any, to be devoted to the purchase of works of art. Praise be – errh, please delete that.' The director coughed once more and placed his hands on his desk to steady himself.

'The collection has been valued for probate at – let me see – between £5,000 and £6,000 and the replacement insurable value is probably in the neighbourhood of £8,000. It includes in the – yes – in the splendid series of British stamps the rarest of all stamps of the United Kingdom: the fivepenny . . .'

There was a clatter from the fireplace. Tongue, picking up his poker, bobbed his head towards the director and bent over the narrow brass fender again. Christ. His wage as assistant foreman was £3 4s 0d a week. He owed Finch – what was it now? Thirty shillings? He couldn't afford a fivepenny stamp, never mind the other. And it was only Tuesday.

Andrew Moncur

The director's secretary just sat there and scribbled down all this stuff. She was the cool, stand-offish sort. Miss Hopkins. What was her other name? Susan? Stephanie? She would hardly lend him a tanner. She wouldn't even look at him. But there was something else – something almost brazen about her. He wanted her attention. He wanted to make her react.

'No. Sorry. That should be the sixpenny King Edward VII I.R. – that's I as in Inland and R as in Revenue. This collection will place the Vincent Museum and Art Gallery in the very forefront . . .' The secretary's pencil flowed over the practised, private shortform. A dance tune was playing in her head: When I Take My Sugar to Tea.

'. . . A valuable and beautiful addition to the Department of Costume is a lace flounce of northern French needle-point lace, generally known as Brussels, circa 1880 to 1890. Together with this has been presented a fan of somewhat deplorable artistic quality, showing the fashion of the sixties and seventies for the acrostic, in that the flowers incorporated in the design spell by their initial letters – one moment.' Dr Mackie, humming quietly, explored another heap of papers. 'Yes, they spell Alice.'

Miss Hopkins turned her page.

'Now . . . Your keeper of the natural history section wishes to inform the committee that – good grief – the leg of an ostrich, recently purchased, has been placed alongside the model of the leg of the extinct Aepyornis, whatever that might be when it's at home – please, Miss Hopkins, ignore that. I'll give you the spelling in a moment.

'On a recent visit to London, your keeper visited Messrs Rowland – that's R-O-W – Ward's establishment, the taxidermists, in search of new material and was much struck by a beautifully mounted leopard. After conferring with your chairman it was decided to purchase the animal through the Scrivens Bequest Fund . . . Dear me, I'm afraid that this is all too likely to be overtaken by events.'

Bert Tongue was standing almost at attention with his poker grounded by his side. Behind him the fire was issuing a thin column of smoke. He cleared his throat. 'Sir? Will that be . . . Sir?'

Dr Mackie waved, describing a vague circle with his bony arm. Like the limb of an extinct Arsebandit itself, thought Bert. Doctor Ostrich in person. Beautifully mounted, mind.

'And a further note, please, Miss Hopkins. A separate heading,

A Good Looking Man

I think. Emergency Contingency Plan. Your director wishes to inform the committee that the – aghh – the emergency work in connection with evacuation in the event of hostilities, is proceeding. I think we should say it is proceeding in accordance with the terms approved by your chairman. The arrangements regarding places of safety are well in hand. And this will need to be dated, let me see – when is the meeting? – yes, Friday, 14 April 1939.'

It was only then that he looked up, first at Stella Hopkins, then at the large, dark-haired man standing to one side of his desk. 'Carry on, Tongue,' he said. He coughed again into his large linen handkerchief.

Miss Hopkins watched, frowning, as the assistant foreman turned at the door and swept up his right arm in a shuddering salute. As he pulled the door closed, Bert Tongue was smiling at her through the narrowing gap.

Chapter Three

The high roof was supported by cast-iron columns, still picked out in the elaborate colours chosen by the Victorian architect who – part influenced by Siena, part by Barry's new Palace of Westminster – had designed the Vincent gallery some hundred and ten years earlier. Up here, on the top level of the museum and art gallery, nobody any longer came to admire the precise detail which had been associated, rightly, with his work in the 1880s. His name itself was now, sadly, just as obscure.

George Benbow fell in love with it at first sight.

This part of the building had been left in its original state, cut off and unseen by museum visitors for almost half of its long life. The upper, or industrial, gallery had been closed to the public at the outbreak of the Second World War.

At that time, the space had been taken over as a temporary home for the Traffic Commissioners. But, with the coming of the blitz and the incendiary bombs, it had been judged unsafe for use as an office. Its part-glazed roof, calculated to allow natural light to flood in from the north, was reckoned to pose an unacceptable threat to the safety of the clerks working in the chilly hall below.

The upper gallery was evacuated again and left to the fire-watchers as a vast mess room and dormitory. They slept there safely, shaken only by blast, throughout the worst of the German bombing onslaught. One incendiary had fallen clean through the roof. It had been extinguished by a volunteer, a postman, who had not even needed to climb out of bed for the purpose. He had simply reached for a bucket of sand and upended it over the device. Then he had fallen back to sleep.

His comrades wanted him to have a medal pinned to his pyjamas – but nothing ever came of it.

Meanwhile, the Traffic Commissioners' staff moved to the relative safety of an Edwardian house on the edge of a golf course. It was miles from any remotely military target. In 1941 that house suffered a direct hit from a landmine. The clerks were blown all over the fairways, which says something about the uncertainties, and the downright unfairness, of modern warfare.

The industrial gallery was not reopened in the immediate aftermath of the war, although it figured in the long-term plans of the Vincent's committee. Its members were seriously excited by the prospect of a brighter tomorrow when shining-eyed workers, with time to spare and a thirst for knowledge, would wish to acquaint themselves with the fine arts, antiquities and the wonders of the natural world.

For the time being there was a crying shortage of heating fuel and money to renovate the place in the modern style which would be celebrated at the Festival of Britain. There were more pressing needs.

So the gasoliers and the cast-iron columns were allowed to remain undisturbed; the patterned ceramic floor was left untouched beneath worn linoleum, still marked by the feet of the firewatchers and their little iron-framed beds. There was even a scorch mark to recall the postman's heroism – although nobody did, of course.

Down below, in the galleries and exhibition halls which were brought back to life after 1945 for the enlightenment of the people, the original columns – built to endure for centuries in the massively confident style of an altogether different age – were hidden away behind false walls of lathe and hessian. Vaulted roofs vanished behind plasterboard partitions, painted pale blue or grey and set with discreet lighting. Marble floors were covered with matting. For many years visitors, touring an exhibition of Pre-Raphaelite drawings or reviewing the boring life of the ship worm (*Teredo navalis*), could have been forgiven for thinking that they had wandered inside a building raised from poor materials in the most austere days of post-war reconstruction.

The committee and its officials had succeeded in obliterating one of the most fascinating artefacts in their possession: a perfectly genuine, late Victorian museum and art gallery.

And yet up aloft the bones were still laid bare. The industrial gallery had been handed over, intact, to the storekeepers. Here was the only sensible place to consign a collection of interesting boat paddles from the Savage Islands; a hornets' nest collected by a retired policeman; the badly worn and frequently shampooed head of a buffalo; or the entire archive of a friendly society whose

A Good Looking Man

long-vanished members were largely drawn from the carriage building trade. It had become the home of what the gallery staff called, simply, the stacks.

These were monstrous and forbidding. Shelves had been constructed to no very clear design along narrow gangways. At some points they towered towards the rooflights, a full forty feet above. In other places they resembled low sheds, with dim interiors hidden by dust sheets. Rough wooden pallets and tea chests stood in untidy piles. There were bookshelves and racks of boxes, crammed with rolls of paper lying end-on.

Occasionally, the attendants had set up some object for their own amusement. In an open space beneath an iron balcony, a stuffed moose cow was being unmistakably mounted by a yellowing polar bear. Hanging from the balcony rail and supported by a makeshift scaffold was a nineteenth-century oil painting, of enormous proportions, depicting a scene from an Ottoman bath-house.

George Benbow stared at this in awe. He had never – not even on holiday in Greece, where there had been a serious misunderstanding with a group of Dutch naturists – seen so much floundering female flesh. Save the Whale, he thought. He was suffused with pleasure. He even forgot the sore point of his chin.

He turned and gave his warmest smile to Dorothy Parker. She was so tall. She could probably give him a couple of inches, even in her low heels. She crossed her arms and stared at him, wondering why he should be so cheerful. Then she wondered why she was staring at this man. And, more to the point, why she, too, was smiling.

'Hey, look at this,' said George, tapping the top of a small glass case standing on a chest. Within, a tiny, fat-cheeked mouse with an extraordinarily long tail clung to a corn stalk, a skilful piece of work by some taxidermist.

'A denizen of the ocean deep capable of penetrating the timbers of a ship's hull with its long, fearsome blade,' George read aloud from the plate inside the case. 'Sword fish (*Xiphias gladius*) donated by Captain R.F.U. Bulstrode, RN, 1902.'

George really was happy. He believed himself to be about as normal as a young man could be, given his family background. His father had once more or less spontaneously combusted in the presence of Her Majesty Queen Elizabeth the Queen Mother. It was almost the last great mishap in a chapter – no, in a three-volume life story of accidents. The old man had died shortly after the fire-raising incident, from causes quite unrelated to it. He was killed by, of all things, a lucky horseshoe.

For understandable reasons, George preferred not to discuss this tragedy, which had happened when he was aged only thirteen. Indeed, it was some measure of his sense of confidence in any new friend whether he would be prepared to discuss his parents at all.

He was burdened most of the time by this appalling sense of nostalgia for things he was too young to remember; he was often distressed about aspects of contemporary life which were the more upsetting because they were so absolutely of his time. He hated the idea that he might at some point be held to account for developments which he had, in fact, deplored. He didn't wish to be implicated merely because he had been there.

At times he felt completely out of touch with his own day and age. He was bewildered when rich men, impregnably set up with their salaries of £400,000 a year and surrounded by all the comforts that wealth provides, could be heard angrily denouncing care workers – on wages of £12,000 – for destroying the fabric of society.

A Remembrance Day service could bring him to tears. Not for the sake of young men dying in current conflicts (he was fairly sure that he could go for several months without thinking of the world's trouble spots at all) but for the Greenjackets of Sir John Moore's rearguard at Corunna. He felt closer to the fleet in mourning after Trafalgar. He was immeasurably moved by the graves of boys left behind in France in the dying days of the 1918 war or by the picture of massed pipe bands leading a victorious desert army into Tunis in 1943.

The fact that he had never been inside a uniform, let alone a trench, enabled him to feel his grief without the intrusion of more complex, ambiguous emotions.

If he went to an Indian restaurant he was Lord Elphinstone, swaying on an elephant's back, surrounded by books from his travelling library. He was borne at the head of a tremendous caravan of palanquins and ox carts, cooks and camp followers kicking up dust, escorted by sepoys and cavalrymen. Usually they were creeping towards Jubbulpore.

Waiters were surprised to be drawn into one-sided conversation about the storming, before breakfast, of the fortress at Ahmadnagaror or Arthur Wellesley's tactics at Assaye. Usually

A Good Looking Man

they assumed that the open-faced young man was, like so many of their customers, simply swaying on a tremendous quantity of beer. They treated him with their habitual gentle courtesy – and were thankful that at least he was good-humoured.

George liked to think they shared his interest. He did not believe that two hundred and fifty years of British involvement in India could be forgotten, written out of the memory as though it had never been, in less than fifty. In this he was, of course, quite wrong.

His flat was a repository for an empire which had all but died before he was born. On the bedroom wall hung a fading photograph of the 1st Battalion, the Scots Guards, drawn up on the the parade ground at Kasr-el-Nil Barracks, Cairo, in 1936. George had no connection with the Scots Guards.

He had been standing on the bed, examining their knee-length shorts and the officers' riding breeches and reflecting on what might have become of them all, when his last lover had told him that she was leaving. She said she hoped they would remain friends.

George could remember thinking there were few things a desired woman could say to a man more hurtful than that she wanted only to be his friend. He was aghast to hear himself, for no accountable reason, replying: 'My biographical dictionary says – and this is about a man whose name is part of the language – "Ned Ludd: a Leicestershire idiot; destroyed some stocking frames about 1782." And that's all . . .'

She had simply stared at him. Then she packed and left.

'The storekeeper's office is over there, by the spiral staircase. I don't imagine he'll be able to help,' said Miss Parker, pointing to the right. 'If you come back to my office afterwards I'll have those acquisition records for you.'

George Benbow smiled again and ran a hand through his hair. 'So sorry about the, you know, the potted flower. Embarrassing . . .'

She had already turned and started to walk away between the looming stacks.

Chapter Four

Between 12 June and 24 July 1939, exactly 11,799 people visited the Vincent Museum and Art Gallery, fifty-six more than the total for the corresponding period the previous year. During that time a number of items joined the collections: a memorial teapot and milk jug bearing the portraits of Princess Charlotte, daughter of George IV; a copper statue of Buddha from Seremban; a preserved budgerigar (Lutino red-eye); the report, in three parts, of Sir Walter Maitland's Great Khingan Expedition of 1926, presented by the trustees of the British Museum (Natural History). Members of the gallery's manual staff were beginning to joke about being called up for compulsory military service.

In London there were IRA bombing outrages and in Danzig Nazi troopers, arriving from the increasingly menacing German fatherland, outraged the Poles.

In his office, Dr Oliver Mackie replaced the telephone receiver. He had arranged with the commissioners for three thirty-hundred-weight trucks to be made exclusively available to the gallery, on standby, from 1 August. His plans for wartime evacuation of the Vincent's treasures were now very nearly complete.

Albert Tongue was not worried about being called up. He had done his bit in the Great War, serving for two years in France with the artillery. If he thought about it at all, he could recall the moment during one bombardment when he looked down and, seeing his trousers wet and black, believed he had been injured. He was, in fact, in a sweat of terror.

Bert had seen good friends destroyed – utterly, wickedly blown away – in France. But he had not once attended a Remembrance Day service, and he certainly never shed a tear.

The lines *For the Fallen* might appear on a thousand memorials to the dead of that war but the words merely filled Bert with anger and contempt. It seemed to him as though the top brass

Andrew Moncur

– a committee of, say, the Imperial General Staff – had sat down after the armistice and tried to put the best possible shine on the senseless, useless destruction of so many young men's lives.

And what did they find to say?

That they wouldn't be growing old, unlike those who had the sense to keep their heads down and stay well out of it. Age would not weary them, nor the years condemn. Anything else? Oh, yes. They would be remembered, morning and evening.

Was that it? Was that all?

Well, thanks a lot, said Bert. Thank you so very much.

He collected from the office of the Keeper of Local History two pieces recently removed from display. They were neatly labelled, respectively: 'A police rattle, of carved wood, carried by Henry Minnis, great-grandfather of the donor, Mr R. H. Minnis, probably about 1810,' and 'Shotgun, 12-bore, engraved with sporting scenes, made in Birmingham, Messrs Carpenter & Dyke, 1906.'

Very carefully, he untied the labels and swapped them, knotting each one firmly. Then he tucked both objects under his arm and, whistling, walked to the stores.

* * *

The chief storeman shook his gingery head again. 'Dear, oh, dear. Ceiling?' And he gave a little snort.

George selected a cavalry sabre – American Civil War, he guessed – from the rack behind the storekeeper's office door. He felt its weight and balance. A couple of swishes, left and right, then, with all his force, he hacked at the back of the man's neck. His first cut lodged in the spinal column. The second passed clean through, sending the head bounding across the floor. It was still piping out a derisive sort of snigger when it collided with the leg of a table and came to a halt.

'Nothing of the sort. May have a plan of it, somewhere over there, if you can tell us where it came from. References. But a Jacobean ceiling, even in bits, well . . .' The head storeman shook his head again and gave George a look of pity.

George Benbow wiped the blood from his blade then, raising his left arm for balance, he sprang forward and prodded the man's breastbone. He stepped back a pace and raised the sabre in both hands. It came down with terrible force. Each half of the plump body fell slowly, left and right. The arm and leg attached

A Good Looking Man

to each of the separate joints waved feebly then slumped and lay still.

'Actually,' said George, 'it came from a manor house in north Norfolk. Egmere Old Hall, at Pudding Norton. There had been some sort of habitation on the site since the year dot but the house which interests me – and the ceiling, of course – dates mainly from the early seventeenth century.

'It was built by a man named Cole. Or, rather, by his master mason called Edge. There was a curious story about Cole's son, you know. When they were building the house he fell from the roof of, I think, the south . . .'

The storeman pulled open the top drawer of a filing cabinet. 'Pudding what?' he asked in a bored voice.

'Norton. In Norfolk,' said George. Christ almighty. Here we are in a world of bloody computers, so much so that even your auntie drops you a line by e-mail, and this great fool still files his records in shoeboxes.

'What name?'

'Cole. C for cow, O for obliterate, L for loathsome, E for encephalopathy. I've some reason to believe that the last owner had a connection with this museum. Her name was Cole-Vincent . . .'

The storeman slammed shut the drawer with pile-driving force and pulled open another.

'It was a beautiful house in its day,' said George. 'There's an engraving, eighteenth century, which gives some idea about the quality of the plasterwork. The ceiling which I'm trying to find was very richly decorated – some great, fat sheep and other things.

'The hall was used as a military hospital during the First World War and fell into decay very rapidly after that. An awful lot of land changed hands at that time, you know. Anyway. Lead stripped from roof. Badly damaged by fire. It was quite a celebrated house at one time; figured in the Dalhousie affair, with which you're probably familiar . . .'

'Pole?'

'No, Cole. Or Cole-Vincent. She certainly meant to leave a number of bequests to the Vincent Museum: some silver and a few peculiarly hideous landscapes. She thought the world of one of those painters who made a living out of moist highland scenes and rampant – what do you call it? – heather all over the place. J.MacIvor, if I recall. John? James? I don't know. There was some dispute over her will in the end . . .'

Andrew Moncur

The storeman wasn't plump, he was downright fat. He hunched his shoulders. George spoke to his resentful back. 'In any event, Oriel Cole-Vincent's last diary notes that the then director of your museum – a Mr Lamprey, I think – visited the house in 1921. Oriel was living in a gatehouse by that time with several goats. She went completely gaga soon after. Convinced she was Sir Ernest Shackleton, apparently. Wouldn't go out without a balaclava helmet and fur boots, and towing a sledge . . .'

The storeman grunted, crashed shut the filing cabinet and without a word hurried off towards the stacks. His feet, in white trainers, slapped about like paddles. George followed, silently baring his teeth at the retreating back.

'Anyway, Mr Lamprey agreed, according to Miss Cole-Vincent's diary, to "make certain dispositions regarding the architecturally valuable portions of the hall". Which leads me to believe that the finest single item in that house may have come to . . .'

The man had disappeared into the second line of stacks. George could hear a series of thumps. He leaned on the hindquarters of a – what on earth was it? He squeezed towards the front end of the stuffed animal, noticing a large and poorly stitched patch on the side of its belly and a powerful smell of old furniture. It was a llama. George squinted into its hooded eyes.

'Hey,' he called. 'This thing's . . .'

There was a ripping, scraping noise from the dim interior of one of the large, box-like storage spaces. The storeman's pear-shaped bottom emerged first; he was pulling something weighty towards the gangway. 'Here you are,' he said, breathing heavily. 'The Cole-Vincent bequest, in its entirety.'

He lifted a corner of the enveloping dust sheet. Beneath, there was a large, heavy wooden sledge, probably English, 19th century, with well-worn shafts.

'Do you know,' said George. 'This llama smokes. There's the remains of a fag end stuck between his teeth.'

Chapter Five

'It's good of you, Mrs – sorry, Miss – Crum Brown, but the most pressing need is for, and I hope you'll understand . . . the most urgent need, in the event of hostilities, is for places of safety for our larger exhibits. Now, the ballroom at Abbot's Hall would . . . Yes, yes, of course . . .'

Dr Mackie covered the telephone mouthpiece and, looking across at Miss Hopkins, raised his eyebrows. 'It's the same thing again,' he murmured. 'They would all be perfectly happy to take care of a few of our French Impressionists . . .'

He removed his hand and turned back to the telephone. 'No, please be assured that our arrangements for the paintings in the Vincent's collection are complete and have been for some time. I'm sorry, but for reasons of, ahh, security I am not at liberty – especially on the tele . . . No, it goes without saying that you enjoy my absolute . . .'

Stella Hopkins collected the small pile of papers from the tray on the director's desk and cocked her head in a little question mark.

He nodded and, as she crossed to the door, he spoke again: 'Well, Miss Crum Brown, we had earmarked for you the entire Athill Collection, a most – yes, I think I can say – prized group of . . .'

The Athill, indeed. Well, you have to laugh, Stella thought to herself. That assortment of . . . 'Uuff!' She couldn't prevent an exhalation of alarm as she cannoned into the man. He was built like a chest of drawers. He did not retreat an inch and her outstretched palms remained flattened against the pale-washed brown of his overall jacket. She could smell tobacco.

'Sorry. I'm sorry,' she said. She was instantly annoyed with herself. Why should she be sorry? He made her so angry – and she was never completely sure why this should be. He had beautiful hands.

Bert Tongue smiled. He was cleanshaven to the extent that his skin seemed to shine; his chin was blue black above his prominent Adam's apple, which bore the mark of his collar stud. He bent and shuffled together the letters which had scattered at their feet and a little way along the corridor. She really had beautiful legs. As he came upright he looked down at the small triangle of pale skin at the base of her throat. She had a scattering of freckles and, yes, a mole right on her collar bone. She also had blue eyes with unusually wide pupils. He could see his reflection in them.

No. He wouldn't mind at all. Not one little bit.

He had a bloody nerve, she thought. He was so unbearably amused all the time. Pencil a moustache on him and he would start to think he was Clark Gable. God, how old was he? Forty odd? She'd had enough of that. Still, he was attractive.

'I was wondering,' he said, 'if you . . .' She was already framing a crushing reply. But Bert, looking over her shoulder, narrowed his eyes and sighed.

Cyril Finch, the foreman, was clumping towards them, making the odd half-gargling sound that rose in his throat whenever he moved at anything above strolling pace. It was a strangely loud noise to emerge from so small a mouth. He had sparse grey hair which he oiled in place with a raspberry-scented pomade.

He was wearing an ankle-length apron which made him look like an elderly, overweight fishmonger. He had, in fact, spent the greater part of his working life as a purser in the Royal Navy. It was said that when he served in Malta most houses around Valletta had ended up painted battleship grey.

Cyril had certainly put aside enough to come home and buy a semi-detached villa, with blue and red stained glass in the front door, as well as a plot of land overlooking a river estuary in Essex. He had built a hut on stilts beside a muddy stretch of beach and now spent weekends there with his wife, Hilda, who was unusually thin.

'Bloody Nora,' he said. 'Pardon. My French.' Cyril had a celebrated line in language. 'They're. Calling up. The Auxiliary. Fleet. Heard it. On the. Wireless.'

'You're well out of it, old son,' said Tongue, watching Miss Hopkins swinging away down the corridor. He felt his top pocket for his packet of Player's Weights.

'Effin' right. I am.' He was the only man Bert knew who actually used the word Effing. 'In the. Last lot. Spent three. Effin' years. Up the bleedin'. Orkneys. Shagging. Seagulls . . . They can. Stuff it.'

The foreman swung round and raised a hand to knock on the director's door.

'What's up then, Cyril?' asked Bert.

A Good Looking Man

'War planning. Meeting. Mate. Our Oliver . . .' He jerked his melon-shaped head towards the office door. 'Doctor Macbollocks. Reckons the. Balloon's going. Up. Putting us. On a. Total. War footing. Load of. Cock. Of course.'

'Start spreading the stuff round the countryside, do we? Plan A, eh?'

'Plan B, Bert,' said Finch. 'Balls-up. From the. Word go. Just you. Wait and. Effin'. See.'

* * *

'I'm afraid,' said Dorothy Parker. 'I'm afraid that ceilings are a little, well, outside my experience. We all have them, of course, but I've never heard of one being carted about the country, as it were.'

George Benbow smiled at her. Finials, he thought. Great, deep mouldings. Roundels, bosses. Fleurs-de-lys and coats of arms. Imagine having the wealth and wit to order some craftsman to immortalize your favourite bull in plaster, up on the ceiling above your dining-room table. Miss Parker was staring at Benbow across her desk, as though expecting him at any moment to head-butt her Anglepoise lamp.

'Sorry,' he said. 'Miles away.'

'I was asking about ceilings. They don't seem very mobile things, if I may say so.'

'Oh, they are. They are,' said George. 'There's a wonderful one, from the Old Palace at Bromley-by-Bow. You know it?'

She shook her head. Her hair was escaping again. It was actually held in a heavy knot at her nape; it was the colour of thick cream, he thought. Her brows, in contrast, were dark – almost as though they had been drawn in charcoal.

'It was made for King James the first – or the sixth of Scotland, of course – probably by Scots craftsmen he imported to London. For his hunting lodge. Funny, isn't it: hunting in the East End. Hounds drew Bethnal Green, took scent – or whatever they do – in Stepney and ran on strongly through West Ham.'

She looked at him steadily.

'Anyway, this beautiful ceiling in the state room, with his arms and initials all over the shop – it's, ooh, about thirty feet by twenty feet. Pretty big. Well, they moved it clean across London to the Victoria and Albert Museum. In about 1894, I think. In fact, they transported the entire room.'

'I must see this some time.'

'Yes. And there's another one, really lovely. From the Casa Maffi in Cremona. Fresco on plaster – you wouldn't believe it.'

'Well, I . . .'

'And the Americans, for heaven's sake, have been collecting English rooms for years. The Metropolitan Museum, in New York, has the dining room from Lansdowne House. It's eighteenth century, astonishingly beautiful ceiling. And they've also got the tapestry room from Croome Court. And they have some wonderful Jacobean panelling from a house in Yarmouth. It's amazing. Mind you, they've shipped entire castles, haven't they, and rebuilt them stone by stone. And what about the old London Bridge?'

'Yes, I see.'

'Have you ever noticed how some men sit in trains? With their legs sprawled wide apart? It's very interesting. There's always some poor woman cramped up beside them, looking fed up . . .' George was dismayed to hear himself, once again, speaking off the top of his head with his brain in neutral.

Miss Parker started to slap together the papers which she had found for him.

* * *

By the beginning of August 1939, preparations for war were far advanced. Ration books had been printed; gas masks were stockpiled for issue to civilians; plans were laid for a blackout, to include an absolute ban on the use of car headlights – a notion which proved so lethally dangerous that, in the event, it would remain in force for only a month when war was finally declared. Instead, drivers would be allowed to use masked headlamps.

The British government, meanwhile, continued to put out feelers, still hoping to find some way to avert bloodshed. Throughout the summer it had remained ready to offer a £1,000 million loan to help Germany cope with the problems of disarmament. It was an utterly forlorn hope; Hitler continued to refine his plans for lightning war.

The Vincent Museum and Art Gallery was also preparing for the worst. The manual staff started to dismantle one of its most enduringly popular island stands: the reindeer in the snow scene had been a favourite of museum visitors since 1912.

Looking back, Stella Hopkins would say that it was only then – as the reindeer was being wheeled away into storage – that she realized war was inevitable and frighteningly close.

Chapter Six

George Benbow's old Morris Minor was packed. His things, carefully stacked at the outset, had been thrown into a chaotic slide. A pile of painted boards had slipped across the floor of the boot, coming to rest between a plain wooden box and a piece of furniture which might originally have been a folding, brass-jointed music stand meant for a bed-bound musician.

The pine chest with the black lid had caught his eye at an auction in a village hall. He wasn't interested in the box so much as in the ancient newspapers with which it was lined. He had noticed that one, a page from the *Sherborne Mercury* of 1851, contained a report about a balloonist's unplanned descent on the front lawn of the Surrey County Lunatic Asylum. He had been very sweetly welcomed by the inmates.

George was by nature a neat man but one who, if pressed, would admit to believing in the dumb insolence of inanimate objects. They needed to be watched.

He checked that the driver's door was locked. Then he turned and walked rapidly up the path to the front door of the small, semi-detached house. The number 41, in chipped silver numerals, was set above the bell push. A newspaper – it looked like a local free sheet – was flopping out of the letter-box. He glanced up at the gable and noticed that the paint was peeling badly. There was a spider's web stretching undisturbed across the left side of the door.

George rang the bell again. The house remained still and somehow hollow.

'It's no use.' A grey-haired woman was stretching to see over the hydrangea in the next door garden. 'Are you from the meals-on-wheels?'

'No, I'm . . .'

'She won't be wanting it this week. I told them.'

'Do you . . .'

'Useless. Might as well save my breath.'

'You mean there's nobody here?' George asked quickly.

'She's still in hospital, isn't she. With her legs.'

'With her legs?'

'It goes in one ear, out the other.'

'Thank you. Thank you very much.' George pushed the newspaper through the letter-box before turning back to his truck.

'And nobody should get any ideas. We have the Neighbour Watch operating round here. Oh, yes.'

George waved cheerfully as he pulled away.

* * *

On Thursday, 10 August 1939, they tested the air raid sirens. The eerie dying wail over the wet rooftops, clearly audible throughout the Vincent's galleries, could have been frightening. But, as had already been found elsewhere – to the surprise of the authorities – air raid precautions appeared to have an encouraging, rather than alarming, effect on the civilian population.

'Look at the state of you,' said Bert Tongue to the heavy, silent creature. 'You're bad for morale, you horrible specimen.'

The Athill Collection had become something of a problem for the Vincent's natural history section. The group of large animals, bearing silent testimony to the skill of the taxidermists of Edwardian England, had come to the museum in 1911 as a gift from the Imperial Institute. Five of the beasts were, by general consent, splendid specimens: a moose, a musk ox, a grizzly bear, an Indian blue bull and a reindeer. Age did not weary them.

The sixth, a wapiti – or North American elk – was gravely disappointing. It was, in fact, a disgrace.

Its hair was falling out. It had been doing so since 1932 at least. One of its legs – rear, offside – had buckled and remained at an improbable angle. The beast had a perpetual and ridiculous lopsided grin. The taxidermists had attempted to renovate the specimen, but all to no avail. It seemed to have decided to play the goat.

'You should watch it, my son,' said Bert, slapping the animal on its moth-eaten rump. 'You're going to be moving out. You and the rest of the herd. Off to fresh woods and pastures new.'

The assistant foreman straightened and started to wheel away his porter's trolley. He didn't hear the faint thud inside the display cabinet.

The wapiti's glass eyeball – the left one – had dropped out. The remaining eye seemed to follow Bert Tongue's progress down the gallery.

* * *

Dorothy Parker had been taught to eat spaghetti with her elbows tucked well in. She caught a skein on her fork, twirled vigorously and raised it to her lips. The tail-end slapped her on the chin, leaving a dribble of sauce.

As if it were the most natural thing in the world, George Benbow reached across the table and wiped away the smear of tomato with a long finger. It should have been a moment charged with significance; it should have seemed one hell of a nerve. Benbow carried on eating a ragged piece of bread. Dorothy took a mouthful of wine and looked at him over the rim of her glass.

She was asking herself whether it had been an entirely good idea to accept his invitation to dinner. He had a strangely disarming directness and, she had to admit, he radiated a sort of benign optimism. Taken one by one his features might have been described as having all the refined perfection associated with the potato. Put together they made a cheerful, quirkily attractive face. She might have hesitated had she not been struck by the intense warmth of his eyes.

'Death rays,' said Miss Parker.

'I beg your pardon?'

'Death rays. Everyone wanted to believe that it was possible to invent something of the sort between the wars. Mainly, I suppose, because they wanted to imagine that all the ghastly machines of destruction which did the damage during the first lot – the weapons which caused the slaughter on the Somme and the Marne – could somehow be knocked out, safely excluded, from any future conflict. Science could break that awful deadlock.

'There were lots of queer schemes and strange claims. And the newspapers did a good deal of agitating, demanding government backing for some pretty loopy people. There was a man called Grindell-Matthews who did a demonstration for the Admiralty and the Air Ministry. It really boiled down to pointing his ray at a motorbike engine and making it stop . . .' Miss Parker felt that she was running on.

'May I be frank?' she asked.

'You may if you wish,' said Benbow, 'but it's a very funny name for a woman.'

She doesn't just smile with her eyes, he thought. She blushes with them.

'Well, then, to be frank, I don't know if I have quite grasped why you should be interested in this particular ceiling. You said in your letter that you were "doing a Pevsner" . . .'

'Did I, Frank?' George was trying to attract the attention of the waiter. He appeared to be the ideal man for the job in every respect but one: he had some sort of fundamental objection to waiting at table. George was convinced that there had been contact – their eyes had met – yet the waiter had immediately glanced away and was now refusing to see anything.

The meal had started in confusion when as soon as they arrived the man had brought two glasses of lemon water ice to the table. George and Miss Parker had assumed that this was some sort of regional speciality or, maybe, a custom of the house. They had eaten a little of the dish when the waiter tried to reclaim the ices, protesting that he had delivered them by mistake to the wrong table.

Next, he brought them the bill meant for a table of three in the window.

'I know what this is,' George had remarked, raising his eyebrows and gesturing with his whole head at the waiter's retiring back.

'Yes?'

'I don't think he's a waiter at all. It's patently a witness protection programme.'

At this point Miss Parker allowed the trailing length of spaghetti to hit her chin.

'I take it that you're writing some kind of guide to buildings. Architecturally interesting ones, I suppose,' she said.

Benbow walked across the restaurant, slid an enormous, square-nosed, black automatic pistol from his shoulder holster and, taking aim at a point midway between the waiter's startled eyes, squeezed the trigger and blew his head off.

'To tell you the truth, I'm flying off at a tangent,' said George. 'It's really a personal obsession. Hopeless. I mean, who's going to want to know?'

A Good Looking Man

'What? Know what?'

'About the vanished bits. The lost heritage, if you like. I found myself starting to catalogue what you might call the Lost Buildings Of Britain. Nikolaus Pevsner gone mad, you see. Then I began trying to track down the parts which, it stands to reason, must remain at large. The missing pieces of the Euston Arch, for instance.' He seemed to have lost interest in the waiter and contented himself with upending the empty bread basket on the tablecloth.

'Do you know, I found a complete panel of plasterwork by Joseph Rose the elder – spears, hunting horns, drums, foliage, a thumping great eagle, the whole works – behind the food counter at a wine bar in Bristol. They hadn't the faintest idea. Thought it had been rescued from a cinema.

'I just knew for certain it came from Henge Hall, in Somerset. You know the place at all? It started to fall into disrepair when Hercules Hervey – that's Mad Hervey – was put away after attacking Prince Albert with his umbrella in Windsor Great Park.'

'Was he badly hurt?' asked Miss Parker.

'No. Although Albert called up a gamekeeper and ordered him to shoot the poor old . . . Oh, I see. No, the Prince wasn't hurt much at all. He was wearing a patent waterproof cap and that took the full force of the blows. Fortunately, the gamekeeper flatly refused to blaze away, both barrels, at dear old Hervey. Albert was said to have been beside himself. Hopping mad.'

Dorothy Parker raised a single finger of her right hand and the waiter – who had been leaning against the corridor wall, reckoning a complicated sum on his pad – glanced up and immediately crossed the room to her side. Quietly, she asked for more bread.

Privately, she was worried. She had spent most of the previous evening and some time that morning working through the Vincent's acquisition reports, which seemed perfectly straightforward. However, she had as well checked the catalogues of the current holdings. They did not, in several instances, add up.

Further, she had – choosing what she felt would be an ideal point of reference – read the director's reports and the committee minutes from 1939 to 1946. It had seemed sensible. The period of the Second World War was the only time in the history of the museum and art gallery that its entire collection had been gathered up and removed, lock, stock and barrel for safekeeping. It had then, similarly, been brought back together again.

Somebody, surely, must have recorded every item and its destination. Then they must have noted the safe return of each piece. It was the ideal point at which she could touch ground.

Miss Parker had expected to find these records on file; the most complete stocktaking imaginable. But she had failed. There were no such lists to be found.

'It's funny, you know,' she said. 'It appears that we did acquire some items from the Cole-Vincents at Pudding Norton in 1922. Including, I think, a decorated plaster ceiling.'

George leant forward. 'Yes?'

'But now – I'm sorry, I know this sounds ridiculous – we seem to have mislaid them.'

There was a brief silence while they both avoided looking at one another.

'I was wondering,' he said, after a moment, 'are you – that is, are you doing anything tomorrow evening?'

'I don't quite . . .' she began.

'You see, Dorothy . . .' he had not thought about using her first name; she now accepted its sudden appearance quite naturally. 'You see, I want to carry out a small burglary.'

Chapter Seven

On Thursday, 24 August 1939, the great national museums and art collections closed their doors to the public and began the task of of dispersing their treasures to places of safety throughout the British Isles. All those capable of being moved, that is.

Even the Coronation Chair – only once previously removed, when Oliver Cromwell was installed as Lord Protector, over the road in Westminster Hall – was carried from Westminster Abbey and taken by special train to an undisclosed destination. It was not so much a matter of ensuring that the chair would not be available to Hitler should he invade. It was more a precaution against the aerial bombardment and gas attack which experts believed would follow immediately upon the declaration of war. They calculated that the Germans would drop up to 100,000 tons of bombs on London in a fortnight (a figure exceeding the total which actually fell on the capital in the entire course of the war); one sober estimate was that the British might suffer nearly a quarter of a million casualties in the first week of hostilities. It was reckoned that bombing during the first two months of the war would leave 600,000 civilians dead and twice as many injured.

Nobody intended that the chair, made for Edward I to hold the stone of Scone he had seized from the Scots in 1297, should also be destroyed.

That war was inevitably coming seemed obvious to all except those in ultimate authority; Neville Chamberlain, the prime minister, and his foreign secretary, Lord Halifax, continued far beyond the eleventh hour to attempt to appease Hitler through a Swedish intermediary. Parliament met, however, and passed an Emergency Powers Act through all its stages at a single sitting.

The following day, 25 August, the Vincent Museum and Art Gallery closed to the general public. Dr Mackie's carefully prepared plan for evacuation swung smoothly into operation.

'Effin' arseholes,' said Cyril Finch, breathlessly. 'Told you. Like a. Soccer match. For one. Legged. Effin'. Aboriginals. Look at. Bloody. Perkins.'

A brown-coated attendant tottered down the corridor clutching to his chest a bundle of ancient rifles tied together with coarse twine. Ernie Perkins, like many of his generation, had been brought up in great poverty. He was distinctly bandy-legged.

'Couldn't catch. An effin'. Pig in. A passage,' said Finch, shaking his fat head without disturbing his crinkly grey hair.

Perkins, peering anxiously around his armful of guns, bounced off the wall opposite the museum foreman and his deputy.

'Mr Finch,' he said. 'Mr Finch. Dr Mackie says all the rifles and shotguns are to stay. They're going to be handed over to the Military Authorities.' He invested the last two words with great gravity.

'If that's. All we. Got to. Fight off. The effin'. Hun then. We might. As well. Stay in. Bleedin'. Bed. Go on, Ernie. Get on. With it.'

Albert Tongue had to get a move on as well. The Athill Collection of large mammals was among the first to be assigned for removal, after the pictures, watercolours and drawings had been packed off to their new, temporary homes.

Each of the animals occupied a separate glass case. Even the one-eyed wapiti still grazed one of his own, although the keeper would cheerfully have evicted the broken-down beast.

It was Bert's job to see that they were assembled in the rear courtyard for collection by the removers, selected by Dr Mackie because of their experience in the exhibition and concert trade; the well-known firm of Luff, Beavis and Cotton.

Half-way down the back stairs, bow-legged Ernie Perkins proved the undoubted truth of Mr Finch's remark about his poor prospects as any sort of a longstop. He was in the lead, struggling with the front end of the large glass cabinet, when he slipped.

The wapiti, as though determined not to leave its ancestral foraging ground, seemed to leap violently and crashed through the side of its case. It ricocheted off the banister rail and plunged down the staircase, followed by Tongue's cascade of abuse.

Stella Hopkins had just been exchanging a bright good morning with Fred Ellis at the staff entrance. She suddenly found herself confronted with a hundredweight of charging elk, thundering down the stairs.

To her credit, she didn't shriek at all. She stepped aside. Not showing a morsel of fear, thought Bert, observing all this as he sprinted down from the landing.

The wapiti hit the ground nose first. It then executed a perfect somersault. And finally, and very gracefully, it demolished Mr Ellis's comfortable little sentry-box.

Its loose rear leg landed last, striking Fred a painful blow on his left temple. Afterwards he would be able to recall seeing the rogue wapiti flying towards him, three legs rigidly upright in mid-air, before his world exploded in splinters of plywood, hide and glass. Very late in life he would insist that it had performed a victory roll.

He would also remember, although he never talked about it, seeing Bert Tongue take Stella Hopkins very tenderly in his arms. And, strangely, they were both laughing helplessly.

Chapter Eight

On Friday, 1 September 1939, they extinguished the street lights, although Britain had yet to declare itself at war. It was only a matter of time, of course; a state of conflict had become inevitable at 4.45 that morning when German troops crossed the frontier to attack Poland. It seemed almost symbolic that the lights should be turned out. Night-time streets throughout the British Isles would remain unlit until May 1945.

The first of September also brought convulsive change into the life of Walter Benbow, then a more than normally accident-prone bloody-kneed ten-year-old.

In company with roughly 1,499,999 others from areas believed at risk – children of primary school age, their teachers and some, but by no means all, mothers of younger girls and boys – he was evacuated to a place of safety. That is to say, he was removed from his family's loving embrace; he was labelled, issued with a gas mask and a bag containing the barest essentials of clothing, a toothbrush and a pink-salmon sandwich; taken to the railway station in a tearfully excited crocodile; and finally carried away by train from an area deemed to be in danger of air attack.

In this way, Wally Benbow was removed from Hayes Avenue, the quiet suburban street which was the only home he had ever known, and set down, bewildered and homesick, in a village hall surrounded by fields of red mud in Herefordshire.

The welcoming party of women was outwardly kindly but somehow dangerous. The children, sensing a crackle of electric storm behind the rising note of the adult voices, remained unnaturally still and quiet. The mud was hostile. Wally and the other town children were simply not properly equipped for negotiating wet fields, ditches and deep-rutted tracks. Wally had travelled in sandals; in his bag was a spare pair of black plimsolls. Nothing had prepared him for a world without pavements.

Andrew Moncur

He was billeted on a farm ruled by a man of uncertain and sometimes violent temper who had two passions: lay preaching in the Primitive Methodist chapels of the area; and, at most other times, killing things. Mr Gilbert was a pale-eyed, stringy man with very few teeth and enormous fists.

He insisted, perversely, on calling his young guest the Orphan Boy. If he used a name at all, it was invariably the wrong one. Walter, on the other hand, became confused from the very start about the proper title of the farm.

'Benbow?' the tall lady had called out. 'Which one's Benbow?'

Wally jumped to his feet, causing the bench on which he had been sitting to catapult into the air. A small girl who had perched on the far end, holding a brown teddy bear, was dumped on the floor. Her squeal was lost in the clatter of falling furniture.

'Right. Yes, come over here. You're going to – let me see – yes, Copse Farm.'

'Cops?' The boy sighed inwardly. He would sooner have been sent to Robbers.

Wally's life was made bearable by the company of a black dog and by the kindness of the farmer's three maiden sisters, all built on more generous lines than their brother and all equally intimidated by his uncontrollable rages. The sisters seemed to think it natural that their lean brother should eat the lion's share of all their rations.

Young Wally Benbow would sit wide-eyed at the kitchen table, watching the farmer devour the greater part of a rabbit pie.

'Wor'sa matter wi'you, Master Willy, my dear? Not heating-hup?' Mr Gilbert would suddenly roar, spitting flecks of pastry. 'Notwithstandin' thou mayest kill an' heat flesh in thy gates, whatsoever thy soul lusteth hafter, haccordin' to the blessin' of the Lord thy God which 'e 'ath given thee.'

'Whatsoever thy soul lusteth hafter,' Wally would repeat silently, lying in his cold, narrow bed and thinking of marzipan and toast, aniseed balls and lemon sherbet. 'Haccordin' to the blessin' of the Lord thy God . . .'

The Gilbert sisters fussed around the Benbow boy in a stiff, unbending way. They found him an odd pair of wellingtons which could be made to fit if the toe of the left boot was stuffed with old socks. They rhapsodized over his modest successes in spelling and arithmetic tests at school and chided him awkwardly but gently for his petty disasters.

A Good Looking Man

The sisters stood by him when he was arraigned for destroying a pedal harmonium. It was by any standards a superior instrument: a Great Exhibition harmonium of 1862 with five octaves, two pedals and an oak case which had cost fifteen guineas, new.

The Misses Gilbert pointed out that the young evacuees had all been asked to lend a hand, clearing chairs and trestle tables from the stage of the village hall on the afternoon in question. Walter thought he was being helpful. He wasn't to know, when he lay stomach-down across the instrument and pushed off with his feet, that it would run out of control – trundling over the stage, gathering speed, before erupting across the footlights and landing on the floor below with one final, shattering discord.

It was fortunate that Wally was able to twist and throw himself clear before the harmonium slipped the frail bonds of earth and, however briefly, flew. It was a miracle that nobody was standing in the landing zone.

'Orphan boy's no musician,' said Mr Gilbert, surveying the wreckage and sucking his teeth.

The sisters Gilbert came to his defence when Walter cooked their brother's favourite hat; when he sawed through the saw bench; and when he rode a bicycle into a lake of wet cement, the foundations for a barrack room on a new military camp close to Copse Farm. Witnesses said that boy and bicycle remained upright for a full minute, wobbling progressively, before eventually keeling over. It was inadvertent, the sisters insisted on each occasion.

Mr Gilbert's labrador bitch, Bess, was implicated in the majority of these incidents. She had adopted the lonely child from the beginning; she would sit, ears down, watching him climb a tree – as though waiting for the inevitable fall. At other times they would play a berserk game together, following a pattern that only the boy and the dog understood.

All three sisters rallied to make his costume when Wally was cast as an angel in the village school's nativity play, that first Christmas of the war.

'An' there shall be an 'ole in the top of it, in the midst thereof,' boomed their farmer brother. 'It shall 'ave a binding of woven work round habout the 'ole of it, as it were a 'abergeon, that it be not rent.'

'What's a 'abergeon?' Wally's muffled voice emerged faintly from the enveloping robe of flour sacking.

Andrew Moncur

'An' beneath upon the hem of the robe thou shalt make pomegranates of blue an' of purple an' of scarlet, round habout the hem thereof; an' bells of gold between them an' round habout.'

'Aargh,' said Wally as a pin from the hem impaled his skinny calf.

'A golden bell an' a pomegranate, a golden bell an' a pomegranate, upon the 'em of the robe round habout.'

The boy and the three kneeling sisters could still hear Mr Gilbert as he clattered off down the stone-flagged corridor to the yard door. 'An' thou shalt put in the breastplate of judgement the Urim an' the Thummim . . . the Urim an' the Thummim, and they shall be upon Aaron's 'eart.'

Wally's teacher was momentarily lost for words when, the following week, the children rehearsed their play for the first time.

'Over here, you Wise Men,' she had called. 'Wise Men, stop being silly! Immediately! No, not you, Walter Benbow. You're not a Wise Man. What are you, dear? Are you a shepherd?'

'I'm a angel an' I got a 'abergeon and a Ummin and a Summin,' said Wally.

'That's nice, dear. Don't touch the piano. We can't afford to lose that . . .' The teacher was casting distractedly around, looking for the Magi.

'An' at Christmas I shall 'ave whatsoever my soul lusteth hafter.'

What he most wanted was his own home, back in Hayes Avenue. He had always thought of his address as one word: Four-tee-one-Hay-Savenue. It now seemed impossibly remote from the mud and the blood, the rabbit skins and pigeon feathers, the dung, the wet flagstones, the warm breath of cattle and the unmistakable odour of freshly drawn pheasant, which characterized life on Copse Farm.

As the weeks passed it began to dawn on the boy that it was also increasingly unlikely that he would ever see his private treasure again.

He could picture it clearly in his mind's eye. Back at home, in his little bedroom at the front of the house, the room beneath the rather fanciful gable, there was a loose floorboard. It was just beside the fireplace, to the right of the hearth. It was easy to remember which one: the board was pierced for the copper pipe which fed the gas fire.

There, on the eve of his evacuation, he had hidden a white cardboard box. It contained his highly prized collection of Dinky toys: little racing cars in red and green; vans and trucks with grey rubber tyres; a tractor and a horsebox. He had not wanted these little vehicles to fall into enemy hands.

* * *

Visitors today see little to betray the fact that Hayes Avenue, like thousands of other unexceptional suburban streets, once found itself in the forefront of a vicious war. A grassy hump beside the rhubarb in the corner of a back garden is all that remains of the air raid shelter. Over there, a few odd tiles on a red roof may show where blast damage was hastily repaired. Every so often a house of a later period intrudes, disturbing the uniformity of the street. It is a safe bet that it occupies a site left empty by a high-explosive bomb.

People living there during the Second World War, defiantly surviving the bombs and the later missile attacks, could not have imagined some of the eventual consequences and the shape of the peace to come.

They could not have known, for instance, that one day their empty road would be filled from end to end with cars, often of Japanese or German manufacture.

* * *

Wally Benbow's stock rose to its highest at Copse Farm because of a family tragedy – an event which would, at the same time, lead directly to his departure from the farm, the collective bosom of the Gilbert sisters and from the rolling, red Herefordshire countryside.

The blow fell out of a clear sky: the boy's father was killed during the blitz. He was a civil servant with the recently formed Ministry of Supply, where he spent the greater part of his brief career covering up one of his own mistakes. He had been responsible for grossly overestimating the demand for snow camouflage capes for the British Army, at the time when the government was planning – for reasons which defy rational explanation – to send an expedition to fight in Finland. It was a simple mathematical error. Some of the excess garments he ordered would, incidentally, still be held in army stores in the late 1980s. They would be lost, at last, in a fortuitous fire.

His death was as inglorious as his career, although his son, young Walter, would never know it. Mr Benbow senior was sheltering in almost perfect safety during a German bombing raid. Unfortunately, he choked on a chicken bone while eating his packed supper too hastily.

When news filtered through to Copse Farm the Gilbert women made a terrific fuss of the now fatherless boy. They had somehow got it into their heads that the poor mite had been dealt this blow due to a brave man's selfless heroism. The late father had been in the government service, after all, no doubt doing his patriotic duty.

'Orphan boy's gone and lost 'is poor ol' dad,' said Mr Gilbert, confusingly. He made it sound as though it was due to another of Walter's errors of judgement that his father had been mislaid.

Wally's widowed mother quickly decided that she wanted her boy home and at her side. And so, with the giving and receiving of awkward kisses and the shedding of a few tears, young Walter left the farm. His little suitcase was packed with cheese in greaseproof paper and half a dozen eggs, hard-boiled for safety's sake.

Mr Gilbert walked him to the railway halt. 'Well, goodbye then, young William, my dear,' he barked, shaking the boy's hand. 'Remember Jeremiah: One basket 'ad very good figs, even like the figs that are first ripe; an' the other basket 'ad very naughty figs, which could not be heaten.'

'Right,' said Wally, staring into the dog's dark eyes. Then, screwing up his face, he looked away along the railway line.

'We best be 'avin' them wellington boots back, then, my dear,' said Mr Gilbert. 'You won't be wantin' 'em where you're goin'.'

So Wally, a little taller now and dressed in a raincoat and plimsolls which no longer fitted, returned to the care of his mother. He brought with him his ration book and a strangely mixed accent. His speech became further mangled when the unfortunate Mrs Benbow took her son to live at her parents' home just outside London. The house in Hayes Avenue was taken over by a family who had been bombed out of their own place.

Walter, the young evacuee, never again set foot inside his old home. There would be no climbing the familiar stairs to his little front bedroom. He did not have the chance to lift the floorboard and retrieve the cardboard box full of toys which he had so carefully hidden.

The tale of Wally's secret hoard became part of family history.

A Good Looking Man

He spoke of it often. When he married and had a son of his own, he liked to take the child by the hand and tell him about the drama of the war and his boyhood's hidden treasure.

He even on one occasion took his son to Hayes Avenue and pointed out the exact house. A strange woman had peered out of the window and the pair of them, standing at the gate, had hurried away like guilty schoolboys.

Walter Benbow thought often of those events of his childhood, so disrupted by war. He was doing so still only moments before the horseshoe brought about his untimely death.

* * *

Hayes Avenue is the sort of street which teenagers, growing up there, feel is unutterably dull. It is only when they return years later, after living in a succession of more or less squalid rooms in the city or in some functional modern apartment, that they come to appreciate the quiet charm of the suburbs.

Twin rows of semi-detached houses, developed in the late 1920s, face one another over neat garden hedges. A laburnum tree nods over every third fence, rattling its pods of poisonous seeds at passing children; marigolds push up between the lavender and the lilac. There is an occasional tiny fishpond and a weeping willow. Here and there concrete has been poured to make a short driveway to garage doors and paving slabs have been laid, to be stained with fats and sauces from the barbecue. It is a peaceful hunting ground for blackbirds and robins. Sometimes a lone jay swoops to the branches of a flowering cherry tree.

Sometimes a single burglar climbs over the creosote-stained panels of a back garden fence.

'You can't – you just can't possibly be thinking of breaking in?' Dorothy Parker stared at George Benbow in disbelief.

Well, all right. He knew it was ridiculous. But he was also clear in his mind that it could do no harm to anybody; and he was sure that there was no risk. The plan had arrived unbidden and with amazing speed, as soon as he had discovered that the house was unoccupied.

Something of the kind had almost certainly been taking shape in his head from the moment he first knew he must visit the Vincent. The museum and art gallery was a mere ten minutes' drive from the suburban street which, he liked to think, remained the ancestral home of the Benbows. While he was seeking a ceiling, why not look under a floorboard as well?

His late father, Walter, had never tried to retrieve the cache of boyhood possessions he left behind in Hayes Avenue at the outbreak of war.

'It was just kid's stuff as far as he was concerned. Part of the – you know, the picture of a happy pre-war childhood he wanted to keep intact. God knows how many times the place must have changed hands. And, anyway, he was too embarrassed even to think of knocking at the door and asking. A grown man with some ridiculous story about toy cars . . .' George sipped his coffee.

'Of course, they would be worth a fortune today. Collector's items.' He neglected to add that, should they survive to pass into his hands, he would never dream of selling them.

It occurred to George that he would like to talk to her some time, in a simple way, about losing his father.

'Oh, lord,' said Dorothy. 'You are going to, aren't you? You're going to break in.'

She started to gather together her papers and her possessions in a brisk, resolute fashion.

'It is, you understand, utterly out of the question that I should be a party to any such . . . such escapade,' said Dorothy. And as she looked up, George Benbow turned his smile directly into her eyes.

Chapter Nine

On Sunday, 3 September 1939, an ultimatum having been delivered and no reply having been received, Mr Chamberlain announced: 'This country is now at war with Germany.' The expected bombing raids failed to materialize.

Eight members of the manual staff of the Vincent Museum and Art Gallery had already been called up, as reservists, for military service. The remainder worked on through the weekend; the Standish Collection of British birds was packed off, consigned to a former school for delinquent boys in the Cotswolds. The government's stirrup pumps and buckets were distributed throughout the galleries and storerooms.

Just before tea time Cyril Finch, former Royal Navy purser and foreman attendant of the Vincent Museum, dropped down dead. It was his heart. Cyril was, said Bert Tongue to Stella Hopkins, possibly the first casualty of the Second World War.

The next day Albert Tongue, formerly of the Royal Artillery, was promoted to the post of foreman in practical charge of the evacuation operation at the Vincent. His wage was increased, with immediate effect, by the sum of ten shillings a week.

That night, on the sofa at her parents' home in Armoury Road, Bert lifted Stella's skirt, revealing her stocking tops, her suspenders and her white, freckled thighs, and entered her with intense pleasure. The fact that she was still wearing her white silk French knickers at the time seemed only to heighten the power of the experience for both of them. She cried out silently and later wept copiously.

* * *

'Here's the record of the original acquisitions from Pudding Norton in, yes, April, 1922,' said Dorothy Parker, passing over a photocopy.

'And this is the minute of the committee meeting where – you see there, the marked passage – they agreed to send their best thanks to Lady Oriel's executors. It's a standard courtesy, of course . . .'

She knew that she was gabbling uncontrollably but there was nothing to be done about it. 'And here's the then director's report on the condition of the items in which – yes, look – he mentions a ceiling "of some antiquity" delivered crated in sections.' She pushed another photocopy across to George, who was sitting at the wheel of his car with a growing pile of documents in his lap. There was still a distinct kink in his tie, about four inches from its wide end.

The dark green Morris Minor was parked in Stanley Park Road, just twenty yards from the corner of Hayes Avenue. The evening light was fading. A lamp-post had, in fact, come to life some time ago but was only now starting to radiate its pale orange glow over the car, washing out its true colour.

George yawned, which was always a sign of nervousness with him. He felt his stomach doing a rapid series of press-ups and he wiped the palms of his hands on his knees.

Dorothy was talking rapidly again: '. . . becomes really quite fascinating. Quite extraordinary to my mind. The director – that was Dr Oliver Mackie, a really nice man, by all accounts; he stayed on beyond retirement, it seems. A paintings man, of course, but then they all are. You don't get anywhere if you're a rude mechanical or in local studies, I can tell you. He died in 1941 or thereabouts, still in harness – he'd been ill for some time but felt the place needed him, what with all the upheaval and the younger ones being away in the forces – quite a difficult time, even if the collection was disp . . .'

'Dorothy,' said George.

'Whaaa?' she almost shrieked.

'It's nearly dark. Another ten minutes or so should do the trick.'

He could sense the close warmth of her. He could smell the faint perfume of her hair and clothes.

Dorothy slumped in the passenger seat which yielded in a comfortable, deep-bottomed way. Her knees were almost above her head.

She really wasn't cut out for this sort of thing. She was an elder sister and had always felt herself to be somehow responsible, not only on her own account but for everyone else as well. It was

A Good Looking Man

as though she had, right from the very start, cast herself as the good girl.

It followed that her younger sister, Helen, must be the bad girl, the other option having already gone. At least, that's the way Dorothy worked it out. She was only sorry that their parents had failed to produced a third daughter, who could have filled the statutory role of lost girl, which had in consequence to remain vacant. They had a son instead, but he didn't count. Dorothy consoled herself with the thought that Helen, being bad, would almost certainly, sooner or later, be lost into the bargain.

Dorothy's was, on the face of it, the less glamorous of the available roles. In contrast, she was by some way the more attractive of the sisters. She had, too, a natural sense of style; the way she dressed and the confidence with which she carried herself had an impact which was impossible to ignore.

Her sister turned out to be completely unreliable. Helen kicked over the traces, wilfully rejecting the part chosen for her and going out at the first opportunity to marry a solicitor of the very steadiest kind.

Dorothy, the good girl, became entangled with a series of more or less unhygienic young men. She then at a relatively late stage – and furtively, at first – discovered the secret, musky pleasures of study.

For three years, the question of being good, bad or indifferent did not figure much in a life largely devoted to academic endeavour. Then, her first degree safely out of the way, she met an Australian cartographer with a passion for rugby and motorcycles. They agreed in a matter of days to move into a flat together. Dorothy, although she did not see it this way at the time, became a sort of fourth interest for the map maker.

It took almost three years for the truth to dawn: that he was a fundamentally dull man and their life together was torpid. 'There are no exciting contours,' she had told him in an effort to make her meaning clear. Since then her encounters with men had been steady, reliable and cerebral.

There had been precious little of what her mother called bedroom activities. There had certainly been nothing like this caper. How had she stumbled into it? The Great Dinky Car Heist, for God's sake.

George, having put the papers on to the back seat, started to feel in the glove box for his large screwdriver.

Andrew Moncur

'What's the collective noun for learner drivers?' he asked her suddenly.

He sensed, rather than saw, Dorothy shaking her head.

'A jumpy clutch.' And he smiled at her again in what remained of the fading light.

Chapter Ten

On the third day of the Second World War, Bert Tongue, in his new role, was charged with the safekeeping of objects too large and fragile to be removed altogether from the museum and art gallery. These were gathered in the basement and strongroom, judged to be the areas least vulnerable to bomb damage.

The life-sized mammoth from the natural history section had to be hung in a sling, passed under its great red-haired belly, and hoisted with the help of a small, petrol-engined crane. Bert had made an arrangement for its loan with the foreman of a builders' gang excavating the site for an air raid shelter around the corner, near the Assize Court.

At one point it seemed that Ernie Perkins was in danger of disembowelment as the hairy beast swung crazily, jabbing the air with its tusks in a playful way. 'Cor!' said Ernie, then toppled backwards over a crate, so escaping the yellowed prong.

In the afternoon a fretting group of mechanics from the science section wheeled over the Towser, an early steam locomotive built for the ill-fated Macclesfield–Warrington line by Humphrey Stephenson (1801–67), the barely-remembered nephew of George Stephenson.

Once the machine was in place they fussed over it, dusting every speck of gravel from its absurd little wheels. Then they greased the entire engine again.

Foreman Tongue later had an angry exchange with the young Keeper of Industrial History who demanded that the sandbag wall, rapidly built around the locomotive by Bert's working party, should be dismantled and shifted a full yard for fear that it would cause damage by penetrating damp. It had to be taken down and rebuilt – but not before the mechanics had returned with their grease guns.

That evening, when the team from the science section had at

last gone home through the blackout, Bert Tongue returned to the museum basement with a ladder, a bucket and a stirrup pump.

Scaling the barricade of sandbags, he squirted two gallons of water down the Towser's tall and brilliantly-polished smoke stack.

Afterwards he went to meet Stella Hopkins, who was baby-sitting for a friend, and was soon further satisfied.

* * *

George Benbow, tugging a dark blue sweater over his head, bent to the passenger side window. 'Tuuquillahh,' he said. Then his head emerged from the muffling folds.

'. . . all perfectly simple. You just sit here – read a book or something – while I stroll around the corner and take a squint at the lie of the land. I won't be long. Bung us the torch, would you.'

It was, in fact, a bicycle lamp. Dorothy, holding it as though it might bite her, passed it through the open window. He strapped the light to his belt.

'You know . . .' she said.

'Wha . . .?' A siren sounded somewhere in the middle distance, possibly an ambulance up on the main road. It was a starless, overcast night.

'You know this is a Neighbourhood Watch area? And, what's more, you know this is damned silly – and possibly even dangerous?'

George bent at the waist as though to lean into the open passenger-side window. His bottom came into contact with the lamp-post, pushing his doubled-over frame forward with surprising force. There was a fraction of a second when it seemed likely that his head would be propelled into the car in the way a performing dog jumps through a hoop.

For once – just once – Benbow caught himself, checking his rapid forward momentum by bracing his forearm against the door. And this time he leaned into the car and kissed Dorothy. Her lips were extraordinarily sweet. They pushed against his own very gently.

'Just a few minutes,' he said. 'I'll be as quick as I possibly can be. Please wait right here.'

He lifted his head and managed to avoid cracking it against the upper frame of the car window.

A Good Looking Man

Dorothy watched as he turned and appeared to walk directly into the lamp-post. She heard a dense smack and a low moan.

'Not very convincing,' she hissed at his departing back.

'Only kidding,' said George as he moved rapidly away from the car into the gathering suburban night.

* * *

'Young man,' boomed Mrs Spratt-Hanbury, standing with her feet planted wide apart in the centre of the rear courtyard at Hanbury Park, in Derbyshire. 'Young man, there has clearly been some mistake.'

Young Billy Beavis, representing the third generation of his family to work for the respected removal firm of Luff, Beavis and Cotton, stopped as though shot. He had a cow-lick of dark hair, which he now flicked away from his eyes.

'I was given to understand by Dr Mackie that Hanbury Park would be receiving into its care a valuable postage stamp collection. Known, I believe, as the A.N. Butler Bequest. And you deliver these . . .' She tapped the side of a crate with her brogue. Three of the boxes had been offloaded in the flagged courtyard. Each crate was about thirty feet long and only twenty-four inches high.

'Let me see – errh, madam,' said Billy, reaching for his clipboard. 'Reference numbers A2093, 4 and 5 . . .'

He walked round the rough wooden boxes, checking in turn their labels. 'Well, all the numbers tally,' he said, brightly. 'That's A2093: a sedan chair . . .'

'A sedan chair.' Mrs Spratt-Hanbury's voice rose dangerously. 'A sedan chair? In a crate shaped like this?'

'Then there's A2094: a pianoforte, concert standard, late eighteenth century, German manufacture. And A2095: a four-poster bed, Regency, with seventeenth-century crewelwork hangings, white Hungarian goose-down mattress and ostrich plumes.'

'Potter! As quick as you can! Quickly, man!' Mrs Spratt-Hanbury, turning on her heel, was already marching towards the walled kitchen garden. She had the voice of a woman born to command. 'Potter! Where are you? Fetch a crowbar and a hammer. Now.'

As the driver spun the truck's steering wheel to swing into the gravel drive, young Billy, looking back, could see them prising open the side of the first crate.

Inside was something which looked suspiciously like the hull of a Polynesian war canoe.

*   *   *

George Benbow walked quickly and confidently to where he knew with certainty he would find the front gate of Number 41. The aristocratic cracksman, in his impeccable evening wear, gave a jaunty smile as he prepared to shimmy to the safe; it would be the work of moments to lift the fabulous Grosvenor diamonds . . . There, to the left, was the outline of a hydrangea bush. Ahead was the dark block of the house and the unmistakable shape of its gable end. Not a light was showing. George took a deep breath.

The gate opened with barely a squeak. He followed the garden path then tiptoed across the tiny patch of lawn towards the open side of the building. He knew that in every case these houses had small side windows at ground floor level. A toilet – or downstairs cloakroom, as the estate agents would have it. Further down the road a dog barked. Another, more distant, replied. Then there was silence. The night air was distinctly cool but he felt a bead of perspiration running in the small of his back.

George, his eyes now accustomed to the gloom, picked out the white window frame. With a thud of elation he saw that the little upper transom was slightly ajar. Very carefully – so carefully – he lifted the dustbin from beside the back gate. Then step by step, with infinite caution, he moved it into place beneath the window. Then he paused and listened. Nothing.

Silently, he climbed on to the dustbin lid and pulled the screwdriver from the waistband of his trousers. It slipped under the lip of the window and – with only a slight tug – sprang it open. Then, pushing the screwdriver down the back of his trousers, he lifted the window and poked his head inside.

God, it was black. With a heave, and still gripping the window frame, he launched himself head first through the narrow gap.

His face, upside down now, inched down the main window pane until his head came to rest on something soft. He brought down one hand and felt around. It was a spare toilet roll on the window sill. George remained there for a few seconds, feeling the blood running into his head and a pulse throbbing in his temple. His thighs rested on the edge of the frame up above, where his legs and feet still poked out of the window into the open air.

A Good Looking Man

He brought down his left hand as well. Taking his weight on both wrists, he lowered himself gingerly; then his hands stepped down, first on to the lid of the lavatory cistern, next on to the seat.

By now his feet were hooked over the window frame. Gently, he allowed himself to slide to the floor. The window dropped shut with a dull thud. George lay still. His heart was thumping with an alarmingly loud beat. Finally, he checked that his lamp was still secure. He could barely suppress an hysterical whinny.

Back at the car, Dorothy Parker, finding herself unable to sit still a moment longer, climbed out and walked towards Hayes Avenue. It was impossible to make out the street numbers. To her relief, she found a plastic numeral on the gatepost of the second house and read – or, rather, felt – the number three. She started to move up the road, counting off the houses.

Chapter Eleven

Dr Mackie felt that Miss Hopkins looked extraordinarily well. It was a wonder that anybody should, considering the hard labour which had been inflicted on the entire staff during the period of evacuation, which was now all but over. He knew that he was exhausted. The time had come to record in full the dispersal of the Vincent's collections. The director had no idea how long the war might last – or, for that matter, how much time was left to him personally. He had done his best.

There were those who were asking how long it would be before the war actually began. Not one of the expected bombing raids had taken place; accidents in the blackout caused the only casualties, doubling the number of fatal injuries on the roads in the first month of the war. The British government seemed to have decided to avoid using its armed services in any capacity which might inflict harm on anybody, least of all the enemy. It took the sternest measures, however, against foreigners living in the United Kingdom. Thousands were rounded up and interned – including many refugees from Hitler's Germany and avowed enemies of the Nazis.

The public had been told to make war by improving their blackout arrangements and by carrying, at all times and in every case, a luggage label marked with their name and address. A wise precaution, it was suggested, considering the very real risk of getting lost in the dark.

Through the country ran a mounting sense of unreality and frustration. If the nation's leaders were committed to anything it certainly wasn't all-out war for a noble cause.

Dr Mackie and his staff had been given precious little leisure in which to observe this official torpor. The director felt that he had driven everyone hard, yet his secretary, for one, was looking positively refreshed. She was really a very bonny girl. Woman, he should say. He gave a dry little smile.

'First, I shall want to record my thanks to the academic staff and, naturally, to the manual workers who have borne the brunt of this exercise. Mr – ahhh – Tongue has been a pillar of . . .'

Stella Hopkins could not prevent herself from looking up. He had, indeed, she thought. And tonight they were going dancing, which he did surprisingly well. Her father was edgy about the whole business – but he simply had no idea. Besides, there was a war on, wasn't there? They could all be blown away tomorrow. She very much wanted to live.

'Then, and this is most important, I want to compile in complete form a record of the exact whereabouts of every item distributed to places of safety,' said Dr Mackie. 'It is of paramount importance. We cannot know what might become of any one of us before this dreadful war is over. And somebody, someday is going to have to reassemble our treasures.

'I'm afraid it means a lot of work for you, Miss Hopkins. I hope that it will be possible to find you some less onerous task in the days ahead.'

Stella, thinking of the nights to come, gave him a smile of great sweetness.

* * *

George Benbow spread his fingers across the face of the lamp and flicked it on. The beam, flying off at all angles, showed him the staircase and the closed doors of what he took to be bedrooms on the landing above. He snapped out the light and, after waiting for a moment to be embraced again by the darkness, began to tiptoe up the stairs. The third tread creaked horribly and he froze. He knew the place was empty but he couldn't help himself. The house remained quite still.

In seconds he was on the narrow landing. He felt a shape – a cupboard or, perhaps, a cabinet – and edged around it towards the door of the front bedroom. His hand found the round knob and, holding his breath, he turned it and pushed. The door inched open and then caught on something. The edge of a rug. George crouched and felt for the obstacle, smoothing it with his fingers. Remaining on his knees, he lifted the lamp and played a brief shaft of light into the room.

As the darkness blanketed him again he reviewed what he had seen. A narrow bed to the right, piled with what looked like a

A Good Looking Man

heap of clothes. A miniature dressing table and a stool under the window. A television set standing on the corner of a shelf, beside a small row of books and something that looked like an overgrown doll. And – glory be! – there was the fireplace, against the lefthand wall. The pinkish ribs of an old-fashioned gas fire remained in place. A piece of cake. Lead me to the diamonds, old fruit, and then it's off to the boat train and Le Touquet . . .

He stepped into the room and quietly pushed the door shut behind him. There was some sort of coat hanging on the back. George crossed stealthily to the hearth – God, what had he trodden on? Some sort of little crunchy animal? A mouse? Why didn't it squeal when his great boot flattened it? He explored under his foot, with extreme caution. There was nothing that felt like blood. It was whiskery, springy . . . a hair curler. And, God, what was that? A hedgehog? He pushed the hairbrush aside.

A tiny red light penetrated the darkness. It was the television, a glow from a switch indicating that the set was live; it must have been left plugged in to the mains and turned on. Careless, thought Benbow. It was firmly lodged in his mind that electrical appliances should be unplugged while you were away from home.

Hold on. Had he left the water heater switched on, back at the flat? No, it was off. He was almost, nearly certain.

George knelt by the fireplace and, taking the little lamp from his belt, propped it upright on the floor. He reached for his screwdriver, still tucked into the waistband of his trousers. Pulling a corner of the rug half over the light, he clicked it on. There was the floorboard, neatly drilled for the gas pipe.

The blade slipped easily between the boards. As he forced down the handle, the plank gave easily and started to rise. Dad, if you could see me now, thought George. In a moment it was three inches clear. His hand snaked into the exposed floor space.

'Jason!'

George was instantly, totally rigid. The hairs on his neck rose and stiffened. His whole scalp seem to crawl forward an inch and settle over his eyebrows. So that's what it feels like when your hair stands on end, he found himself thinking. His face set in a hideous rictus. He was the animal in a trap. His free hand, unbidden, had the presence of mind to snap off the lamp.

'Jason?' hissed the voice from the bed again. 'Me mum'll kill me.'

Bloody, bloody, bloody, bloody, bollocking hell. In the paralysis of alarm, George could only open his mouth and allow the silent string of words to fall out.

As his eyes became used to the dark, he could make out a tousled shape rising from the heaped duvet, propped on one arm. That was it. There had been a sort of warm sleepiness about the room and he had known it from the moment he stepped through the door. Nobody in the damned house? That wretched neighbour was clearly insane.

'Don't turn the light on. And keep quiet, for god's sake.' It was a young woman's voice.

'Gurrr,' he said, softly.

'You said it wasn't worth it.'

She's talking in her sleep, thought George. Please let her be talking in her sleep. No, she bloody well isn't. She's bloody wide awake.

'You said, you said. Not the first time you stayed in me mum's place, you said. Not with her ears. She got ears like a hawk, you said. You mad sod.' The girl – woman? – was whispering huskily and urgently.

'Yurr,' said George. So, there wasn't only this female in the house. There was also her mother and Jason, a mad sod. Probably a fighting fit mad sod, trained in the martial arts and capable of tearing limbs off people.

'Come on, then. It'll be all right . . . It's warm in here. Come on – but quietly.'

Christ in heaven, thought George. If I make a run for it, she'll scream the place down. If I go anywhere near her she'll soon know I'm very definitely not her Jason and she'll scream the place down anyway.

At any moment she'll switch on her bedside light. Then try saying that you only popped in to look for a Dinky car . . .

'Hang on,' the girl whispered. 'Loo. Gotta go.' And she slid out of bed – a pale, naked shape – and flitted to the door. 'Don't go away,' she hissed, touching him on the very top of his head with the tip of her finger as she passed.

'Wurr,' said George. He could feel the radiant, sleepy warmth of her body as she passed. Then she was gone. Ohmygawd, muttered George. Don't go? Don't bloody well go? As soon as he heard the bathroom door latch he flew across the bedroom for the landing. Then he raced back for his lamp and screwdriver. Christ, where's the screwdriver?

A Good Looking Man

You, you absolute tool, he moaned venomously. Where was the bleeding screwdriver? He felt the hairbrush and, in panic, stuffed it under his sweater. Screwdriver? Screwdriver? It would have his prints all over it – including the prisoner's buttock prints, m'lud. Then, his hand touched the plump plastic handle.

Thank you, God. Thank you. Thank you so very much. The floorboard remained on end – and he left it like that. He skittered on to the landing, remembering just in time to dodge the cabinet, and raced on tiptoe helter-skelter down the stairs.

'Judy?' It was an older woman's voice. 'Judy? What the hell's going on?'

George had a last glimpse of a line of light appearing under the back bedroom door. So mum really was all ears – and, for poor old Jason, there was going to be hell to pay.

Dorothy Parker was waiting, tense with anxiety, on the pavement outside the silent and unlit Number 41. Suddenly she saw a man's form erupting from a front garden six doors further up the street. Slabs of light appeared in the dark mass of that building.

She shrank back, taking a sharp prod in the ear from a broken twig. The man's figure came tearing towards her like the clappers of hell, as her father would have said. Then, apparently spotting her dark shape in his path, he veered wildly across the street.

'Oh, bugger, bugger . . .' he seemed to be saying as he hammered off into the night, in the direction of Stanley Park Road and a waiting Morris Minor.

Chapter Twelve

Bert Tongue, driving with one hand on the steering wheel, the other high on Stella's thigh, allowed the van to slow and drift into the kerb. He pulled on the handbrake and then reached across to her. Her reddish hair fell heavily across his arm, cushioning her head, as their mouths closed hungrily in a long kiss. Bert cupped his hand and felt the beautiful, soft weight of her breast.

Stella's hand closed around his and pressed it harder against her. So hard that, at any other time, he would have been frightened of hurting her.

'I'm hungry,' she murmured into his throat.

'Yes,' he said, in a thick, choked voice.

'No. I mean I'm hungry.'

'What, you mean hungry?' said Bert, drawing back and looking into her face.

'Yes. Hungry.'

'Hungry hungry?'

'Yes.'

'You should have said.'

'I did.'

He looked around, taking in for the first time the small town shopping street where the van had come to rest. He had pulled in just short of a road junction. On the far corner stood a grocer's shop with a window rendered more uninviting by the failing light.

Bert adjusted his tie as he crossed the road. The shop had that sweet smell of raisins and preserved fruit and biscuits and brown sugar, stacked in thick paper bags. A schoolgirl in gymslip and blue beret was standing behind the counter, her serious face set in pale determination. Bert gave her a broad smile of greeting.

'Lovely day,' he said. 'Which are you going to bring in first, food rationing or thirty bob's worth of free credit for all your customers?'

The girl's entire expression was a blank space of utter incomprehension.

'We don't give credit. Only the feckless and undeserving would ask for it,' she said, as though echoing some absent adult. She must have been about fourteen and, by the sound of it, she had been taking elocution lessons. 'We have been told that butter, sugar, bacon and ham will be rationed . . .'

'I was only . . .'

'Will be rationed from January. Butter will be limited to four ounces, sugar to twelve,' she continued, raising her voice and showing every sign of disapproving – no, deploring – the interruption.

'I was only joking,' said Bert.

The child looked completely lost again. 'I don't understand,' she said after a moment. 'Credit isn't a joking matter.'

'A joke. You know? Nothing to be frightened of . . .'

'I'm not frit. It's cash only.'

Bert looked at her steadily.

'What's your name, little girl?'

'Margaret Roberts.'

'And what do you want to do when you grow up?'

'I would like to introduce some extra grocery lines – more bottled meat and fish paste.'

'Well, good luck to you, Margaret.'

Bert settled back in his seat, looked in the van's rear-view mirror and drew a deep sigh.

'That's the trouble with this country,' he said. 'What sort of ambition can a girl have, growing up in a grocer's shop in a place like this? Whatever sort of future does life hold in store for her?'

'Don't let it get you down,' said Stella, adjusting the road atlas on her lap. They were on a tour of inspection, visiting some of the country houses pressed into service as safe havens for Dr Mackie's beloved artefacts.

The director had decided that Stella could do with a break. Who better to take care of her and to check on the gallery's possessions than Foreman Tongue.

'What is this place anyway?' asked Bert.

'Grantham, I think,' said Stella. 'God, we're miles off course.'

* * *

A Good Looking Man

'Well, how was I to know you were there, lurking in the shrubbery?' George, the morning after his bungled burglary, was feeling unusually defensive. 'When I got back to the car and there was no sign of you, I naturally assumed that you'd got the wind up. I thought you must have decided to go home. Didn't mean to leave you there. Of course not. Never crossed my mind . . .'

Dorothy drew herself to her full height. 'It took me over an hour to walk – to walk, mark you – back to my place. I've never been so cold and miserable. Stupid, ridiculous nonsense. In all my life, I've never felt . . .'

George made as though to approach her but she stopped him dead with a look of concentrated, arm's-length disapproval.

'I'm sorry. Really,' he muttered. 'Dreadfully sorry.'

He noticed that she had a nasty scratch on her ear lobe. 'You weren't even in the right house. You came charging out of Number 57, or something, as though the hounds were after you – and just hared right by me. I mean, Benbow. How could you be so . . . so bloody hopeless?'

George had been thinking about that. It occurred to him that, approaching the house on foot – he had previously reconnoitred the road only in his car – he must have misjudged his distances. He had remembered the scale of things as seen through the eyes of a small boy. Now, with the legs of a grown man, he had simply overshot. And all the damned houses looked exactly the same.

'Of course,' he said, 'it goes some way to explaining why there was nothing under the floorboard. I find that quite, you know, encouraging.'

Dorothy's glance could only be described as cold; whole mammoths could successfully have been preserved in the permafrost of her gaze.

'Well, as far as I'm concerned you should be encouraged to forget it,' she said. 'I'm perfectly willing to help with your inquiry about the Pudding Norton ceiling, so far as I'm able to be of any assistance of a, let's say, legitimate nature. But as far as anything else goes, you're strictly on your own. I don't want to know about it. You can damned well play the . . .'

And that was how Miss Parker's secretary, who just then entered the room, came to tell her friend in the textile workshop that she had witnessed an incredible bollocking, yes? A bollocking delivered, what's more, to the man who on his previous visit had been laid out across the keeper's desk with a blow to his frankly attractive chin.

Chapter Thirteen

At the end of March 1940 Bert Tongue began speaking to Stella Hopkins about marriage – and about his other great plan. By this time they were out together on their jaunts roughly once a week, roaming the countryside to examine unlikely storerooms and, later, each other in soft down beds.

Stella's father, who had treated Bert with mistrust at first, now seemed to be well disposed towards the gallery foreman. The two men were both aware that they were very nearly alike in age. Mr Hopkins had visibly warmed to Bert when he discovered that they had served in the same section of the line in France in 1917. They spent a couple of evenings recalling battered landmarks and billets – and plotting where, in this show, the trench lines might be bogged down by, say, 1943. If the shooting match ever got started. God, the troops out there today didn't know they were born.

Mrs Hopkins had treated Bert like a son-in-law from the beginning. She had clearly decided to regard him as a mature twenty-five-year-old, in need of good, plain cooking and motherly advice.

Since Bert's own mother had died when he was seven – he had never known his father, who had apparently left before he was born – he took to this regime rather well. He was soon calling Mrs Hopkins mum. And she called him son. Considering that she was three years his junior, this amused Bert no end.

He had been married before; a disastrous, brief affair in the bewildering days of 1918, when he was aged only nineteen and was gripped by panic about the appalling prospect of returning to France. They had one leave period together and he never saw her again. His young wife had, he learned later, taken up with a merchant seaman. They had apparently decided after the war to settle in Canada. He had been relieved at the time – and he was again now.

He was also, without question, deeply in love with Stella. She was unafraid; she was intelligent and funny and she was endlessly kind. She also had a beautiful body; he loved to watch her walking naked around whatever hotel bedroom was theirs for the night. Her skin was so soft and unblemished; her breasts were young and as sweetly shaped as, well, as the statue of Giannetta Baccelli, a mistress of the third Duke of Dorset, they had seen in its packing case in the orangery of a country house only that morning.

Bert, raising himself on his elbows and looking down at her face, surrounded by the fan of her red-brown hair, started to tell her of the plan that was taking shape in his mind.

She began moving to a strong and beautiful rhythm, which soon shut him up. But not before she had noted, again, that Mr Albert Tongue, foreman attendant and remarkably controlled lover, was a very smart man indeed. That night he wept, which surprised and strangely gratified her.

* * *

George Benbow was considering what he should do with the plastic hairbrush in his jacket pocket. He thought about posting it back to Hayes Avenue but then, on reflection, replaced it in his pocket. He looked out of the window, across the wet slates. He hummed a little tune.

He had tried to make it a rule always to have an absorbing project on which he could fall back at times of crisis. It helped when coming to terms with any failure, or the sort of empty ache left behind by the crash landing of a promising friendship with an attractive woman.

There had been ample opportunity to develop his interests. He was a naturalist with a particular concern for the wildlife of the sea shore. He was a reasonably good cook. He wrote letters to the newspapers under a variety of more or less unlikely pseudonyms.

One of George's greatest strokes had been to start a lively row in the readers' letters columns of the *Daily Telegraph*, involving increasingly angry exchanges between no fewer than three correspondents entirely of his own invention.

The dispute had started over a feature on the fashion pages. Off went an opening shot, which soon appeared in print.

'Sir, your staff writers are clearly unaware of the fact that the blazer, a most useful garment, derives its name from the crew

A Good Looking Man

of the Royal Navy ship HMS *Blazer* who, in the mid-nineteenth century, wore distinctive, striped jackets of this kind. I remain, yours etcetera, Captain R.S.J. Legge RN (retired).'

A day later came a withering response.

'Sir, your correspondent, Captain Legge (yesterday's letter), is quite mistaken about the derivation of the word blazer. The name simply means brightly coloured and showy, as in blaze. Flared trousers are so called for similar reasons. Yours faithfully, Squadron Leader Ivor Lympe RAF.'

A stinging reply appeared in the following day's issue of the *Telegraph*.

'Sir, Why does your correspondent Ivor Lympe (reader's letters, yesterday) find it necessary to sign himself Squadron Leader, followed by the initial letters RAF? Who else, apart from the Royal Air Force, employs Squadron Leaders these days? Unless the Midland Red bus company is taking them on. Nothing I can possibly say will dispel his invincible ignorance on the question of blazers. Yours, etc . . .'

Then, breaking in on these exchanges, came a letter in another hand.

'Sir, Both Captain Legge and Squadron Leader Lympe (yesterday's letters to the editor) are sadly confused about the origin of the jacket we call a blazer. In fact, the name derives from the French: *le blason*, meaning coat of arms. This is the obvious source and points to heraldic origins. Yours faithfully, Chas. Dashwood (Very Revd).'

The next issue brought another angry riposte.

'Sir, Dean Dashwood (letters, yesterday) is no doubt well informed about matters biblical. I do not, however, recall any significant figure in the New Testament wearing a blazer. Perhaps he might correct me if I am wrong. Otherwise the Reverend gentleman, who is woefully ignorant about the origins of this garment, should stick to what he knows. Yours faithfully, I. Lympe (RAF) . . .'

And so on. George had taken considerable interest when, some weeks later, he noticed a letter from Squadron Leader Lympe appearing in the *Spectator*. The strange thing was that Benbow had not written it.

He peered out of the window of his flat again. It was still raining.

Oh, well, he sighed. There was really nothing for it. He would have to try, once again, to undermine BBC radio's Test Match Special cricket commentary team.

* * *

The process of evacuation to places of safety involved, for some, a good deal more effort than any journey to the tranquil, muddy countryside. A significant number of women and children were shipped overseas in the early months of the war.

Roughly 11,000 took passage on ships leaving British ports, in most cases bound for North America. There was only one really basic test to determine which children should be given the chance to avoid the blitz or a German invasion: the ability to pay.

This flight wasn't exactly calculated to appeal to the mass of British people at a time when the nation was supposed to be united in common sacrifice. Those sending their children abroad included members of the government.

'Restores your faith in human nature, doesn't it?' as Bert Tongue remarked to Fred Ellis and Ernie Perkins at the Vincent gallery. 'You shall fight to the last man and the last round of ammunition – and don't take any notice if, meanwhile, we slip out the back door.'

The royal family would have none of it. The Queen explained their position with great simplicity: 'The children can't go without me. I can't leave the King – and, of course, the King won't go.'

* * *

Kenneth the cat, who lived with Dorothy Parker in her small, terraced house, had some curious characteristics. While she had taken the trouble to install a cat-flap in the door to the back garden, he would only use it if somebody held it open for him. Dorothy knew that this was ridiculous and avoided speaking of it to her friends, who were thoroughly sensible people.

He was the only cat she had ever known who liked to eat black olives. He also lay in her bath with his legs in the air, sometimes – during his brief periods of physical activity – juggling with the soap. Kenneth vanished, naturally, if threatened by even the faintest sound of running water. And he slept with her, lying on the bedcover and curling himself into the small of her back. All in all, sleeping was the thing that Kenneth did best.

A Good Looking Man

The cat was attacking the flowered cover beside her left ankle, stretching his forelegs and clawing upwards in a series of savage steps. He stopped, looked up at her with complete indifference and then flopped sideways.

It was a great shame. Dorothy had known as soon as she first saw Benbow that there was something risky, even dangerous, about him. But he was bright – and, above all, he was alive.

Apart from anything else, he had also captured her interest in his damned ceiling.

Chapter Fourteen

The price of petrol in the calm but uneasy spring of 1940 was one shilling and ninepence halfpenny a gallon. Fortunately, the Vincent Museum and Art Gallery was prepared to pay that exorbitant price to keep its Austin van, and its foreman, on the road.

The van was coasting along a lane, overhung by banks of cow parsley and blackthorn, somewhere north and west of Hereford. There had been rain but now the sky was Canaletto blue with a brightness that gave new life to every leaf, branch and gnarled root at the roadside.

Stella was whistling. It was surprising, thought Bert, how few women you heard whistling really well. He did not believe he had ever been happier; if this was total war, he couldn't get enough of it. He was the foreman of a museum and gallery that had nothing to put on display. It was his duty to swan around, examining pictures racked up in dusty ballrooms or glass cabinets crated and left in barns.

Careless talk costs lives, eh? Or, in this case, careless driving will get us lost.

'Ask that boy over there, in the gateway,' he said. Stella pulled over and beckoned the child.

The boy, aged about eleven, was sitting on the timber platform where the milk churns were left out each morning. He was swinging his legs; his knees, emerging like sticks from the wide legs of his shorts, were scratched and bloodied. He appeared to be wearing an odd pair of wellington boots. At his side sat a black dog whose flapping tongue looked like half a yard of pink flannel.

'What's your name?' asked Stella, smiling warmly.

'Wally . . . Walter,' the boy replied gravely.

'Well, Wally Walter, we're lost.'

'It's Wally Benbow.' The boy sniffed noisily. 'I been evacu . . . I been sent here for the bombing.'

'That's nice,' said Stella. 'Where's your mum and dad?'

'At home. So's my things . . . toys an' that. I hid 'em.'

'That's a good boy.'

'One day I shall 'ave whatsoever my soul lusteth hafter haccordin' to the blessin's.' The dog looked into the boy's face and yawned.

'Can you help us . . .'

'I seen Farmer Gilbert kill an hen. Pulled 'er 'ead off.'

'Did you? Well, we're looking for a place called Hopton Malpractice . . .'

''E's an bugger, Miss Enid says.'

'Have you any idea, which way . . .?'

'She says she wished Mr 'Itler would bomb 'im to blazes. An' do for his damn old mare, an' all. That's Stella.'

'How funny. That's my name.'

'No. It's an horse, what bites.'

Bert Tongue could no longer contain himself. He rocked forward and back: 'Stella. An horse what bites. Oh, dear. Oh, dear.' He pulled out his handkerchief.

Stella gave him a cool smile. 'Bye-bye, Wally,' she called.

Bert leaned from the van window as they rolled away, gathering speed. He shouted back along the tunnel of the lane: 'Remember where you come from, son. Always remember . . .'

* * *

The package of photocopied documents arrived at George Benbow's flat by messenger, a youth in motorcycle leathers, massive boots and a helmet of streamlined design which emphasized the extreme stringiness of his neck.

Since there was no reply at Benbow's door, the messenger approached the immediate neighbour, Mrs Dashwood. ''Etter ur Missur Elbow,' his muffled voice seemed to say, as he pushed the parcel into her reluctant hand. 'Sigh 'ere.'

Mrs Dashwood took the offered ballpoint and put a tremulous signature on the paper attached to the delivery man's clipboard. Then she retired inside her flat and triple-locked the door, finally slipping the security chain into place.

She had already dropped the package unopened into the waste paper basket under her little hall table.

A Good Looking Man

Mrs Dashwood neither knew nor cared that it contained papers laboriously collected by Dorothy Parker, Keeper of Local History at the Vincent Museum and Art Gallery. She was not to know that these dealt in detail with the dispersal of that institution's collection during the war of 1939–45. It was a matter of complete indifference to the old lady that also tucked into the parcel was a conciliatory note in Miss Parker's looping hand, offering careful words of regret to Mr Benbow and her hopes that they might be able to work together further on his interesting project concerning a missing ceiling.

It was sadly the case that Mrs Dashwood didn't remember the Second World War at all. She had lost track of the name of her next door neighbour although he had, in fact, been looking after her patch of garden for more than two years. She frequently failed even to recognize Mrs Lympe, the home help, and Nurse Legge, the district nurse whose visits enabled her – but only just – to keep her independent life.

The motorcycle messenger, had he taken the trouble to glance at his clipboard, would have seen that the old lady had signed herself: Elizabeth Regina.

* * *

The Austin van was fairly bucketing along. Bert was angry about the surly exchanges he had had back there, in the farmyard at Collingbrook Castle, in the Vale of Evesham.

'Why did he think it was my fault? I wasn't driving the delivery lorry. I didn't run it off his precious road on to his precious asparagus bed. Why did he have a go at me?' He was still cross.

'Anyway, what was he moaning about? They delivered the stuff in the end, didn't they? All he's got to do is store it in that bloody great barn. I told him. I said it's only a lot of old junk anyway.'

He pulled out to pass a company of soldiers in ugly, ill-fitting khaki, marching in full battle order with steel helmets and rifles. The men looked hot and pink but cheerful.

'We should be looking for somewhere to stay,' said Stella, soothingly. They were driving beside an apparently endless estate wall. 'What's the name of this place?'

'Oh, I don't know. It could be Badminton.'

'Look, Bert. Look at that funny old girl.' An elderly woman, wielding a little hatchet, was attacking the ivy on an ancient oak at the roadside. A green Daimler was parked a little way down the lane, a uniformed chauffeur at the wheel.

'She looks exactly like Queen Mary,' said Stella.

'Don't be ridiculous,' said Bert.

They were glad to find a small hotel beside a village green just outside Swindon. It had been a long day.

'You liked that boy we met this morning, didn't you?' Stella was lying on her elbow, looking intently into Bert's sunburned face.

'Good boy,' said Foreman Tongue, taking a deep pull from his cigarette. He reached for the ashtray on the bedside table.

'Perhaps we should do something about that,' she said.

Bert turned back and tried to fathom her eyes.

'You might want a boy of your own. Someone to strangle chickens for . . .'

Bert took her in his arms. 'Come on, Stella, my little mare,' he said. 'Come and bite me.'

* * *

Dorothy Parker was surprised by the absence of any response from Benbow. She would, at least, have expected him to acknowledge safe arrival of those wartime papers which she had parcelled off – even if he didn't feel the need to answer her own little letter.

Two days had gone by without a word. Not a peep.

It was strange that she should have misread him so badly. She had believed he was a kind man, if nothing else. He possibly deserved penal servitude, transportation and judicial amputation of one or more limbs, but he was still kind. Or so she had thought.

'Gail,' she called, glimpsing her secretary as she hurried past the open doorway of her office. 'Gail, when you have a moment, would you mind just checking with that bike firm to make sure Mr Benbow's package was delivered on – when was it? – yes, Wednesday. Thanks. That's very . . .'

The secretary was already walking rapidly away, giving a brief wave over her shoulder.

Dorothy was a busy woman who liked efficiency and energy in others. She had chosen Gail for those reasons alone; she had noticed that many men, when appointing staff, were moved at least to some extent by other factors – most especially, in the case of women employees, by age and appearance. They would always deny it

A Good Looking Man

but she knew it was true. She, on the other hand, had selected for business-like qualities alone. Gail had repaid her by becoming an unfailingly reliable assistant but one so brisk Dorothy felt she hardly knew her.

'The dispatcher checked his records. Yes?' said Gail, referring to the notebook she had flipped opened on the corner of Dorothy's desk. 'He says the package was delivered to the lady of the house. Right? He got out the docket. Yes? It was signed by somebody calling herself Regina. OK?'

Dorothy Parker sat quietly for a moment after she had been left alone.

Well, she certainly hadn't reckoned that there was a woman in the case. And why on earth, she wondered, had she been so stupid as to overlook that possibility?

The BBC radio broadcasters' box at the Oval cricket ground is perched high on a balcony of the endearingly ugly pavilion. Members of the commentary team, working in relays, have a perfect end-on view along the length of the famously fast-paced pitch.

It is a tight squeeze in the box when a cricket test match is in progress. At any one time there is a commentator at the microphone, giving a ball-by-ball description of events taking place below; a former player of international stature sits in the next seat, ready to offer an expert opinion on the play and the balance of the game; a scorer occupies the third place, recording or calling up the endless numerical data which surround this most statistically stalagmitic of sports.

Close by sits, or stands, the producer, who is responsible for keeping the commentary flowing throughout the five days of a full test game. Other members of the team crowd in, waiting to relieve a colleague completing his standard twenty-minute spell on-air or pausing to watch some drama develop on the pitch. The men have nicknames for each other; they have all known – and, in some instances, loathed – one another for years.

There is always an undercurrent of conversation at the back of the box; bottles are uncorked; letters are delivered and opened; juvenile jokes are exchanged; visitors come and go. The atmosphere is masculine and clubby. There is often a scent of cigar smoke.

It was shortly before 3pm on the second day of the first test match, England versus Australia, that a parcel was brought to the door of this busy and crowded box. The producer opened it

Andrew Moncur

to find inside the parcel – to nobody's great surprise – a large and elaborately decorated fruit cake. It had been piped with green and white sugar icing, laid out in the form of cricket field placings.

The BBC cricket commentary team is notoriously fond of cake. Its match reports are frequently punctuated with remarks about particularly splendid cakes baked by listeners and sent in for the enjoyment of everybody involved in the broadcast.

This particular cake arrived with a card saying: 'To the Test Match Special boys. Baked with you cheerful chaps very much in mind.' It was signed 'Uva Crotch (Mrs)', a name which gave rise to much amusement on the crowded back bench of the box.

Yes, said Benbow to himself, that should do very nicely.

Chapter Fifteen

Early on Friday, 10 May 1940, the German military command ended the phoney war by invading Holland and Belgium. The Germans were doing so, they claimed with an unblushing contempt for the truth, to protect the neutrality of these two small kingdoms. In the face of a crushing advance by the Wehrmacht, and heavily outnumbered, the Dutch army had no choice but to capitulate after five days; the Belgian forces yielded thirteen days later.

By that time their French and British allies were in utter disarray and facing their own, by now separate, military disasters.

At the Vincent Museum two members of the manual staff, who were spring cleaning in the storerooms, discovered a neglected marble bust of William Camden, sixteenth-century antiquary and headmaster of Westminster School. It bore a label, undated, with the brief and unhelpful inscription: 'Nose destroyed by rioters.'

They also unearthed a bronze mortar, believed to have been used for firing fireworks at the peace of Aix-la-Chapelle in 1748; a long-forgotten long-eared bat (*Plecotus auritus*), preserved and mounted in a cabinet with cracked glass; a mortally wounded painting, catalogued 'Dead game birds, hares and fruit: Jan Weenix, Dutch school', whose canvas appeared to have been either slashed or trodden on; a dozen sets of false teeth of American manufacture, shown at the Great Exhibition of 1851; and a German infantryman's *pickelhaube* helmet of Great War vintage.

The spike-topped helmet was transferred to the mess room and used as an ashtray for the duration.

* * *

George Benbow had already mowed the tiny lawn in Mrs Dashwood's garden and was weeding dandelions and dead poppies from her flower bed. It was then that he started to realize he was being observed.

'Hello, Mrs Dashwood,' he called at the frail figure, glimpsed in the dimness of her ground floor sitting room. 'I'll be in for a cup of tea in a minute or two. I say, I'll be in to see you in a couple of . . .'

By then the pale shape had disappeared. It had become a Saturday morning routine for George to spend a little time in what, privately, he called Dashwood Park. In reality, the plot was about the size of a tea tray. Most weeks he managed half an hour's work in the garden and then a chat with the old lady, on a day when she would not otherwise have any visitors.

Sometimes she recognized him and asked vague questions about his work. He had, along the way, contrived to lead a number of his friends to believe that he played some leading role in the National Trust's higher policy-making circles. This was not entirely true. George did not try overwhelmingly hard to disabuse them.

If pressed, he would talk about the guide books to two lesser properties which he had researched and written. It was somehow more interesting, more the sort of thing people expected to hear. Who wanted to be told about the trust's shops and garden centres? Yet that was the direction in which his career had, in fact, taken a turn over the last three years.

George's heart was in old buildings, even if his remaining organs were now in the sweet-scented commerce which paid for their upkeep. 'Especially the nose,' he would say to himself, when surrounded by the heady fragrance of lavender bags, soap and piety which hangs over many of the Trust's retail activities. He could tell friends that he was working on the Woolsthorpe Manor Collection, which carried a pleasing hint of academic connoisseurship among artefacts touched by the very hand of Sir Isaac Newton. In fact, the collection was a new range of toiletries being introduced to Trust shops, including the Isaac Newton Falling Apple brand of tangy male fragrances.

George often reflected wryly on how much public esteem the National Trust would continue to enjoy if people could see some of the business dealings, the cheese-paring – and the downright ruthlessness – which went on behind the scenes.

Sometimes Mrs Dashwood failed to recognize him, or affected not to know him at all, when he called at her door. It

A Good Looking Man

was difficult to know how she might react from one week to the next.

It was difficult to tell with women full stop. George felt once again the small lead weight in the pit of his stomach; it had been lying there for long enough now to have become familiar.

* * *

Colonel Ryder was not an unreasonable man. He would have liked to have been doing his bit in this show. But he knew he was, at eighty-two, pretty well past it. The Hun had poured into France; the Frogs had legged it; the British and the Canadians – God bless 'em – had their backs to the wall. And still the War Office allowed him to remain in his cushy billet, out of the firing line. Shame and all that, but what could he expect?

His sole contribution to the war effort had been to provide a safe home for one consignment of thumping great pictures from the National Gallery – a load of fancy foreign muck – and three blasted great crates from the Vincent. The least he could do. Jessore Park wasn't exactly a stately home but it had some half decent stabling – as any fool might expect in Leicestershire – a library, a billiard room and a servants' hall with damn all servants. So why not? Very devil to heat the place, of course, but in times like these everyone must make sacrifices, mustn't they?

The only trouble was, he liked to have things straight. Which was why he was interviewing this chap – a ranker and a damned old soldier, you could tell – about the junk from the Vincent. All he wanted was to get it sorted out.

'I was told, you see. Your director wallah. Came to see me best part of a year ago. He had me down for a collection of war canoes from the Marquesas Islands. Frog territory. Looked it up . . .'

Bert, standing uneasily at attention, slid the manila folder from under his arm. The Colonel made an impatient gesture.

'Bloody suitable for an old cavalryman, I said. He didn't seem to get my drift. Anyway. There they are. And they ain't, are they?'

Bert opened the file and ran his finger down the page. 'Yes, sir. That's what you've got, it says here . . .'

Colonel Ryder fixed him with a yellowish glare from one rheumy eye. 'Look at them, man. For God's sake.'

Craning round the door, Bert could make out in the shuttered gloom the shapes of, variously, a sedan chair, a grand piano and a box-like structure surmounted by – well, they looked like plumes.

'I told the old bugger. I said, right out: "Well, I wouldn't fancy paddling off to war in that little lot!"' Bert explained to Stella later. Having seen her Mr Tongue's prickly, defensive attitude towards those he saw as figures of authority, Stella somehow doubted that his response had emerged quite like that.

'But, don't you see, it just proves the point of what I was saying, doesn't it?' Bert was completely earnest now. 'Nobody seriously knows where everything's gone, do they? We've got a better idea than anyone. We've seen it on the ground. We know who's got the delftware when they're supposed to have the bloody stuffed birds. Old Cyril let the whole lot get out of hand, didn't he?

'We know that, sooner or later, the chaos will have to be sorted out – and nobody's going to be too particular about how it's done. They're not going to fuss over the odd item here or there, are they? They'll only want to get enough of it back in one piece to fill up a few frigging galleries. Then it's back to business and Bob's your uncle.

'Your Dr Mackie thinks he knows. Putting away those precious lists you did for him, all top security – can't let this fall into the hands of the beastly Hun, and all that. Or the beastly committee, come to that. But even he hasn't got much of an idea.'

Bert took her hand and spoke softly, but very clearly: 'And you're his secretary, aren't you? The one he trusts with those records – his all-important, secret bloody files. And I'm his foreman who's gradually sorting out what's really gone where. We're in – yes, I think that's the way to put it – an extremely interesting position.'

Stella smiled wryly. 'Don't you know there's a war on?' she said – and then lay back.

* * *

'Hello, Dorothy?' Benbow was smiling broadly into the telephone mouthpiece. It was, by any standard, a ridiculous thing to do – but George was perfectly unaware that he was grinning at all. 'Hello? Is that you?'

'Hellooo?' said the woman's voice again.

'Dorothy?'

'It's her mother, dear,' said the woman. 'If it's Dorothy Parker you're phoning, that is.'

A Good Looking Man

'Yes. Yes. Please may I speak to . . .'

'She's not here, dear. Could I take a message?'

'It's her parcel,' said George. 'I've had your daughter's parcel and her letter. The old lady next door put them out with the rubbish. And I'm so very, very pleased . . .'

'I see. You're pleased that an old lady put my daughter's parcel in her rubbish. I'll tell her.'

'Hold on. I'm pleased . . .'

'Yes. I've made a note of that. And what, Mr umm – what was my daughter writing to you about?'

'The ceiling. Oh, yes . . .'

'I'm sorry, you'll have to speak up. I thought you said something about a ceiling . . .'

'I did. A plaster ceiling.'

'A ceiling?'

'Exactly.'

'I see. You have been corresponding with my daughter about a plaster ceiling?' A note of coolness had crept into Mrs Parker's voice.

'That's right.'

'Are you a building contractor?'

'No, you see. It's a missing ceiling . . .'

'Have you been in touch with the police?'

'Goodness, no. That wouldn't be . . .'

'I understand. Apart from mentioning your interest in rubbish dumping, I am to tell my daughter that you have lost your ceiling but you don't want the police involved.'

'Lord, no! I'm searching for a Jacobean ceiling. I wouldn't have known a thing – but then, luckily, I found all this stuff from your daughter. In the bin.'

'I see. So you've been in the bin?'

'Yes. You see, it's a memory problem. Sad really. The old lady didn't know me from Adam . . .'

'Who is Adam?'

'No. Look. I'm sorry. Adam doesn't come into this. I'm not explaining myself very well.'

'This old lady you mention, does she have some interest in the plastering trade?'

'Good heavens, no.'

'And when did you last see your ceiling?'

'Oh, no. I've never set eyes on it . . .'

'Right. Very well. I'll let my daughter know that you rang, Mr umm. Thank you very . . .'

And the line went dead with a decided click.

* * *

More than a million men had enrolled as Local Defence Volunteers by the summer of 1940 when, at Mr Churchill's suggestion, the pitifully ill-armed force was given a new name: the Home Guard.

'Tell me, bonny lad,' said Sergeant Storey, speaking with a softness that was infinitely menacing. 'Tell me what, precisely, you have there.' Robbie Storey was a man of considerable size and presence; his chest was enormous.

Private Smith M. looked down and read the label. 'It's a shotgun, Sa'rnt. Errh. A 12-bore, with sporting scenes, made in Birmingham.'

'A shotgun,' whispered Sergeant Storey. 'Tell me, laddie. Just tell me, straight out. Feel free. Don't be bashful, now . . .' The volume of his voice was swelling to a terrifying parade ground roar, '. . . am I forever to be surrounded by fucking idiots?'

With a crunch of gravel he performed a crashing about-turn and stamped off, his boots striking sparks, towards the company HQ, a tar-coated shed. That morning Mr Fucking Lieutenant Fucking Pilgrim had signed for a delivery of twenty-eight rifles and shotguns, all museum pieces – which was very appropriate, seeing as how they had come from a moth-eaten museum.

And now this arms consignment turned out to consist of the following: twenty-seven rifles and shotguns and a palpable, wooden, carved rattle. English; early nineteenth century.

* * *

Benbow listened to the cricket commentary on his portable radio. He was beginning to feel that something was amiss. But then, at last, one of the broadcast team took advantage of a lull in the afternoon's play to say a few words of thanks.

'We've had the most splendid cake, here in the box,' the commentator said. 'It was a real corker, wasn't it, Fred?'

'Absolutely. It were, absolutely. Absolutely. I've never seen nothing like it, I 'aven't,' said Fred.

'So there's a big thank you from all of us here to the cake baker,

A Good Looking Man

Mrs Crotch. Thank you very much. That's, let me see now, Uva Crotch, Fred.'

'Cor, dear. Dear, oh, dear,' said Fred, with a spluttering, smoke-pickled little laugh.

At that moment the cake exploded, showering fragments of raisin, candied peel, marzipan, icing sugar and retired international cricketer all over the square in front of the pavilion at the famous Oval ground . . .

No, it won't do, Benbow said to himself. There had to be a more plausible alternative. There had to be a way of getting at them which would be so simple it would seem like . . . well, like, a piece of cake.

Chapter Sixteen

Without question, it did not add up. George hoisted the pillow behind his head and picked up once again the top photocopy from the small pile resting against his knees.

Dr Oliver Mackie, then director of the Vincent Museum and Art Gallery, had reported to his committee on Friday, 29 September 1939 – the same day, incidentally, that the poor Poles surrendered Warsaw to the Wehrmacht's armoured divisions. His attention had been fixed on events closer to home.

Dr Mackie had set out, in laborious detail, the practical steps taken to secure the safety of the possessions in his charge. 'Following upon the crisis of September 1938, your director initiated inquiries to ascertain the best methods of dispersing the collections and of obtaining transport for this work. At the end of April 1939, he was able to complete preliminary arrangements with a number of householders selected for the purpose of providing secure accommodation for items of value.

'These persons were approached on the basis that their properties, set in rural positions, could be regarded as safe from the risk of damage by aerial bombardment. Their houses or other properties were also of a size to permit of the safekeeping of items, many of a considerable size or requiring the construction of temporary storage frameworks and racking on a large scale.

'Your director was successful in obtaining the services of Messrs Luff, Beavis & Cotton for the task of transporting the collections. This company's previous experience of handling valuable works of art in connection with the larger loan exhibitions at this gallery qualified them specially for . . .'

Blah, blah, thought George. He picked up the next sheet of paper.

'. . . in the afternoon, the first vanload left the gallery. This consisted of the entire collection of Old Master drawings. From

Andrew Moncur

that date continuously, with the exception of Sundays, evacuation continued until Friday, 15 September 1939. The gallery is now entirely emptied of its contents so far as the pictures, watercolours, drawings and the industrial, local and natural history collections are concerned, with the exception of objects too large or fragile to be moved.

'A very small proportion has been stored in the basement and sandbagged. In some instances, objects of value had been sandbagged only at the foot; it was felt that more comprehensive protection of this sort could create greater danger of deterioration by damp than there was risk of damage by enemy aircraft. The Henry Proudfoot fresco, on the ground floor, has been boarded up in situ and protected by sandbags . . .'

And the art critics were unanimous in declaring that this was a distinct improvement on the appearance of the ghastly old thing, thought George. Then he sat bolt upright as he read: 'A complete record of all objects and their several destinations has been kept by your director.'

George marked that passage with his felt-tipped pen, which he then laid beside him on the bed. So the movements of his ceiling must be noted, along with everything else. It was simply a case of finding that record.

The director's report rolled on. It pleased George to find that, despite the turmoil of war, the everyday life of the museum and gallery continued. New acquisitions were being reported to the committee, even as Europe erupted in flames and the Vincent's own possessions were scattered across the nation.

Four early bicycles of a previously unknown design, made in Coventry, had been presented to the museum on 19 September. The director had succeeded in obtaining a Dutch seascape, with cockle boats, attributed to Albert Cuyp (1620–91). The academic staff had been particularly pleased to acquire a copy of the important Britannia road map book of 1675 by John Ogilby, a former deputy master of the revels in Ireland, whose survey of England and Wales was based on the statute mile of 1,760 yards as opposed to the so-called customary mile, which varied locally on a scale ranging from 2,035 to 2,500 yards.

The work of clearing the storerooms had revealed some previously unrecorded items: a fine wooden club from Fiji (a valuable addition to the ethnographical collection); a damaged painting by Weenix the younger, tentatively dated 1705, which was now being

A Good Looking Man

assessed for repair and restoration; an item of Burslem ceramic ware, believed to be part of a flushing water closet; a collection of Blue John ornaments and fluorspar, as found in nature.

The director regretted to inform the committee of the sad death of Mr Cyril Finch, foreman assistant. He had been a tower of strength in the period preparatory to the evacuation. Further, he would be remembered as a man who always had a kind word for everybody. The committee might wish to record its sympathies to his widow, who had, he believed, temporarily moved to their holiday home on the East Coast for peace and quiet at this difficult time.

He was pleased to say that the assistant foreman, Mr Albert Tongue, had been appointed to succeed the late Mr Finch. A Miss Masters, an assistant on the staff of this gallery, had resigned her position to take up work with the Postal Censorship, at Liverpool. A Mr Organ had joined the staff as a junior assistant, at a salary of £325 per annum. 'To do what, for heaven's sake?' George asked himself, aloud.

The director had to inform the committee that the watchman's box at the staff entrance had been somewhat damaged in an accident believed to have been caused by the outside firm of removers. The estimated cost of repair was £27 and a bill for this sum would be presented to Messrs Luff, Beavis & Cotton.

George adjusted his pillow. He was allowing himself to be sidetracked.

On Monday, 13 November 1939, the committee met and received one apology for absence and the director's report on the evacuation. On that day, for the record, the first bombs of the Second World War to fall on British territory were dumped on the Shetland islands.

George read on quickly: 'The chairman asked the director to convey to his assistants, secretary and staff the committee's appreciation of the special efforts made by all . . .' Yes, yes, said George.

'The committee noted the list of names and addresses of all those who had kindly volunteered to act as temporary custodians of the Vincent's possessions. The chairman said that he felt sure that members would understand the necessity for this list to remain confidential at present, for obvious reasons of security. It was agreed that letters of . . .'

A list of names and addresses? Nothing about a catalogue of the possessions they had received. Dr Mackie must have decided that it was sufficient for the committee merely to acknowledge their thanks to the hosts; the more important document – the one mentioned in his report – must have remained in the director's own hands.

George reached for his pen again. A round patch of blue ink was spreading across his duvet cover.

* * *

The British experienced two escapes of near miraculous proportions in the first year – give or take a few days – of their war with Germany. On 23 May 1940, when the Anglo-French military alliance was already in tatters and the British army was falling back on Dunkirk, the Germans halted the advance of their encircling heavy armour. The British were allowed to get away. By 3 June almost 340,000 men (more than a third of them French) would be removed from the beaches and carried to England.

Then, in early September, when RAF fighters had given everything in the Battle of Britain, the Luftwaffe appeared to be poised to inflict the decisive blow. The Germans came desperately close to turning the battle by destroying the home bases of the Spitfires and Hurricanes. But on 7 September they switched the target of their assault and turned instead to bombing London. The British fighter aircraft remained airborne; a German invasion was postponed, indefinitely as it turned out.

Civilians in, principally, the cities would continue to bear the worst of the air attacks. By September 1941 the Germans would have killed more British civilians than combatants.

The people proved far more resilient than the pre-war planners and policy-makers had believed possible. The factories were back in full production within days of even the most horrific raids, including the notorious attack on Coventry. Many civilians became used to shelter life; yet more preferred to stay at home, choosing to remain in their own beds through the worst of the blitz. Others decamped to the countryside each night.

'Poor old Hilda Finch is back,' said Stella Hopkins, as a series of dull crumps reverberated through the Anderson shelter. Her father was sitting in his old greatcoat, thrown over his pyjamas, and wellington boots. It had become his standard outfit during air raids; his own version of the siren suit.

A Good Looking Man

'Hilda who?' he asked. Outside, shrapnel splinters hissed down over the sour little gardens of Armoury Road.

'Widow of the previous foreman at the Vincent – my old boss,' said Bert Tongue. 'When he passed on she went to live right by the coast. Essex somewhere. Near Clacton, I think. Ridiculous. Course, the army took over her poor bloody old seaside hut. They put a concrete pill box slap on top of it. And so she comes back here, just in time for this lot.'

'Someone said she's going to sell up here and go to stay with her sister. Near Bristol, I think.' Stella tightened her coat belt and gave Bert a significant sort of look. So did her mother, sitting on the far side of the shelter.

He cleared his throat.

'Go on, for God's sake,' Stella whispered.

Bert looked at his big hands. 'We've been thinking, me and Stella,' he said. 'We think we ought to give it a go . . .'

'Give what a go?' asked Mr Hopkins. On the heath the guns opened up again in a thunderous, ragged salvo.

'Banging away, all bloody night,' said Bert.

'You what?' asked Mr Hopkins, by now bolt upright.

'On and on. From bedtime till half past bloody breakfast.'

'What are you saying?'

'Those guns. Banging away at the wide blue yonder.'

'No. About you and Stella?'

'We want to get married. We thought we might have a go for Hilda Finch's place, if it's coming up. What do you think?'

And at that his future mother-in-law, three years his junior, stood up – as much as the curved roof of the shelter would allow her to stand up – and gave Bert an enormous smacking kiss. Simultaneously, a stick of high explosive bombs destroyed five houses (Numbers 12 to 20, inclusive) on the western side of Armoury Road and buried the Hopkins family's garden shelter under a landslide of timber, slates and dusty house bricks.

*   *   *

The next photocopy had been marked in what George Benbow was coming to recognize as Dorothy's generous hand. 'Compare and contrast,' he read.

It was another report to the Vincent's committee, only this time dated 3 May 1945. George noted, without much thought, that the name of the director of the museum and art gallery was now given as Dr Hilary. The section headed 'Accommodation' was marked for his attention.

'Your director is pleased to report that, repairs and cleaning having now been carried out, space is available here – at long last – to accommodate possessions at present stored in a further four of the private houses which have been used as wartime repositories. Your director has made arrangements for the partial return of the collections, as follows: On 28 and 29 June, Hanbury Park and the Collingbrook Estate will be cleared of their wartime charges. On 5 and 6 July, Timberlakes House and Saint Philibert's School will be similarly disembarrassed.

'The task of assessing the extent of the damage caused by the unfortunate fire at Maze Hall, in Warwickshire, is still in progress.

'As your chairman is aware, the director has been working at something of a disadvantage since no complete record of the dispersal of all the Vincent's collections is extant . . .'

George laid the paper on his knees and looked up at the ceiling. Well, well. No complete record. He continued reading.

'It has been necessary to rely to a large extent on records assembled originally in a somewhat piecemeal manner but which, thanks to the diligent efforts of Mr Tongue, foreman assistant, are now in a more complete and satisfactory form. The objects left in storage at the Vincent are, of course, well known to the committee (see Appendix A) . . .' George found that page: the Towser locomotive; a carpet weaving loom; a stuffed wapiti (left for repair); a full-scale reconstruction of a mammoth and so on. Nothing about architectural remnants from Pudding Norton. He turned back to the director's statement.

'As for the dispersed possessions, the absence of full original documentation gives yet more cause for regret regarding the untimely death of the former director, Dr Oliver Mackie, whose loss is sorely felt for so many other reasons, not least his scholarship. His contribution to the better understanding and appreciation of the followers of Cornelius Van Hoogwimpell (the younger) was valued by those who felt that this was a sadly neglected school of seventeenth-century Dutch maritime painting.

'It is clear that in the difficult days of the onset of war there was every incentive to concentrate on the physical wellbeing of the collections at the expense of less pressing clerical tasks. The dispersal was also attended by some misunderstandings over the correct designation of certain objects. A full record of the houses providing storage facilities (Appendix B) is in your . . .'

Well, a bit of posthumous back-stabbing going on there, thought George. Obviously old Dr Mackie had lost his wretched file – or he'd never, in fact, got round to drafting the thing.

Funny that he should have told the committee so, back in September 1939. What was it? 'A complete record of all objects and their several destinations has been kept . . .'

Patently it hadn't been. You could imagine, reading between the lines of Dr Hilary's 1945 report, that they must have got into a proper stew trying to work out where everything – thousands of individual items – had ended up.

Perhaps it wasn't so very surprising that a Jacobean ceiling, which ought to have been in their possession before the war, appeared to have gone walkabout some time since. Most probably, you had to feel, at some point before the museum and art gallery was reassembled in the summer of 1945.

As though following the same train of thought, Dorothy had attached Appendix B: a page of addresses. There were, in all, sixteen country properties which had acted as temporary storage places for the Vincent's collections on their long out-of-town holiday.

First on the list was the Dower House, Hopton Malpractice, Herefordshire.

Chapter Seventeen

Sergeant Storey's patrol was deployed on invasion alert, which is to say it was out harassing civilians.

'I'll need to see your Identity Card, sir,' said the sergeant, heaving his vast chest into its parade ground mode.

'Give over, Robbie. You know me,' snapped Bert Tongue.

'I said, I'll be needing to see . . .'

'Look. For Christ's sake. I've just come from the bloody hospital. At six o'clock this morning I was being dug out of the bloody rubble. I'm not in the mood.'

'I'm sorry, sir. I still have to see your ID. I'm under orders: proof of identity or hand 'em over to the civil authority . . .' Sergeant Storey had had a bad night as well. That pillock Pilgrim had managed to lose an entire field kitchen in the space of twenty minutes. Map reading? He couldn't read his own bleeding horoscope.

'Bollocks,' said Bert. He had left Stella at the hospital where she was waiting for her parents, who were being treated for shock; her father was especially knocked up. She had told Bert that it was nothing to do with the bomb blast; simply the surprise of his proposal of marriage. They had lost their home but they were, at least, alive.

'Smith! Over here – at the double,' roared Sergeant Storey. Private Smith M., who had been tinkering with the chain of his bicycle, came trotting across.

'Sar'nt . . . Oh, hello, Bert,' he said.

'Morning, Michael.' Bert nodded.

'Enough of that!' The sergeant's cheeks and forehead were the colour of boiled beef. 'I want two men over here to hold this man in close arrest. You, Smith, take the unit transport and contact the Civil Authority. That's the constable up there – see – directing the traffic on Wakefield Street. Move it.'

Andrew Moncur

'Funny-looking bike,' said Bert, looking across at the unit transport section. 'Looks like something out of a museum. And what's this . . .'

Private Smith looked sheepish. 'It's the front line warning system,' he said.

'Looks like a bloody old football rattle,' said Bert.

Sergeant Storey let out a primitive, strangled cry. 'Bert Tongue,' he piped. 'Why don't you just fuck off out of here . . .'

* * *

Dorothy Parker telephoned late in the afternoon, which pleased Benbow for at least two reasons. First, he had almost lost hope of hearing from her. Secondly, her call helped him to find his cordless phone. While making the bed he had somehow buried the handset at the foot of his duvet.

'Never mind the lost ceiling. Your mother must have thought I'd lost my marbles,' he told Dorothy when, finally, the bed had stopped ringing and the phone had been retrieved.

'Your message was, well, just a little confused.' From the way her mother had described their conversation, it was clear that Benbow had suffered by some way the worst loss of marbles since the seventh Earl of Elgin's agent visited the Parthenon at Athens with a masonry saw in 1801.

'How did you know it was me that rang up, anyway? I don't think I actually managed to leave my name . . .'

There was a significant moment of silence on the line.

Where could she begin? It might surprise him to learn that relatively few people made phone calls which left a lingering impression – if only an impression – that they had recently been let out of some institution. In everyday life, hardly anybody called up respectable women in order to speak about missing ceilings.

'It could only have been you. I don't imagine there's another person in the country – no, in the entire known world . . .'

'Really?' said George. 'You amaze me.'

And she did, too. He wanted to see her. More than that, he wished she would join him on a tour of country houses.

'Why, exactly?' she asked.

'Because I want the pleasure of your company. Why do you think?'

'I see,' said Dorothy. 'I had somehow got it into my head that the

A Good Looking Man

trip might have something to do with your missing masterpiece in plaster.'

'What on earth gave you that idea?'

* * *

Bert had not felt at all afraid in the shelter, which – when he thought about it later – seemed bewildering. In France, where he had, in reality, never come so close to being buried alive, he had known fear all too well. He had expected almost daily to die.

This time all his attention had been directed towards Stella. He could remember the flood of relief as he reached for and found her. His hands measured the slight width of her back and felt its surprising strength. Why did men, moved to describe women's bodies, tend to draw on the animal kingdom – or, at least, on its more acceptable divisions? Her heart fluttered like a trapped bird's. She was as alert as a startled deer. Well, all right. At times like this you wouldn't want to start comparing a woman with, say, a vegetable – or a fish.

He hadn't felt a moment's doubt that they would be safely dug out. Stella, the woman who had faced a runaway elk, was hardly going to flinch in the face of anything the Luftwaffe could throw at her.

Her mother sobbed a little but then became calm. A Civil Defence unit, working steadily and with not a little courage, had soon reached them.

A little ferret of a man, covered in plaster dust, had stuck his head through the shelter doorway, cheerfully upside down.

'Got a cup of tea, Missus? I'm as dry as a bloody temperance rally.' Stella had picked her way to the door and kissed him, smack between his eyes. Bert had not minded a bit.

'Good luck to you, pal,' said Bert Tongue, as their grimy rescuer and his companions moved on to tackle another skewed heap of rubble and shattered rafters further down the street.

* * *

'I'm a plaster man, myself,' said George. 'There's something about fine plasterwork that simply fascinates me. I think I would like to have been a craftsman working in – oh, the eighteenth century, ideally.'

Dorothy could not help but wonder what damage he might have done to the stately homes of England, given a bucket and spade and half a ton of wet plaster. Anyway, he would probably have been transported as a housebreaker. He had avoided telling her about his chat at the bedside of a naked young woman. The penalty for that in the time of Adam and Nash, it is probably fair to assume, would have involved a certain amount of stringing-up.

They were dining on Sunday night in the sepulchral restaurant of an hotel. It had one conspicuous virtue: it was midway between his flat and her house. It had seemed at first a bad mistake. Only two other tables were occupied in the entire room, which could comfortably seat a hundred and fifty.

'Do you have a reservation, sir?' the waiter had asked. It baffled George when it was assumed that only a man – never the woman at his side – possessed the power of speech.

'No. We were hoping that you might have a spare table,' he said, making a great show of surveying the vast, empty dining room.

'I shall have to check, sir. For how many?'

'There's just forty-seven of us,' said George. 'And, please, could we have a table within easy reach of the lavatories? Most members of our party are, sadly, chronic incontinents.'

'Yes, sir,' the waiter replied solemnly. 'There's a table for two just over here . . . if the young lady would like to step this way.'

The food was, to be fair, better than they had any reason to hope or expect. Even the waiter unbent during their meal, treating them to a sardonic sort of commentary on his working life.

'It's so quiet in here,' said George, 'it almost reminds me of a retreat.'

'What? You mean like Dunkirk?' the waiter asked.

'No, I don't mean that at all.'

'No?' said the waiter. 'Then you obviously haven't seen what's going on in the kitchen.'

Benbow went to refill Dorothy's glass. Their eyes met and held steady for a long minute. George saw then, just for a moment, that it wasn't really a matter of choice at all. When two people were brought together at the right time, at the point of being ready, then there was no choosing to be done.

'You know,' he said. 'You know . . .'

Then, to his dismay, he heard himself adding: 'There's a fabulous house in Northumberland called Wallington. Wonderful ceilings and walls. Winged sphinxes, fruit, garlands of flowers, swags,

A Good Looking Man

swathes, you name it. All finished about 1743. Work of a bloke called Pietro Francini – the Italians were the masters, of course. And do you know how much it cost?'

'I really haven't the remotest . . .'

'Plasterwork: sixty-eight quid and a few shillings. For a masterpiece. I ask you.'

Dorothy straightened her back and looked away from him, casting a glance around the room. She cleared her throat.

'George,' she said at last. 'You're not related, by any chance, are you? To Benbow. Admiral Benbow, I mean. John, wasn't it? I have a feeling he came from Shrewsbury, or somewhere.'

'I don't know. I had an Uncle John. He was in the navy. But I think he ended up running a tobacconist's shop in Cardiff.'

It was a strange thing, but he had been about to tell her – he had felt a real need to do so – about the day his father died. It probably wouldn't have been a good idea anyway, George told himself later.

There was a moment, at the front door of Dorothy's pleasant house, when they might still have stepped across the line that they knew – they both knew – lay just ahead. There was a hum of potential in the night air.

George started to tell her: 'It's as though my life is only now . . .'

And, just then, a sharp pain burned into the back of his leg. 'Jesus!' It came out like a steam train whistle. Dorothy stepped back smartly in alarm.

'Kenneth,' she said, swooping to detach the cat from George's trouser leg.

And the moment was gone, for now. George, waiting on the main road and waving a sheaf of papers like a flag of surrender, as though already resigned to failure in his attempts to hail a cab, wondered whether he had droned on too much about ceilings.

Chapter Eighteen

There was an atmosphere of purposeful disorder in the streets after a night's bombing. People picking their way through broken glass beside shattered buildings were constantly surprised, not only by the immediate scenes of destruction but also by their inability to remember what had gone, blown away, to open up some new and unexpected vista.

It had been entirely natural, once he had cleaned up at his neglected digs, for Bert Tongue to walk to the register office and inquire about arrangements for a wedding. Later he caught a bus out to Cyril Finch's old home to see the poor old boy's widow, Hilda. Bert had to walk the last half-mile. The main road had been blocked; sappers were working to clear an unexploded bomb.

The ruby-red glass was missing from the front door. It had been replaced by a patch of linoleum. Oddly, blast had stripped every tile from the neighbouring house while her roof remained largely intact. A gang of roofers, over from Ireland – the neutral republic, that is – had already started work up aloft.

She had been very kind, although she had to tell him that there was no chance of taking over her home. She had already been in contact with the housing authorities and the property was being requisitioned; a homeless family was due to move in the following Wednesday.

Hilda was glad that Bert had called. There were one or two old things of Cyril's that she would like him to have, since they had been such friends, she said. Anyway, she didn't know what else to do with the stuff now that she was moving to her sister's. It was only a small bungalow.

Then she took him out to the garden shed and showed him a neat line of tea chests standing on bricks.

'What am I supposed to do with five-hundred-odd oiled wool sweaters? White, roll-neck, submariners for the use of?' Bert was walking with Stella that evening, taking her to her grandmother's house where she was staying for the time being. He caught Stella's elbow and swung her to face him. 'I wish we were effin' effin',' he said – and they both laughed.

He had saved the best news for last. It was only as he was leaving Hilda's place that she remembered that there was a house – a really nice house – falling vacant only two streets away. A young widow, said Mrs Finch. It was, she thought, available for rent. Reasonably new, three bedrooms and a decent kitchen.

Within 20 minutes the resourceful Albert Tongue had been round and secured the property.

* * *

'Will you look at that?' spluttered George, gesturing wildly through the Morris Minor's split windscreen. An enormous articulated lorry had cut sharply across their bows into the slow lane of the motorway, very nearly removing their battered front bumper.

Its wall-like rear end displayed, in letters four feet high, the words: 'Old Farmer Shire's Rustic Bake'; then the smaller message: 'The authentic taste of the farmhouse kitchen'. It belched a blue cloud of exhaust fumes.

'I'll bet it comes from some bloody factory in Dagenham or Falkirk or somewhere,' shouted George. His foot slammed down on the accelerator. The Morris wheezed and juddered as the red needle, flickering, crept up to and passed fifty miles-an-hour on the dial. 'Or Barking. Some place like that.'

'What are you doing?' Dorothy looked up from the road atlas. When she had agreed to spend her next weekend on a trip to the country, she had reckoned on at least a pleasant and peaceful journey.

'Just want to see where that great bugger comes from,' yelled George over the rising whine of the engine. The needle was wobbling violently now, showing a speed of anything from fifty-eight to sixty-seven mph.

The Morris was slowly drawing alongside the long vehicle. Dorothy, looking up at the truck's rear wheels, noted that each of them seemed larger than the entire car, which was now bucketing down the central lane.

'Bloody hell, Benbow.'

'It'll have an address on the cab door,' he shouted. Dorothy's

A Good Looking Man

arm shot out, clinging to the dashboard with whitening knuckles. George started to sing. The Italian ace, Dario Frascati, expertly spun the wheel of the eight-litre Maccheroni Mark IV and flashed a dazzling smile at the elegant Contessa, his navigator and engineer for the 24-hour . . .

'Benbow. What's that smell?' There was a sharp odour of hot oil. The steering wheel was bucking in his hands. George was suddenly aware that the image of another huge truck, its headlamps blazing, was filling his rear-view mirror. There was a sound like a ship's fog-horn. That lorry didn't just want the Morris out of its way – it was going to drive clean over it. Well, no going back. The only way out of this was forward. His right foot was flat to the boards, trying to push itself and the pedal clean through the floor. Unaccountably, the windscreen wipers started up.

They were now creeping level with the bakery truck's smoke stack of an exhaust pipe. He could – very nearly – make out the wording on the cab door . . . There was another deep-throated blare from the lorry behind. Christ, it was about six inches off his tail.

'Ah, ha!' George nearly screamed in triumph. 'Unit 14, Airtex Industrial Estate, Biller-bloody-icay, Essex. I told you!' For no very good reason he leant forward and waved two fingers at the driver's door, looming over his nearside wing.

'Please, Benbow. Please let me out . . .'

Oh, God. The Morris was suddenly silent. The windscreen wipers stopped, as they had started, of their own accord. The needles were dropping back to zero. Only the temperature gauge continued to register: maximum – but it had been like that since 1987. The old thing had died. Croaked, under the very wheels of a forty-ton load of Danish bacon hammering up his backside in the hands of a kamikaze with a heavy goods licence.

There was another trumpeting roar from behind, accompanied this time by an appalling squeal of air brakes and the noise of rubber being laid in black ribbons down the motorway. The authentic taste of the farmhouse kitchen came surging by on the inside, the driver signalling vigorously with a single, raised finger.

George allowed the Morris to coast into the inside lane. His face was burning. The bacon truck hurtled through, its driver struggling to bring the monster under control. And up yours, too, thought George.

The car let rip with a monstrous back-fire. It gave a lurch and then the engine spluttered back to life. The windscreen wipers began to plough across the screen again. George hugged the steering wheel. 'Yes!' he whooped. 'We have the bloody technology . . .'

Dorothy, looking every inch the Contessa, folded her arms and stared deliberately out of the passenger side window. George discovered that he could read quite a lot in the back of her head.

* * *

Lieutenant Pilgrim was an exceedingly tall, thin man with lank black hair which he kept at an unsoldierly length; his profile resembled nothing so much as a seagull's. He walked as though bouncing along to the slow beat of an dance band, unheard and unseen by anyone else in the world.

Big Rob Storey had identified him at first sight, from a range of almost five hundred yards, as an officer, a gentleman and a complete prat.

'Good morning, sir,' he had boomed. 'You'll be the new gentleman, taking over from Lieutenant Sparks after his misfortune with the cement mixer.'

'You'll have to excuse me,' said Mr Pilgrim, 'I'm actually on my way to Boots' library for my wife's books.'

'Right-ho, sir. Of course, sir,' bellowed Sergeant Storey at the officer's thin back. Then he added, at lower volume: 'We'll just send a signal to the Boche: Dear Fritz, Regret unable to fight today. Lieutenant Pillock unavailable for hostilities until the new Ivy Compton-Burnett has arrived safely at Boots' circulation library. Fuck me.'

Chapter Nineteen

Stella Hopkins had precious few belongings to move into her new home. She used to say in later life that she had arrived with a pot of jam, a pound of rice and her ration book – and, to be truthful, there was little else. Some sticks of furniture were salvaged from Armoury Road. Bert had some bits and pieces from his digs, where he had lived in a state of guerrilla warfare with his landlord for over eight years. Just habit really, he said. They were able to stock their new house in time with pots and pans and with furniture bearing the government's utility mark.

At first, though, they rattled around in largely empty rooms. Bert had no objection when she suggested that her parents, now homeless, should move in as well. So far as he was concerned, they were his mum and dad, too.

The black out material served as curtains and Bert's newly-inherited tea chests turned out to be surprisingly useful. Upended, covered with an old cloth and set with a bunch of asters in a jam jar, a flimsy wooden box can pass for a table. Stella Tongue, as she became after a brief ceremony in December 1941, had a great gift for brightening up a place.

Mr Hopkins never went into an air raid shelter again. He insisted that if a bomb had his number on it, then he would wait to receive it in his own bed.

He would refuse to budge even when the doodle-bugs were dropping in during 1944. If anything, he seemed less anxious than the other members of the family. Mrs Hopkins suffered from her nerves and would sometimes sit for hours at her bedroom window staring into the street.

Stella and Bert were simply happy, right from the start. They did not mention to anybody the three small boxes that Bert brought home after a long trip to the country, in the Vincent's Austin van, early in 1942. Nor did they discuss the manila envelope that Stella removed from the office and placed for safekeeping in her suitcase, in the cupboard under the stairs.

She did so on 15 November 1942, as church bells pealed in Britain for the first time since 1940, when the threat of invasion was imminent. They were rung, at last, for the desert victory at El Alamein.

The death on that day of Dr Oliver Mackie, director of the Vincent Museum and Art Gallery, passed largely unremarked. He left a widow and three grown-up children. It was decided that a memorial service would be held at some later date.

* * *

George Benbow pulled up by the side of the lane, where a farm track cut through the overgrown hedgerow. A tangle of weeds covered what looked like a pile of rotting planks beside the road.

'My dad was evacuated somewhere round here during the war,' he said, reaching for the coffee flask on the back seat of the Morris Minor. 'Actually, I think it was a touch closer to Hereford – the old man was a bit vague about where, exactly, he'd been. He used to talk of living with a family of complete eccentrics. The farmer was some sort of psychopath. Always on the lookout for small fluffy animals . . .'

'That's nice,' said Dorothy.

'Except that he wanted to blow out their brains.'

'Oh.'

'Don't know why he didn't join the Army and put his tendency to some use. He could have been a commando. Or, better still, a butcher in the Catering Corps.'

The Dower House – or, at least, the hamlet of Hopton Malpractice – was, according to her atlas, about three miles to the west. The road was not dignified with a colour on the map and seemed to bend impossibly, although that could have been the crease where the page slipped into the fold. It was one of Dorothy's firm theories that the geographical location sought was always, without exception, in the fold of the map.

They put away their coffee cups and George, starting up the car, wondered why his father had never wanted to return to his temporary wartime home. You could be happy in a place like this, among the fields and the black polythene bags.

A Good Looking Man

'What on earth are those things?' He pointed at the line of fat, plastic-wrapped bundles, each about the size of his car.

'They use them for making silage, or something. Haven't you noticed? The countryside's full of them,' said Dorothy. 'The British farmer can make a sow's ear out of a silk purse any day of the week.'

Then, to George's total surprise, she put her long arms around his neck and kissed him with great abandon.

The old Morris, springs creaking, trundled into the shadows of the deep lane. About 150 yards on it bounced into the bank, lifting a clump of poppies on its nearside front hub-cap. Then it stopped altogether.

* * *

Private Smith M. was wearing a thick white polo-neck sweater beneath his battledress tunic. Sergeant Storey started to open his mouth, then checked himself. What the hell. It was perishing – and there was more sense in having a sentry improperly dressed but alive than one who was following King's Regulations all the way to the mortuary slab, ready frozen.

'Now, let's have no mickey-taking with these poor unfortunates. They're feeling pretty pissed off, I believe.'

The Home Guard had flung a defensive cordon around the gun battery on the heath. Although quite who should wish to attack it, apart from the outraged fathers of several teenaged girls in a five-mile radius, was not entirely clear. That wasn't really true anyway. The gunners stationed there were always pathetically hard up and they could seldom get out at night, when they were supposed to be banging away at Jerry.

They wore ugly uniforms and brutal haircuts and, having been recruited more or less straight from school, they didn't know much about girls in any case. But it cheered them up to think of themselves as licentious soldiery. The mildest of them could imagine, after a couple of weak beers at the Hare and Harrow, across the way, that he was no end of a dog.

The gloom which had fallen across their miserable battery was, in fact, entirely self-inficted.

'They've only had one confirmed kill in the entire campaign, haven't they?' said Robbie Storey. 'Shame it had to be their own fucking colonel.'

Sadly, this was the case. They had been blazing away for many months, more in hope than realistic expectation. They had claimed a Dornier 217, brought down on allotments a couple of miles away. But the pilot, under interrogation, had insisted that he had merely suffered a fuel pipe blockage and had been forced to ditch. There certainly wasn't a scratch on his fuselage, other than those caused by bean poles and a number of ramshackle sheds which the twin-engined bomber had comprehensively demolished. Credit was denied.

The gun crews drew comfort from the fact that, while they might have thrown several thousand pounds worth of explosives into the air to no great effect, Jerry had – on this occasion – wasted far more in order to destroy an already blighted crop of winter greens and Brussels sprouts.

There had been a number of similar incidents, which did not exactly improve morale.

Anyway, the unfortunate business with their commanding officer had happened the previous night. He had stalked off to the perimeter of their position to observe the pattern of their fire. A dud shell had looped out of a barrel and, skittering off head-over-heels, scored a direct hit.

'Sad sort of way to go, isn't it?' Sergeant Storey was in an unusually chatty mood.

'Oh, I don't know,' said Smith M., reflectively. 'He'll be buried with full military honours, won't he? They'll fire a salvo over his grave . . .'

'Or right into it, knowing the marksmanship of this mob,' said the sergeant. He was already working on a scheme to persuade Lieutenant Pilgrim to patrol the perimeter of the gun site, well within range of their low-flying duds.

'Tell me, bonny lad,' he said. 'Where did you get that bloody hairy great sweater?'

Chapter Twenty

'Hello,' called Dorothy Parker. 'Is there anybody in?'

She had walked round to the back yard of the Dower House after failing to gain any response when she hammered on the front door. George had parked on the gravel drive and was now leaning against the bonnet of the Morris, staring up at the frontage of the house. Splendid, he said to himself. Really splendid.

Hopton Malpractice had turned out to consist of half a street of cottages, three pairs of council houses, an Early English church, a Methodist chapel and a post office and stores. 'Socks,' said a poster displayed in the shop window. 'One of the largest selections in Herefordshire.'

The two elderly ladies in the shop had directed them to the Dower House, whose drive ran for more than a mile through woodland. At intervals of roughly a hundred yards they had been forced to slow down as one suicidal pheasant after another scooted first into, then out of, their path.

'God in heaven. Who are you?' A large, square-cut sort of person had appeared from the corner of the stable block. The brown corduroy trousers, of a generous cut, the Viyella checked shirt and the heavy brown boots were all pretty standard lines for any self-respecting menswear shop in the average English county town.

She also had a short back and sides and an untipped cigarette was screwed into the corner of her mouth. Dorothy couldn't actually see whether it had a filter tip or not. But she just knew, at a glance, that it hadn't.

'If you're some sort of a rep, then it's by appointment only,' the woman snapped. 'If you're anything to do with the church, the Women's Institute or the Boy Scouts' bring-and-buy, you can bugger off. Or the Press. You're not, are you? From the Press?'

Dorothy explained that, no, she wasn't in any way involved in any of these groupings.

'Had some ghastly reporter person round here a couple of weeks ago. Asking impertinent questions about the Master.'

'The Master?' Dorothy wasn't quite following. Was this some kind of religious community, she wondered.

'The MFH,' said the woman, as though dealing with an idiot.

'I'm sorry,' said Dorothy. 'What's the Emmeffage? Is he your leader? Should I be speaking to him?'

'Well, I wouldn't if I were you. That's half the trouble. He's bonked his way round half the bloody county – which is why the johnnies from the papers have been sniffing about. He had to go, of course.'

Dorothy tried to conduct a review of information gathered so far. The bonking Emmeffage, whilst being revered as the Master, was obviously being expelled by the community because he had attracted the attention of the newspapers.

'And has he now gone?' she asked, politely.

'Who? The bloody reporter?'

'No. The Emmeffage?'

'Well, not entirely. You can't get a new Master of Foxhounds overnight, you know. And there's the cubbing, of course.'

'Wolf cubs?' asked Dorothy.

'Look, who the hell are you? And what do you want?'

'I think it might be better if you spoke to my friend. He's waiting round at the front door.'

The atmosphere did not improve entirely when George explained their mission. 'You're looking for a blasted ceiling? What are you? Some sort of plasterer's mate? If you're looking for work you can sling your hook. We can't afford to use half our rooms as it is – and there's no chance of putting 'em in order now.'

George, feeling misunderstood, went back to the beginning again.

'War. The last war? Stuff stored here? Why didn't you say so in the first place?' The woman was now treating him as though he were simple-minded. George did not have the energy to say that he had now, twice, taken her through this preamble. In English society there are those who have always to make an effort to be pleasant and polite, to make themselves acceptable. And there are those who, on the basis of their caste, never remotely consider

A Good Looking Man

the notion. Not once, in an entire lifetime, is it necessary for such people to put themselves out.

'You shouldn't be wasting my time. You should be speaking to my mother.' The woman threw open the front door and then, slamming it shut in their faces, disappeared into the house.

'These devout religious people are sometimes rather tricky to deal with,' said Dorothy. George was momentarily lost for words.

It was a full six minutes later that a tiny flower of a woman, in a straw hat and carrying a shallow basket, appeared from the side of the house. She was, Dorothy guessed, at least eighty-five years old. She smiled at them from under her hat brim. Her eyes were the pale blue of forget-me-nots.

God, thought George, how did she give birth to that cart horse? And, in sympathy, he turned his own smile upon the elderly lady.

'Are you from the museum?' she asked in a faint, twittery voice. 'Have you come to collect your possessions? We've taken good care of them, I can tell you. Such beautiful things.'

Dorothy and George allowed their eyes to meet above the little woman's head. So, here – at the first attempt – they had found part of the Vincent's scattered collection still at large. And after, what, fifty years of peace?

'We won't let them come to any harm, you can be sure.' She smiled again. Her cheeks were like dried rose petals.

'No. We know you won't,' said George, gently.

'If Mr Hitler himself comes up the drive we'll give him what for,' she said. 'We'll call out the Yeomanry. We'll stick him, just like we did at Ypres. Dear boys. Dear, dear boys. Mr Churchill is wrong, you know. Quite wrong. About the Dardanelles . . .'

George placed his hand on her painfully thin forearm. 'We've come about the museum's possessions . . .'

'What possessions? They took them away years ago. A big vulgar man came. Sent him straight to the back door. And then a lot of trucks – all gone. It was the American soldiers to blame, you know.'

'Americans?'

'For the black babies. Young Annie Blunt had one, you know. Just the other week. She was always a flighty piece . . . I couldn't keep her on, of course. No followers.'

Dorothy laid her warm hand in George's as they meandered back down the long drive.

'Well, that leaves just fifteen more places,' she said. The thin sun caught her face and he noticed that her eyes, half-closed, were shaped like almonds.

* * *

If there was one thing in this conflict which reminded Bert Tongue of his own soldiering days, in the Great War, it was the sight of munitions dumps springing up on roadsides in rural areas. They were soon widespread; shells in huge quantities lay in store around the countryside as British industry responded to – and exceeded – the production demands of Mr Churchill's war cabinet.

'If you ask me,' said Bert to Stella, who hadn't asked him anything. 'If you ask me, we're making more of the damned things than we'll ever need in this little war.'

'Oh, yes,' said Stella, brushing her thick, strong hair. They were sitting side by side at the foot of the bed in their new bedroom.

'On the Somme we banged off millions of shells day and night, on and on. This time the factories must be turning out even more but we don't seem to be shooting anybody much. There'll be bloody enormous piles of them left over at the end, just you wait and see.'

And on this point, as with some others, Bert would be proved absolutely right.

* * *

There was a restrained hum of conversation in the tea-shop. It was a long room, more heavily timbered and beamed than any Tudor builder would have believed necessary, or even possible. A few couples, all of pensionable age, were scattered along the twin rows of tables. Their murmurs were punctuated only by the odd scrape of a Windsor dining chair or the clatter of a steam-heated teapot lid being juggled and dropped by scorched fingers.

There was an aroma of toast. Dorothy and George were suddenly alive with healthy, young appetites.

'Hot buttered toast,' said George, his eyes lighting his entire face.

'And poached eggs,' said Dorothy.

'And more buttered toast.'

A Good Looking Man

God, thought George. I want her. I want this woman. Most of all, I want her to want me. Look at her throat and her breasts – and that hair. Think about the skirt, riding up on those beautiful, strong thighs . . .

'I'm so hungry,' said Dorothy. 'I'm as hungry as a woman could be.' Her lips parted. He could see the pale tip of her tongue.

The effect was instantaneous. George felt a stirring of monumental exuberance in his trousers. He was washed with a hot, overwhelming ache of lust. His loins had a life of their own. If loins could paw the ground and trumpet, his would have done so at that moment.

'Come on. Let's go and sit over there,' said Dorothy.

'What?'

'Over there. We can look out of the window while we're waiting for our tea.' She was already on her feet.

'Hold on,' said George. The note of panic should have been audible over seven counties.

It was too late. She had picked up her bag and was already threading her way between the tables.

What to do? He couldn't just sit there like a beached whale. He couldn't immediately get to his feet and follow. Benbow stole a glance down at his lap. Dear God, he moaned to himself. It's all but making a tent out of the tablecloth. There's something architectural and gothic about the structure.

Think of cold, wet days. Think of downpours and drizzle. Think of England, for heaven's sake.

'George?' Dorothy, having reached the window table, was signalling a question the width of the tea room. He was surprised that his raging embarrassment of an erection wasn't visible to her from that range – or, for that matter, to shoppers passing in the street. It was completely beyond his control.

Oh, please. Oh, come on. Come on, he started to plead silently.

Benbow snatched up the menu, a flimsy thing made of pink card. He stood and in one swift movement brought it round in front of himself at waist height, like an apron. Then, doubled over in a strange half-crouch, he headed off towards the distant table.

'Excuse me,' the voice came from somewhere almost level with his left ear. 'Excuse me, young man.'

'What?' George almost jumped backwards.

'The menu. May I?' the elderly little man had the air of one who had spent a long lifetime expecting to be obeyed. The woman on the far side of the table gave George a sharp, appraisive glare over the top of her spectacles.

'Wurr,' said George, trying to move on.

'Thank you,' said the little man, gripping the top edge of the floppy card. 'I'll just take that . . .'

'No,' said George, in an unnaturally loud voice.

'What's he saying, Henry?' snapped the elderly woman.

'He's going to give me the menu, dear,' said her husband, who had turned an angry shade of red.

Dorothy, looking back, could see a short, grey-haired man rising to his feet and apparently fox-trotting for a few paces with Benbow. A chair went over backwards – although she was not aware of any sound. Then the elderly man stepped clear, waving a torn menu card as though in triumph.

Dorothy watched, her eyebrows arched in the Norman style, as Benbow dived and scooped up the fallen chair. He advanced across the room, holding it at waist height.

At last he reached her table in the window and flopped down with exaggerated sighs of relief. George, still trying to compose himself, sat opposite her with the chair legs rising – slightly suggestively, she thought – from his lap.

'There. That wasn't so terribly hard, was it?' said Dorothy. 'Tell me, though. Why the extra chair?'

'I wanted to point out that it has interesting turned legs and, look, it's got bowed stretchers,' murmured George, bouncing the piece of furniture on his knee.

'I see.' She shrugged off her herring-bone jacket, placed her elbows on the table and brought her fingertips together in a decided way. It was clear that the chair was finished as a topic of conversation.

Even so, George told himself, there's hope while you can still find arousal in an English tea-shop.

Chapter Twenty-One

Bert Tongue's van was held up on the Lincoln road. A military policeman in a glistening cape was waving through an apparently endless column of US Army trucks. Now and then a soldier hanging over a tailboard sketched a casual salute as the convoy went grinding by. Bert sat back and lit a cigarette.

'Where are they heading, pal?' he called to the white-helmeted policeman during a brief lull in the noise of engines.

'Berlin, I guess.'

Oh, yes? The cavalry will come over the hill. The cowboys will beat the Indians. And it will all be over by Christmas, thought Bert. Where have I heard that one before? He flicked his cigarette end towards the ditch, then stretched and yawned.

He was only a mile or two short of his destination, a great house in the high Victorian style standing in open country north and east of Lincoln. Even on a fine day it had an air of isolation and coldness. Today, under a leaden sky, the tall buildings looked forbidding.

It had been occupied since the end of the Great War by St Philibert's, a girls' boarding school with one hundred and twenty-nine pupils and eleven teachers, many of them now past the usual retirement age. The house was also serving as a safe haven for a number of possessions dispersed from the Vincent's collection.

The headmistress's study was bathed in a watery light. Bert Tongue's pen nib scratched across the page. A faint cry and the distant shrill of a whistle broke the silence.

'There you are,' he said at last. 'Confirmation that these items, left in your care, have now been properly handed back to the Vincent museum – that's me – to be reassigned to another place of safety. All right?'

The plump, grey woman held the paper close to her face and squinted at it with her right eye.

'So, you're only taking those wee bits and bobs?'
'Yes, Miss Scott. We feel . . .'
'Not the carriages?'
'No. The director believed that they could be allowed to stay at St Philibert's, despite the slightly increased risk.'
'They're extremely inconvenient, you know.'
'Well . . .'
'Having a brougham down there is all very well but the landau – and the Duke's carriage. There really isn't much gymnasium left. I hesitate to say it, but my girls aren't getting a proper programme of dance and exercise.' She started to pace in front of the window.
'I don't suppose your director could be persuaded to leave the Butler collection here and remove the carriages, and the rest of it, for safekeeping elsewhere?' She peered across the room at Bert.
'No. I was rather afraid that might be the case.'
'I'm sorry, but Dr Mackie is quite adamant about this arrangement. It's a matter of priorities, you see. The Butler Bequest is of national significance. We simply can't take any risk, however slight.'
'My dear man, it's only a runway – and it's a good three miles from the school.'
'It's going to be a base for heavy bombers, Miss Scott. There's no question about it, it's a military target. We . . .'
'I have assured our parents that St Philibert's is a safe haven, a place of calm and tranquillity in a dangerous world. I would have hoped that you might have accepted the same assurance.'
'I'm sure that your girls are well out of harm's way,' said Bert, soothingly. 'Now, if you'll let me collect my items. Perhaps, when I get back to the museum, I can persuade them to do something to solve your problem with those old carts – carriages, I mean.'
Miss Scott, leading the way down a corridor that smelled of carbolic soap and chalk dust, stopped abruptly. 'Might I ask where it's going? The Butler collection?'
'I shouldn't tell you this, for reasons of security. But, between the two of us, I'm moving it over to Warwickshire. A place called Maze Hall.'
'No military bases there?'
'Safe as houses,' said Bert.
At that moment a dozen girls, in blue gymslips, erupted from a side passage. They were followed by a harassed-looking young

woman holding a pile of exercise books to her bosom. The girls fell silent as they passed in file.

'One moment, Miss Kennedy,' barked the headmistress. 'One of these girls is wearing perfume! Line them up over there and – and, yes – inspect them.'

Glancing back, Bert could see the teacher bending to sniff the first of the pupils. She seemed to be pink with embarrassment. He was sure he heard a squeal of laughter, instantly suppressed.

Later, as he was about to leave in the loaded van, Miss Scott beckoned him.

'Mr Tongue, will you please give my warm regards to Dr Mackie, your director,' she said.

'I will indeed, Miss Scott.' Some fine day, he thought to himself.

* * *

Dorothy Parker wanted to know whether Benbow had ever met an upper-class person who was in any way gifted as a mimic. 'You hear some Sloaney woman putting on what she thinks is a cockney accent – and it's always, invariably bad. Terribly badly observed,' she said. 'Isn't it?'

'The truth is, I don't know many upper-crust people,' said George. 'Hardly a soul, really. If that.'

'But do you think mimicry is an upper-class idea of fun? Because I don't. Mimicking is the little man's way of getting back at the big and powerful. It's impertinence, isn't it? I'm not sure that the upper classes are interested enough in other people. They don't pay attention; certainly not to the point of being able to imitate anyone with real accuracy.

'That woman at Hopton Malpractice, she was really so rude. It was as though she had never – not once in her life – had to show deference to another soul. You can't imagine somebody like that ever worrying about hurting another person's feelings, or wanting to make them laugh. When she started talking about her master, bonking his way around the hunting set, she didn't seem to see the funny side of it at all . . .'

George watched her from the sides of his eyes. The night had been passed in a restless thrashing of discontent. They had taken separate rooms in a cold and unwelcoming hotel and parted at an early point in the evening when, to Benbow's surprise, she had suddenly announced that it was time for her to make some phone calls. She would then go straight to bed.

Dorothy had stopped at the door. She had turned and, holding her hair back, bent quickly to kiss him. Then she was gone.

If only he had found the right words . . . No, not now. Just pay attention to the road. His lips could still feel the yielding warmth of her mouth.

'That's it. That's it. That was the turning.' Dorothy swivelled in the passenger seat to look back down the road. Her plait now lay across her lips; she chewed it a little while regarding Benbow in a level, steady way.

The ill-proportioned gothic pile, rising from the flat Lincolnshire fields, soon filled the windscreen. 'I always think the whole of this area smells of cabbage,' he said.

'Leave this to me, George.'

The colourful figure approaching on foot in the middle of the drive proved, on closer inspection, to be male. He was wearing a wraparound skirt and a loose shawl; his head was completely cropped but for a scalp lock which dangled over his right ear.

'Excuse me,' she said. 'Is this St Philibert's?'

'This is the Divine Mission for Global Guidance.'

'Oh,' said Dorothy.

'Of the Seventh Coming.'

'Really? We're looking for . . .'

'We are all seekers, sister.'

'Yes. In this case . . .'

'You wish to see the Master?' The red-robed man seemed to genuflect.

'Of foxhounds?' she asked, cautiously.

'This is a place of sanctuary for all living creatures,' he boomed.

'Your Master . . .' Dorothy paused. The man quite definitely bobbed at the knee whenever that word was mentioned. 'Your Master . . .'

'He will grant audience in his private chamber to a noviciate who yearns to know the steps to divine ecstasy.'

'I see . . .'

'And the secret of the seventh coming.'

'Indeed?'

'Do you wish to open yourself to his ministrations? If so, follow me . . .'

'Look. Your Master – I'm sorry to have to ask this but one

hears strange stories about people doing that job. Is he, you know . . .'

'Ask, sister. All questions are but lights to guide us.'

'Right. Does he . . .? That is to say, is he a bit . . . does he bonk a great deal?'

The car finally came to rest beside a spinney about a mile from the old school building. Dorothy was still apologizing.

'I'm sorry. Really, I am. How was I to know that their community is strictly celibate? I've never been called a fornicator and a harlot before. I didn't know anybody actually used those words any more. In fact, I've never heard them mentioned outside the Old Testament. Oh, George. I'm awfully sorry about the dent on your bonnet. It goes surprisingly fast in reverse, doesn't it, for an old car?'

George was desperately pushing aside thoughts of fornication – oh, God, please not now. Had he said the *seventh* coming? Forget it. For goodness' sake, leave it alone . . .

One thing was for sure: they hadn't come this far only to be thrown out on their ears. There had to be another way of approaching the old St Philibert's school.

Chapter Twenty-Two

The voice on the telephone was querulous. 'I am particularly anxious, young lady. Those possessions were in my trust and now I am worried about the propriety of what has . . .'

'Please, Miss Scott. I can assure you that everything is perfectly in order,' said Stella Tongue.

'It's just that the man assured me that he was following the express instructions of Dr Mackie and now . . . and now I find myself reading Dr Mackie's obituary in the *Telegraph*. I immediately felt that there had been some awful mistake.'

'There's no cause for . . .'

'He signed a note of confirmation for me. It's on official notepaper from the museum and art gallery, so I assumed that it was perfectly in order . . .'

'It is, Miss Scott. The collection has now been safely installed in another house in the Midlands. As I say, everything is in order.'

'You are sure, young lady? I would hate to think . . .'

'I'm the director's secretary, Miss Scott. At least, I was secretary to the late Dr Mackie and I'm now holding the fort until his successor is appointed. I can assure you that the gentleman who visited you was following his instructions to the letter.'

The headmistress's sense of relief, and of a difficult duty discharged, came clearly over the telephone line.

'That's all I need to know. Except . . .'

'Yes, Miss Scott?'

'I mentioned to your man that I was a wee bit concerned about the collection of horse-drawn carriages. They are, as you might imagine, something of an inconvenience in a school of this kind. It's a matter of size, you see . . .'

Stella looked at the ceiling. 'Yes, he did mention that, Miss Scott. You have my word that just as soon as the new director is in place, I will draw this problem to his attention.'

'That's good of you. I would be most . . . It's such a help, to know that one's dealing with somebody reliable. Someone really trustworthy . . .'

* * *

George peeked around the end of the kitchen garden wall. Across the broad path, on a strip of lawn, a man in shorts threw himself into the air and brought his tennis racket down in a furious swing. 'Yee-hoo!' he yelled and, losing his footing, crashed on to his bottom. He was wearing white shorts and a red, short-sleeved shirt. He had very whiskery dark legs. He also had a full head of hair.

The ball bounced against the wall and trickled back towards him.

'Ah, hello,' said George, stepping on to the path.

'G'day.' The man, still sitting on his backside, appeared to be scratching his groin. 'Bloody Agassi, eh? Gordon Bennett.'

'Tricky shot . . .' George was relieved to have found somebody so apparently normal. 'Do you, uhmm, live here?'

'S'right. Nearly – what is it? – three years now. Seems longer . . .' He laughed and then coughed. 'We come here first when it was still a bloody school. They was selling up. The place was on its last legs.' He paused and squinted at George. 'You joining up with this mob? You'll need a bloody haircut.'

'No. Not exactly. I was actually just making a few inquiries . . .' George launched into his now familiar explanation. It had never, from the word go, occurred to him that anyone should find it at all bizarre that he was doggedly pursuing a lost ceiling.

'How the hell d'you hump around a bloody ceiling?' The hairy-legged man was back on his feet now. There was a long grass stain on his left buttock.

'In sections, I suppose,' said George. 'It's certainly been done before. There's some particularly fine examples at the Victoria and Albert Museum, including a lovely painted one from David Garrick's London house, in Adelphi Street . . . No, Adelphi Terrace, I think. Late eighteenth century. They've got the whole of his drawing room . . . Sorry. It's a bit of an enthusiasm of mine.'

'No. 'S'interesting,' said the man, twanging his racket against his knee.

'I'm fairly sure this one – which is a lot older, of course, would have been in a series of quite substantial crates. And the fact is, it seems to have gone missing. At some point during the Second World War, I guess. I'm visiting some of the houses where it could have been stored – and where it might just have been left hanging around, so to speak.'

The tennis player looked into the far distance. 'It's not here, I can tell you.'

'Can you be absolutely sure?'

'Abso-bloody-lutely. When we arrived, they'd stripped out everything. There was just a few old desks – and they was busted. And a big steam-heater sort of hotplate thing in the kitchen. That blew up the first time we touched it. Otherwise, nothing. And there's no fancy ceilings here, I can tell you.'

'Well, that's all I need to know,' said George, giving him a generous smile.

'Sure you don't wanna stick around? We could play some tennis . . .'

George shook his head, regretfully. He offered his thanks, waved vaguely and headed for the car, parked just off the back drive by a stand of crooked, ivy-covered trees.

Picking up his tennis ball, the Master of the Divine Mission for Global Guidance (of the Seventh Coming) continued his solitary game.

* * *

'What do we do? I'll tell you exactly what we do. Nothing.' Bert Tongue took his wife's hand and smoothed the pale skin of her wrist.

'We simply have to wait. There's going to be a bit of a fuss when they try to sort out the whole bloody works – but that's all down to your Dr Mackie, isn't it? And poor old Cyril, I suppose. Administrative difficulties in time of crisis. It explains a lot, doesn't it?'

If Stella was worried, she did not show it.

'Then we just sit back until, eventually, we think the time's right. You understand? It could be several years.'

Stella kneaded the small of her back to ease the ache which troubled her most days now.

'And then we'll be modestly rich, won't we? We want our boy to have the best possible start, don't we, eh?'

Mrs Tongue was far from certain that she was going to have the son that he so clearly desired. She had not yet told him so, but she felt a growing conviction that it was going to be a girl. Stella knew that, however things worked out, Bert would be pleased.

'First, though, I've got one more job of work to do – on our own account,' he said.

She looked at him, showing a trace of anxiety for the first time.

'It's nothing, girl. I've just got to arrange a little accident.'

Chapter Twenty-Three

D orothy Parker was apologizing again.
'Please don't,' said George, resting the phone more comfortably against his chin.

'No, really. I am . . .' Her voice seemed disturbingly distant.

'I've just said. You don't need to keep saying you're sorry.'

'I'm sorry I keep apologizing,' said Dorothy.

She had fulfilled her promise and returned to 41 Hayes Avenue, an address which could still make her feel as uncomfortable as any early Christian being taken to the lion show at the Coliseum. This time she was, as a mature adult, approaching by way of the front door and not, as she put it to George, the tradesmen's entrance.

No. On this occasion she was going not only to the correct house but also to the point by the most direct route. It was simply a matter of telling the householder that some items, of purely sentimental value, were believed to have been left in that property many years ago. She was now, on behalf of the family concerned, returning to collect them.

'. . . And can I come in, demolish the fitted carpet and prise up your bedroom floorboards?' said George, at his pre-mission briefing. Dorothy had given him a chilling look.

'I shall just say that I want to make a small inspection, causing no disturbance whatsoever, at a time which is mutually convenient. No climbing through lavatory windows at dead of night and risking twelve years in jail for aggravated burglary, going equipped for crime and possessing an offensive weapon. Namely, an old bicycle lamp. In fact, no fun at all.'

George had agreed to let her try the eminently civilized approach.

'I'm sorry, Benbow,' she said.

'Look, how many more times do I have . . .'

'She was just impossible. She wouldn't even take the front door off its chain. I had to talk to her through this narrow crack – and she was as deaf as a post. Or, at least, she pretended to be.'

Deaf, eh? How interesting.

'She seemed to think I was some sort of social worker. She wouldn't let me explain at all. She kept saying that she was all right now, after the operation. She didn't need any interfering cow – that's what she said – poking about in her house.'

'Did you find out, by the way, what her name is?' he asked.

'It's Mrs Smith. Very original. Her neighbour said that she's in her mid-eighties – and she keeps herself to herself.'

'And does she, uhmm, live on her own?'

'Yes, she does . . .' An awful possibility was starting to dawn. 'Forget it, Benbow.'

'There's something I wanted to know, Dorothy. Are you any good at baking cakes?' George asked.

There was a silence on the line.

'Why?' Her voice was laced with suspicion.

'I've got to cook one. It's something I'm doing for a group of cricket lovers. I hoped you might be willing to lend a hand.'

* * *

On 7 May 1943, Mrs Stella Tongue left her job as secretary to the director of the Vincent Museum and Art Gallery in order to prepare for her first confinement. Since there was no director yet in place – a Dr H.R.K. Hilary had been appointed but he was still, under the terms of his previous contract, at work in Edinburgh – the presentation was made by the Keeper of Local History, Mr Spriggs.

Stella's friends had pooled their clothing coupons to buy her a baby's gown and matinée jacket. Sherry was provided for a small celebration in the vacant office previously occupied by Dr Oliver Mackie. Mrs Tongue had a single glass and barely sipped it.

Her husband, Albert, made a short and witty speech. He was later teased by members of his manual staff who insisted that he hadn't been home frequently enough in the recent past to claim any responsibility for the coming happy event. Remarks were made about the milkman, the welcome guests of the US armed forces and Italian prisoners-of-war. Mr Tongue took all this in good part.

* * *

A Good Looking Man

For the next four days Dorothy Parker was hard at work preparing, among other things, for an important exhibition: Years of Victory, the Home Front. She was concentrating on the selfless labour of the unsung workers – many of them women, of course – who in Britain, alone among the combatant countries, were conscripted and directed to help the war effort. She had found some fascinating pictures of bomb damage, including one showing devastated buildings and what looked like a pantechnicon upended in an enormous crater. She also found time to dig out more material from the archives for George Benbow.

George had to see his publisher to ask for more time to complete what he called his Heritage guide. He visited three more sites and took a large number of photographs which, he realized later, tended to linger on the detail of various plaster mouldings.

Because he was in that part of the country anyway, he took the opportunity to call at Hanbury Park, in Derbyshire, which figured on the Vincent's list of wartime repositories.

He was greeted warmly by a pair of Labrador retrievers, called Nelson and Towser – a name which seemed vaguely familiar, although he could not think why. He was less well received by the owner, a Hugh Spratt-Hanbury, who came close to denying any knowledge of the Second World War, let alone the modest role played in it by his elegant Queen Anne house. He kept George standing outside in the rain.

'Pudding Norton? Never heard of it,' he snapped when George patiently explained the nature of his inquiry. 'Never eaten it, come to that.'

He was the sort of youngish, softish, pear-shaped man who still wore suits of a cloth – brown and yellow check tweed – and of a cut popular in about 1928; he wouldn't dream, thought George, of being seen in his own kitchen without a tie and waiscoat. His shoes looked as though they had been buffed by a soldier-servant. His face was pink and unlined but it already slipped easily into an expression of extreme petulance; his eyes were as cold as a wet fish's. George suspected that he might have a tuck-box somewhere upstairs in his dormitory; there could well have been a matron, and possibly a house master, on the premises to keep him up to the mark.

'It's quite definitely here on the list,' he said. 'This is Hanbury Park, isn't it?'

Spratt-Hanbury looked at him as though he had taken leave

of his senses. He was the sort of English landowner who, on meeting a Bedouin tribesman in the scorching depths of the Qattara Depression, expects him to know that Longbottom Meadow is prone to flooding in winter and Wednesday is early closing day in Hanbury Parva.

'Who, if you don't mind me asking, would have been here during the war?'

'Which war?'

'The last one. You know, 1939 to 1945.'

'We were, of course. And in the Great War – and in the Wars of the Roses, come to that.'

'Yes. But who?'

'The Spratt-Hanburys,' he snorted.

'But which Spratt. Or Hanbury? Or both?'

'What?'

'Oh, never mind.'

George selected a long bamboo cane and swished it experimentally, taking a couple of savage cuts at vacant air. Then he reached out and with the very tip of the cane flicked aside the tail of Spratt-Hanbury's jacket, exposing his ample, tweed-covered buttocks. The bamboo made a fearful whistle as it flashed down, bending with a supple . . .

'My mother was here, naturally. My father was with his regiment.'

'The Barrage Balloon Corps?'

'The 17th–23rd Light Dragoons, actually. Princess Louisa of Battenberg's Own.'

'Really? Whose side were they on?'

'I beg your pardon . . .'

'And is there any chance that anything – the most unlikely sort of crate or box – might have been overlooked and left here after the war? That's all I need to know.' George knew that he would reach out and garrotte the man if he remained here much longer.

'Certainly not. Had any such thing been abandoned here my mother would have seen to it that it was burned.'

And that about captures the attitude of the Spratt-Hanburys towards the creative arts across the ages, George surmised.

'Thank you, Mr Pratt. I can't begin to tell you how helpful you've been.' George made as though to sweep away with great dignity. The effect was slightly spoiled by having first to remove a large, wet dog from the driving seat of his car.

A Good Looking Man

'Good chap,' said Spratt-Hanbury. He was talking to the dog. He shouted at George: 'Careful. He's a valuable animal.'

And a sight more intelligent and sexually alluring than his owner, bellowed George – but only when he was safely out of earshot.

Chapter Twenty-Four

In July 1943, the newly installed director, Dr Hilary, conducted a tour of inspection of his new – and largely empty – fiefdom. He required the presence of his foreman assistant, Mr Tongue, who on arrival in his office gave him a gratifyingly military salute.

'That won't be strictly necessary, Tongue,' he said.

'Sir,' shouted Tongue, just too loudly.

'At ease,' said Dr Hilary. In truth, he rather missed the sort of service courtesies which, but for his chronic asthma, he would have enjoyed as a King's officer. He never doubted that he would have attained senior rank, probably on the General Staff.

He was a stickler. In the Upper Gallery he even spotted the broken pane caused by the incendiary bomb which plunged through the roof lights and gave that postman his finest hour – or, at any rate, his most memorable experience in bed. That, the director told Tongue, must be repaired.

In the basement, he insisted on climbing the sandbag walls and inspecting the hairy mammoth, the carpet weaving frame, a fairground steam organ and other large pieces that Bert had largely, and thankfully, forgotten. He stared at, then ignored, the three-legged, winking elk. Then Dr Hilary took a longer look at the venerable locomotive from the Macclesfield–Warrington line.

'It's in a bad shape,' he told the foreman. 'Signs of severe rusting around the firebox. Pretty poor show.'

'I tried to tell them, sir . . . I'm sorry. It's not my place to pass comment.' Bert Tongue shut his mouth, manfully.

'Come on, Tongue. Spit it out.'

'Sorry, sir. You won't catch me criticizing the academic staff. Not for one moment.'

'Come on, man . . .'

Bert sighed. 'The Keeper of Industrial History was very hard-pressed when we were putting these into mothballs, back in '39.

Anyway, why should he listen to my advice about oiling and greasing? I'm not a university chap. Sorry, sir. As I say, it's not for the likes of me to voice opinions . . .'

The new director merely nodded and moved off to examine the boxed-in fresco upstairs.

'A good man, Tongue,' he confided to his wife that night. 'He was determined – absolutely determined – not to breathe a word of criticism about his superiors. Virtually had to tear every last syllable out of him.'

'Yes, dear,' she said, turning the page of her novel. Dr Hilary paused, with one leg in his pyjamas, one out.

'You know,' he said. 'I like loyalty in my staff – especially loyalty among colleagues.'

* * *

'Has it occurred to you that there might be more to this than mere muddle and incompetence?' asked Dorothy. She was sitting on the very edge of George's sofa. It was the first time that she had visited his flat.

'I'm not the world's greatest housekeeper, but I didn't think the old place was in that much of a mess,' he said.

'The missing things from the collections,' she said, in what he had come to recognize as her keeper's voice.

She had been looking more closely at the pre-war catalogues of the Vincent's possessions and the more recent versions, compiled since 1945. A sort of before-and-after comparison.

Without question, a number of items had disappeared from the records. She handed over the list that she had drawn up.

'These are the ones which I can't trace. That's to say, there's no record of sales, release on loan or disposal by any other means. It's all high value stuff. Look.'

His eye ran down the page: it was mainly silverware, including, he noticed, a tea and coffee service by James Young and Orlando Jackson, hallmarked in London, 1774; also five pieces of jewellery; and, finally, what sounded like a fine clock, in silver, crystal and gilt-brass, dated 1630. Eleven items in all.

'How about this?' said George. 'A silver cup and cover; shaped as a gourd on a twisted trunk; hallmark 1602–1603; from church of St Benet Fink, City of London.'

Good morning, madam. I'm the Rector of St Benet Fink, coupled

A Good Looking Man

with St Agatha's Within the Wardrobe, by which you come to Pudding Lane, and I wish to observe that you're a fruity piece. George, in his mind's eye, advanced a stockinged leg and made a sweeping bow.

'Is there anything else – I mean, bomb damage or anything – which could account for this?' he asked. 'Did one of the galleries get blown to bits before they could move the contents to safety?'

'That's the funny thing. They went through that entire, massive evacuation exercise – and the museum and art gallery escaped without a serious scratch throughout the whole war. They could have left everything there and carried on as normal, although they weren't to know that, of course.

'The only disaster happened at a place called Maze Hall, where there was a fire. The director finally reported on that in 1946, way after the event. The only losses he mentions specifically are a few rather boring old stamps. Postage stamps. Reading between the lines, you can tell that he wasn't much bothered. It would have been a different matter if he had lost his beloved paintings, of course. No mention of silver being melted in the blaze. Or jewellery. You can't burn diamonds anyway, can you?'

George had to admit that he had never tried. But he didn't believe you could.

'Oh, my God,' he said. 'I'm going to burn your supper.'

Dorothy kept talking to his hunched back, visible through the kitchen door. 'You see, I think we ought to consider another possibility, however far-fetched it may seem . . .'

'Do you like your baked potatoes well done?' asked George. 'In the style of . . . well, cannon balls?'

'I mean, Benbow, supposing this was crime? Somebody might have walked off with a very tidy haul. And, if that's the case, they got clean away with it.'

George's head, looking parboiled, appeared round the kitchen doorway.

'Are you saying someone nicked my Jacobean ceiling?'

'Somehow, although you may find this hard to believe, I think not,' Dorothy said. 'It's very difficult, in criminal circles, to get a hot ceiling off your hands.'

The meal was, Dorothy said later, interesting. He had gone to an enormous amount of trouble.

'I just want you to be happy,' he said. And she reached across the table for his hands. She brought them to her face and kissed them. Then, very gently, she led them to her breasts. It was an act of such simple, open desire – so honest and so unexpected – that he went completely still for an unmeasurable moment; he could suddenly hear his blood pulsing loudly.

George, in his urgency, stood up, rocking the table – and a bowl of figs, floating in a syrup of his own invention, tipped into Dorothy's warm and waiting lap.

* * *

Dr Hilary wanted to visit his outstations, as he chose to refer to the country houses whose owners, in some cases with growing impatience, were playing host to the collections in his charge.

Firstly, he wanted to see the pictures. These were, he explained, the very foundations of the temple; the source of the light that was, just as soon as victory was secured, to flood into the lives of the newly liberated generation.

'You mean, like lifting the blackout?'

'That's very good, Tongue. Very good indeed,' said the director, making a mental note to include the line in his next report to the committee. This was to be a seminal work; a charter for the post-war development of the Vincent; his own Beveridge Report, if you like.

Meanwhile, he wanted a tour of inspection. And he wanted Tongue to organize it. 'We'll take my car,' said Dr Hilary. 'You will drive us.'

He had always liked the idea of having a chauffeur and a staff car. He imagined himself touring the front with a couple of cap badges pinned to his beret. Right, you men, gather round. I'm going to explain the plan of campaign, he would say. You may smoke.

'Will that be all, sir?' asked Tongue. 'I should be planning a route.'

'Carry on,' said Dr Hilary. 'As you were. At ease. Stand easy.'

Bert threw him a rattling great salute.

Chapter Twenty-Five

George surfaced with a burning pain in his left hand. He came awake, groaning, with an action replay of the previous evening's events tracking through his head. It hadn't been the pudding mishap, as such, which wrecked the big night. The worst of the mess had been sponged from Dorothy's skirt when George scalded his hand on the boiling kettle. She had dressed the wound and then gone home looking fairly cheerful, all things considered.

The idea of visiting the offices of Luff, Beavis & Cotton plc, the removers, had also taken shape in George's head at some stage during his disturbed and uncomfortable night.

'Luffbeaviscotton-how-may-I-help-you?' sang the telephonist when he rang, just after nine.

'Errh. It's about a ceiling...' George was already kicking himself as he heard the words set off down the line.

'Sea Link? I'll put you through to shipping.'

'No, wait!' It was too late. An electronic travesty of 'Greensleeves' started plonking in his ear.

'Trying to connect you,' chirped the operator.

'Hold on!' screamed George. The ghastly music had returned. He waited for what seemed like an hour and a half.

'Who was it you wanted, caller?'

'Don't go away,' yelled George, seized by a dreadful panic.

'Hello. Hellooo,' said the woman.

'I want to speak to somebody about the war. Don't put me on hold!'

'The war?' She sounded as though he had made an indecent suggestion.

'Yes. The Second World War.'

'What number have you dialled, caller?'

'It's you I want . . .' said George, desperate now to make himself understood.

'I beg your pardon?'

'You moved everything in September 1939, when the Germans invaded Poland . . .'

The line went unmistakably dead.

George circled the area with a growing sense of despair before eventually lighting on a parking space, conservatively estimated to lie a day's march from the removal firm's new headquarters. He locked the car and bent to peer at the parking meter. Then he inserted a coin and looked at the meter again. Quietly but firmly he smacked it around its little head.

The mechanism seemed to be jammed. Benbow had parked on the perimeter of a square. At its centre was a railed-off patch of dusty, urban park, with a pair of tennis courts visible behind a bank of shrubs at the far end. 'Private gardens. Residents of Felton Square only,' read the sign on the gate. George rattled the meter once again, then shrugged and walked off.

Felton? There had been an army officer called Felton who killed the first Duke of Buckingham with a tenpenny knife in — when was it? — about 1620-something-or-other. Hanged at Tyburn for his trouble, the poor sod.

Benbow walked with his hands deep in his pockets. The Toy Town School of late twentieth-century architecture, he thought, when he eventually approached the headquarters of Luff, Beavis & Cotton. The front door was surmounted by a blue triangular pediment resembling a child's building brick.

'How may I help you?' The receptionist gave him a smile of dazzling insincerity. It was rapidly switched off as he explained the nature of his inquiry.

'I'll have to speak to Mr Luff. Please take a seat, sir. Won't keep you a moment.' Her smile flicked on and off again, as though somebody had thrown a switch.

She swivelled her chair away and ducked her head over the phone but he could still hear distinctly: 'There's a loony out here, Peter . . .'

He was in luck. Old Mr William — Mr Beavis, senior, that is — came in only once a week now to help with the books. And today was his day at the office. He had been with the firm at the beginning of the war, before he was called up for service in the

A Good Looking Man

Royal Air Force. Further, he was quite happy to see Mr . . . 'What was the name again, sir?'

'Benbow,' said George, shaking the offered hand firmly.

'Beavis,' replied the tall, elderly man. George guessed that he was aged about seventy. He had fine white hair and a spruce moustache. He led the way to the cramped first-floor office which was set aside for his occasional use; George noticed that he limped badly.

'War wound?' he asked. 'Sorry . . . don't mean to . . .'

'No. Wardrobe,' said the older man. 'Walnut. Twin mirrors. Fell on me from a first-floor landing. Broken in three places. The leg, that is. Wardrobe was perfectly all right. Laid up for nearly four months. Still, if you haven't got a sense of humour you shouldn't be in the business, I always say.'

George started from the beginning again: the 1939 evacuation of the Vincent's collections; the dispersal to country houses; the part played in this exercise by Luff, Beavis & Cotton; the indications of confusion; the missing pieces. 'And, above all, I wanted to know whether you had any records – especially any relating to a Jacobean ceiling . . .'

'Remember it well,' said Mr Beavis. George looked at him, eagerly.

'Not the ceiling, I'm afraid. The operation as a whole. What a palaver. Made bombing Hamburg seem like a doddle in comparison. Bit of a balls, if you understand me. I can remember being chased down the drive of some house – where was it? Derbyshire? Nottingham? Somewhere like that. Dreadful woman. Livid about getting the wrong load of goods. Canoes from the Cannibal Islands or some such nonsense.

'We took crates and crates of stuff. It was non-stop for the best part of three weeks. I seem to recall there was a bit of a barney about the destruction of the watchman's box at the Vincent. They claimed we'd dropped some bloody stuffed animal on it from a great height. Rubbish, of course. Their porters were trying to shift the blame after having a prang. A ceiling, eh?'

'Yes. It would have been crated in sections, I expect,' said George, trying to remain hopeful.

'Well, it could have been amongst the rubbish – sorry, the items – we moved. Tons of it. We didn't know what half the stuff was. And, between ourselves, I don't think the museum knew either. The organization was a bit, well, haywire.'

He offered his packet of Silk Cut and then lit up, taking an enormous drag.

'What about records? Did the company keep any documentation from that period – anything that might give us a clue?'

'We did indeed. Unfortunately Jerry did for the whole damned works in January '43. Daylight raid. Smashed up the old depot and the trucks. Paperwork, accounts, everything scattered half-way to kingdom come, naturally. Course, I was in the forces by then – doing much the same thing to their removers and storers, I dare say.'

George, feeling his eyes begin to smart from the blue haze filling the room, tried his last shot: 'And afterwards? When they reassembled the collections. Would you have any record of the items you picked up?'

'Didn't get the job, I'm afraid. My father had been pretty close to the old director – same lodge, you understand – but he was gone by then. The new chap gave the job to . . . who was it? Yes, father went on about it for months. Crammond and Dyer.'

'Would they be . . .'

'God, no. Went bust about 1959. We had quite a party that night.'

He limped to the door with George. 'There was a chap at the museum, you know. He had more sense than the lot of them put together. Name of Tongue, if the old memory serves. Mainly in cheek, I recall.' He shook Benbow's hand again.

'Take my advice. You should try to find him. Assuming he's still alive, of course – which, come to think about it, isn't very likely.' And he roared with laughter.

The parking penalty ticket had been taped to the windscreen of the old Morris. Benbow swore in a low, moanful way as he tore it free and attempted to rip his way into the enveloping plastic bag. His scalded hand was aching. He was hungry.

It was at this point that he noticed the flat tyre. He looked at the sky and took several deep breaths. He was visibly making an effort to bring himself under control. At last his shoulders relaxed and he exhaled evenly, calmly. There was a moment of complete peace.

Then he kicked the rear wheel violently and pounded on the roof of the car. The hub cap bounced noisily into the gutter.

George opened the car boot and started to heave the contents on to the pavement. A pine chest filled with magazines was lifted

A Good Looking Man

out. Two pairs of boots, a bucket and a terracotta flower pot were placed on the lid. He propped a pile of square sign boards against the railings of the Felton Square private gardens. A bundle of tools wrapped in an old towel was laid on the kerb.

Finally he pulled out the spare tyre and the jack. George, kneeling at the roadside, worked quickly and angrily to change the wheel. The heap of goods from the pavement almost flew back into the boot. George drove away without looking back.

He did not notice the single sign board he had left leaning against the garden fence. He didn't see the two young women, each with a pushchair, who next approached the spot and stopped to read the sign. He didn't see them exchange a few words and then carefully move the board to a more prominent position right beside the garden gate.

The women then turned away and started to push their children towards another playground a block away.

By then George was too far away to see the square itself or the gardens. He would never miss the sign board.

'Little terns nesting. Keep away!' it said. 'Please keep well away from enclosure. Keep your dog on a lead. Do not disturb nesting birds.

'The little tern, smallest and rarest of our British terns, has become even rarer in recent years. The sand and shingle beaches on which it nests are visited by many more people and if the birds are disturbed they may desert. The nests themselves are very inconspicuous and it is all too easy accidentally to step on them.

'Disturbance of little terns is an offence under the Wildlife and Countryside Act of 1981.'

Chapter Twenty-Six

Dr Hilary, director of the Vincent, was sitting in the back seat of his Humber, surveying the countryside with a great feeling of wellbeing. It was a time for looking forward, for rebuilding and shaping a better world; a world in which . . .

'Thank God they've started putting back the road signs,' said Bert Tongue, without turning his head. 'It was a proper game before, sir. I remember stopping one place – last year sometime – completely lost. And do you know what?'

There was silence from the back seat.

'They'd only gone and removed the village name from the war memorial, hadn't they? Chipped it off the stone. To the glory of God and in memory of the men of Blank who'd given their lives for King and country. Worried about Jerry dropping in and seizing the bus shelter and Scout hut, I suppose. Still, they'll have to get the stonemasons back after this little lot, anyway. A few additions, I mean.'

A time to replace the signposts, guiding the feet of a new generation to the broad uplands of knowledge and fulfilment, thought Dr Hilary. Chipping away at the old stone walls standing between the working man and infinite possibilities for self-improvement. The state as enabler . . .

'Goes well, doesn't it, sir? Got a bit of horsepower under the old bonnet. After the war we'll all be wanting motors, won't we? They'll be queueing up. Everyone'll want to be taking the kids to the seaside – the old funfair, the dodgems . . . bit of the other down in Brighton.'

Dr Hilary glared at the back of his chauffeur's neck. 'I trust that the people will have wider horizons than that, Tongue,' he said, stiffly.

'You mean abroad, sir? Hardly seems possible, does it?'

The Humber rolled on through the high hills of north Staffordshire.

* * *

Detection? Detective work? The great detective, as he (it was usually a man) figured in so much crime fiction – and in the minds of some police officers in real life – was always something of a joke. Anyway, that was her opinion, for what it was worth, said Dorothy Parker.

This time she was driving them into the country in her smooth white Audi. The contrast with Benbow's veteran motor was extreme.

'All that scientific police work, from Sherlock Holmes onwards, makes me laugh,' she said. 'Ha, ha.'

'You have an extremely infectious laugh,' said George Benbow, speaking in a tone of unrelieved misery. He turned to face her with an expression of gravity so profound that it would have brought tears to the eyes of an undertaker's hardened mute. 'I only said this search for the ceiling was like a detecti . . .'

'It's such a good example of the way things work,' said Dorothy. 'For hundreds of years the domestic servants, the parlour maids, must have known precisely who was doing what. And with what. And to whom. They would have seen all the signs.

'You can't hide much from the person who makes the bed. She notices the marks on the sheets, doesn't she? When you rely on other people – servants, launderers – to remove the bloodstains from the carpet, it's pretty difficult to cover things up, isn't it?

'But, of course, nobody thinks anything of it until some terribly important man comes along and points out what the parlour maid has known all along. Then it becomes a science. Ha, bloody ha.'

George gave her a smile calculated to warm the bluest extremities of Scott of the Antarctic.

'That's a condescending smile,' she said. 'It's the most condescending bloody smile I've seen for some years.'

'Drive on,' said George. 'This is no time for idle talk. Don't you know I'm looking for a ceiling?'

It was one of those Welsh sheep dogs, black and white and tireless, which win all the trophies in obedience trials. And it was showing George its teeth.

'Good girl,' he said. 'What a good dog.'

'Hhuung,' said the dog, somewhere deep in her throat.

George noticed that she had one pale blue eye, one yellowy brown. Now she was revealing her back molars, too.

A Good Looking Man

'I'm sure she only wants to play,' George called back to the car.

'Yes, but what? Hospitals? Doctors and nurses? It's probably rabid.' Dorothy was very definitely sitting tight.

George made as though to open the farm gate. The dog danced in, snapped at his trouser leg and then sprang back. She dropped to her stomach, watching for the first hint of movement.

'Tore my bloody trousers. Did you see that?' his voice rose in protest.

Dorothy shut the car door. 'Tell it you're an important detective,' she called through a crack of window.

George stood very still. He suddenly knew what it felt like to be an old ewe.

The gate bore a mud-spattered sign: Castle Farm, Collingbrook Estate. Another was visible, lying askew in the hedge. It was resting on a rusting coil of barbed wire, tangled with stinging nettles and brambles. 'No trespassers. No public right of way,' it read. There were several barbed strands stapled to the top of the gate.

'This is really stupid,' shouted George, still playing statues. There seemed to be no way either to advance or retreat. 'I'm sure this isn't even the main gate. There must be a proper entrance somewhere . . .'

For a moment he thought he was hearing the dog's growl again. Then he realized it was the sound of a diesel engine. A Land Rover came surging over the brow of the rutted track. It braked in a flurry of mud clods and slewed to a halt on the far side of the gate.

'Could you call off your dog?' George tried to keep his voice level and calm.

'Errh?'

'Your dog. She seems a bit aggressive.'

'Doing 'er job,' said the man, who had come sloshing round the side of the vehicle and was now fiddling with the chain slung around the gate-post. He was wearing a green waterproof coat, blackened with age, a camouflaged hat and wellington boots. He was in his mid-fifties and bulky.

'Is this the Collingbrook Estate?'

The farm-worker, or whatever he was, gave George a long stare from beneath his hat brim. 'Can you read?'

'I'm looking for the house which was used as a store for valuable items during the war, up until 1945,' George knew he was talking too quickly.

The farm-worker didn't say a word.

'Is this the place?'

The man swung open the gate, narrowly missing the Land Rover's wing. The driver had judged the distance perfectly.

'You see, I'm looking for something which may have been left behind accidentally . . .'

The Land Rover pulled out of the gateway. George noticed, for the first time, that there was a teenaged girl at the wheel. The farm-worker secured the gate and climbed back into the passenger side. 'Hupp,' he called – and the dog vaulted into the open back.

'I just want to ask a few simple questions,' said George, approaching the vehicle. He jumped back as the driver hit the accelerator and, with a roar, spun on to the road, heading towards Halfpenny Wick and Evesham.

'Do you know what that man said to me?' George was pale with anger when he returned to the Audi. 'He said I could fuck off – and next time they'd run me over and . . .'

'And?'

'And feed me to the chickens.'

Chapter Twenty-Seven

The first three properties that Dr Hilary visited were repositories for the collections that he valued most highly: the pictures which had sovereign place in his plans for the post-war revival of the Vincent.

He spent hours examining each piece with minute care. In every case, the householders who had granted space to these treasured possessions joined the director at the beginning of his round but soon tired of the slow pace of his meticulous inspection.

After at most an hour they found some pressing need to be elsewhere, performing other duties.

Bert Tongue grew bored as well but he had nowhere else to go. He had to lift each painting from its storage rack and adjust the lighting to Dr Hilary's instructions. The director was totally absorbed.

'Everything seems to be in tip-top condition,' he announced at last. 'Considering the circumstances – and the state of some of these places – we've been remarkably fortunate.'

And so had the householders, thought Bert. Quite early on, word had got about that those offering safe custody for works of art could obtain help with the expense of heating their homes. Some of the bigger country houses probably hadn't been kept at such an even, comfortable temperature for years, if ever.

Dr Hilary made a great fuss of the hosts, thanking them profusely for their work, as he put it, of national importance. One elderly woman broke down and wept.

'You'd have thought it was King George himself come to dish out the decorations,' Bert told Stella the next day. Her term was now complete and all her attention seemed to be turned inward.

'Next Monday we're off to Maze Hall,' Bert told her. 'I don't imagine he'll spend so much time there.'

She did not even look up from her knitting.

* * *

Andrew Moncur

That night George Benbow and Dorothy Parker stayed in an ancient hotel in the countryside just outside Worcester. They booked separate, single rooms. Dorothy, apologizing for making a fuss, told George that she had to telephone her neighbour. She wanted to be assured that Kenneth was safe indoors for the night. She had also promised to speak to her mother.

George said that he would have been surprised if she hadn't checked up on the cat. He would have thought something was wrong. Was it wise, though, to attempt to deal with her mother on the phone? He had thought of writing to the newspapers on this topic.

'She was out,' Dorothy explained later. 'Odd, really. You know she's heavily involved with her conservation group? Well, she is. My father was just telling me they're helping to protect a most unusual nesting site. They say it's under threat.'

George went to fetch her a gin in a tall glass. He had a broad back, she noticed. And he made the barman laugh.

'Have you ever heard of little terns nesting in a town-centre childrens' playground?' she asked, frowning, when he was seated beside her again. 'No, nor have I.'

They dined quietly in a room lit by a crackling log fire. A clock ticked solemnly. There were few guests. The Young Farmers were meeting in the public bar but their cheerful noise barely penetrated the dining room. It was raining heavily and a wind stirred the great oaks. Inside, they felt warm and wonderfully protected.

'Well,' said George, setting aside his coffee cup. 'I suppose we should be getting to bed. I've got a pair of trousers to mend.'

'Yes,' said Dorothy, looking at his hands. 'We've got to make an early start.'

They climbed the stairs together and walked side by side to the door of Dorothy's room. The polished floor seemed to dip just there. An eccentric chest of drawers stood on the far side of the passage. There was a scent of beeswax and wood smoke. Another clock ticked.

'So . . . goodnight,' said George. She bobbed her head and gave him a swift kiss. Then her door was closed.

George grimaced at the yellowed ceiling. He couldn't even handle a female sheepdog, he thought bitterly. Why could he never, never, make the right move at the right time? It should be so simple. He should be able to reach out. He ought to be

A Good Looking Man

able to tell her. When he said goodnight he didn't mean, well, goodnight . . .

He tapped on the door.

'Yes?'

He could hear his own pulse.

'I've come to brush your hair,' George said. He was surprised that his words emerged with such clarity.

'Come in, then.'

The brass doorknob spun uselessly in his hand. At last the heavy door swung open. The room was warm and still.

She was sitting in the low light cast by a small lamp on the chest of drawers. Her face, reflected in the mirror, was lost in shadow.

'Lock the door.'

She was wearing a white, silky chemise. George stood behind her and reached over her right shoulder. He began to draw the brush through her hair, working from the sides of her head, behind her ears and in steady, deliberate sweeps down over her shoulders, the full length of the cascade of hair.

Dorothy began to sway back, following the rhythm of his gentle but firm strokes. Her chin rose and her long, strong neck caught the light. Her hair was unbelievably sweet smelling.

George dropped the brush and, reaching down, slipped the narrow straps from her shoulders. His hands cupped her breasts.

'Come, now.'

She stood and turned towards Benbow and the narrow bed. She was so tall. So slender. So fair. And she was so naked.

For a moment he simply looked at this beautiful, tall woman. She was lovely. Her face held him. He folded her in his arms, then allowed his hands to sweep over her hips. Her skin was like warm silk. She stirred against him, a slow series of little nudging bumps. A murmur – an urgent exhalation – was whispered in his ear. Then another.

'Oh, God. Benbow,' she said in a low sigh. 'Oh, God . . .'

'Yes?' His voice was hoarse. His whole body was suddenly trembling.

'It's nothing,' murmured Dorothy. 'I just trod on the bloody hairbrush.'

Then she drew him to her in an embrace of astonishing warmth.

Chapter Twenty-Eight

On the night of Saturday, 18 September 1943, fire broke out in the library of Maze Hall, near Kenilworth, in Warwickshire, the home of Sir Richard Trembath and his wife, Amelia.

Sir Richard was chairman of Farmers' Shires Bakery Limited, a company formed in 1927. It was based, strategically, at Billericay, close to the sprawl of London, and made steam-baked bread on mass production lines. It was hugely profitable. Lady Trembath was involved with the Girl Guide movement, the Women's League of Health and Beauty and the Conservative Party.

The fire spread to the dining room and the conservatory before the alarm was raised by Sir Richard's butler, Stone, who smelled smoke as he was reading in bed. He had reached the book of the prophet Isaiah, chapter 43, verse 2: 'When thou passest through the waters, I will be with thee; and through the rivers, they shall not overflow thee: when thou walkest through the fire, thou shalt not be burned; neither shall the flame kindle upon thee . . .'

Sniff, sniff. His elderly legs flew downstairs. He set to work with a stirrup pump while, at the same time, crying in a thin voice: 'Fire! Fire!'

Mrs Compton, the housekeeper, soon arrived on the scene. She burst into Lady Trembath's bedroom, where she was surprised to catch a glimpse of the portly Sir Richard dressed in a low-cut satin ballgown. It was pale pink. Lady Trembath laid aside something resembling a length of rubber hosepipe and, very calmly, told Mrs Compton to assemble the staff in the front quadrangle. This order was promptly carried out.

Meanwhile, Stone made a valiant attempt to enter the library, which contained numerous unremarkable volumes of Sir Richard's. It also, however, provided a temporary home for a variety of items from the Vincent Museum and Art Gallery. These included a number of early books and illuminated manuscripts; some exquisite embroidery panels and wall-hangings; several rich military sashes of the Civil War period; and the A.N. Butler Bequest, a remarkable collection of British, Dominion and Colonial stamps, recently transferred to Maze Hall for safekeeping.

He succeeded in salvaging a dozen bound volumes of the *Sphere* magazine, a cushion cover made by Lady Trembath's mother, a half century of editions of *Wisden* cricketers' almanack and three postage stamp albums. These, sadly, contained some of Butler's more commonplace specimens and first-day covers.

Poor Stone suffered burns to the hands and feet. For the rest of his days he remained a devout member of the Methodist congregation, his religious convictions only strengthened by this great trial of faith.

Just as soon as the telephone line had been restored the following afternoon, Sir Richard attempted to contact the Vincent to report the losses. It being a Sunday, he was unsuccessful.

At 4.30am that day, 19 September 1943, Mrs Stella Tongue was safely delivered of her firstborn child. Bert Tongue, in the manner of fathers at that time, was nowhere to be seen. Stella gave birth, relatively easily, to an 8lb 9oz boy, Roger Albert. It was some months before she realized that his initials were a little unfortunate. But by then she loved him so much it did not seem to matter.

* * *

Dorothy and George lay together for a long time as the sun rose and slowly flooded the room with light. George eased his arm from beneath her head and tiptoed to the window. The distant Malvern Hills, shadowed fleetingly by passing clouds, dominated the skyline.

They made love again. Afterwards they told one another how they had known, right from the start, that this was bound to be; it was right; it was the best thing, ever, to have happened.

'I was just waiting to see whether the stairs would collapse or anyone would throw a bowl of blancmange all over me,' she said. Then she lifted her arms to him.

Later they measured their bodies against each other and laughed a great deal. She was a good three inches taller; his hands and feet were bigger; she was amazingly longer from hip to knee. She was so much rounder and softer, especially here.

A Good Looking Man

Later they were ravenous. They wolfed breakfast. Then Dorothy, in what was a remarkable act of generosity, found a needle and thread and patched his trouser leg. For as long as she could remember she had loathed sewing. George phoned her neighbour and, after some initial confusion, confirmed that Kenneth was well and out patrolling the neighbourhood.

That morning they were to drive across to Warwickshire to visit the next property on their list: Maze Hall.

The remaining furniture from the dining room was spread across the lawn when Dr Hilary and his driver, Tongue, pulled on to the gravel forecourt. Smoke had blackened the walls above the library windows; the glass in the conservatory was cracked and stained. Water was still lying in the entrance hall. There was a dreadful acrid smell. It reminded Bert of the incinerator in the back yard at the Vincent where, in the old days, they had disposed of the rubbish left by visitors and school parties with packed lunches.

The director and his foreman had been in high spirits during the morning's drive. Dr Hilary had congratulated Tongue warmly on the birth of his son and promised a celebratory drink at some stage on the return journey. Bert had come the old soldier, spinning yarns about his army days, which the director seemed to enjoy.

'It's good to keep in with the chaps,' Dr Hilary had told his wife. 'When this war's over we are going to have to work together to win the peace.' She had given him a silent, appraising look before turning back to the crossword.

Dr Hilary, arriving at Maze Hall, was stunned. He walked to the front door as though in shock, making little bleating noises. Bert leant against the back of the car and lit a cigarette.

Lady Trembath swept from the house, taking Dr Hilary by the arm. 'There has been a terrible fire. But we must be thankful. It could have been a great deal worse . . .' Bert lost the rest of her words as she propelled the still-dazed little man towards the tack room, where the remnants of his possessions had been laid out to dry.

Bert began to whistle a cheerful tune. He strolled round to the kitchen entrance, where he found Mrs Compton drinking tea with the cook and the daily woman, taking a break from the salvage operation. They cheered up no end when Bert told them his good news. Mrs Compton insisted on finding the key to Mr Stone's pantry and bringing a bottle of Sir Richard's light ale. She poured it expertly.

'They think it was caused by a coal from the library fire,' she said. 'Poor Mr Stone was ever so brave – he's nearly sixty-nine, you know. Has trouble with his chest at the best of times. He saved the household, really, which is what he would have wished.'

'He's not badly hurt, is he?' Bert Tongue's manner was unusually serious.

'Ned will be all right, bless him,' said Mrs Compton. She was pleased, and a little touched, to see that Mr Tongue was so relieved. 'Here. Have another beer – to wet the baby's head. How much did you say he weighed?'

Dr Hilary was still looking shell-shocked when he returned to the Humber. They had driven four or five miles before he spoke.

'Thank God it wasn't any of the pictures. Think, man . . . it could have been a disaster.'

'Quite right, sir.' Bert Tongue smiled to himself – well, he had cause to be happy, hadn't he? – and drove on.

George turned another page of the scrapbook. The *Leamington Morning News* had carried a full page report about the 1943 Maze Hall fire, including pictures of the damaged wing and of Mr Nedabiah Stone, the heroic butler. You could see, in fuzzy black and white, that his hands were bandaged extravagantly. He was photographed sitting, very stiffly, in a wheelchair.

The report was vague about the extent of the damage. It merely said that 'certain works of art and objects of historic value were believed lost or damaged in the fire'. They were understood to include 'Sir Richard's valuable George III commonde'.

'What's a commonde?' he asked, turning his smile, in its most brilliant form, on Mrs Trembath, sitting on the far side of the fireplace.

George's mind was filled with the image of another woman. He was happy. He could feel it, right there, deep in the pit of his stomach. He didn't know when he had ever felt so protectively committed to another person.

'You'll see that my mother-in-law added a note there. At the foot of the page.' The middle-aged woman was dressed as she must have been for the past thirty-odd years, since she was first allowed to go shopping by herself in Sloane Street. Her hair, greying now, was still swept away from her face and held back by a girlish

A Good Looking Man

band. Her ankles were slim in dark green tights and her shoes were neatly buckled. She could well have afforded to dress more extravagantly. Her husband, through his holdings in the food and brewing industries, was a millionaire many times over.

'Yes, I see . . .' The hand-written lines explained that the fire had damaged books, manuscripts, items of needlework and a number of postage stamps stored at Maze Hall by the Vincent Museum and Art Gallery. Some of these had been salvaged but the majority had been destroyed. An inspection had been carried out, two days after the event, by . . .

'. . . by Dr Hilary, the director, accompanied by his foreman, Mr Tongue,' George read out loud. So, Tongue again. He was right in the middle of all this, wasn't he?

'More coffee?' asked Mrs Trembath.

'Thank you,' said George, passing his cup. 'There doesn't seem to be any mention here of a Jacobean ceiling . . .'

'My mother-in-law was always meticulous. Had there been anything of the sort stored at Maze Hall, she would have noted it. You can be sure of that. I only wish I could be so thorough.'

George was suddenly anxious to go. There was nothing more to be learned here. More importantly, he had left Dorothy at the parish church. She had wanted to tour the graveyard and examine names on memorial stones. Sometimes, he had told her, you are a very curious woman.

Now he wanted more than anything to be with her. Mrs Trembath was politeness itself as he thanked her and climbed into the car. She did not once raise the matter which had been troubling her throughout: why was the jagged tear in his grey trouser leg mended with pink thread?

He found Dorothy in the north aisle, peering at a marble slab set high on the wall. It bore, lettered in gold, the words: 'Sir Richard Trembath KBE, 1885–1973. Husband of Amelia; father of Rupert. "Give us this day our daily bread".'

'Why on earth did they choose that?' asked Dorothy, snaking her arm under his. 'I'll have something much more exciting put up for you. But not just yet.'

'Forgive us our trespasses,' said George, 'sounds appropriate.'

Chapter Twenty-Nine

Albert Tongue, in extravagant mood, bought drinks for his friends at the Duke of Wellington.

'Do you have any more of those sweaters? The white ones?' asked Smith M. 'Bloke I know in the market says he could shift a couple or three dozen. Say eight pounds for . . . wonderful weather we're having for the time of day, isn't it . . .'

'Ah, Robbie,' said Bert, playing the welcoming host. 'What's yours? A pint or something short?'

Sergeant Storey eased his enormous frame on to a bar stool. 'Yes, please,' he said, clapping the shoulder of Roger Albert Tongue's proud father. Bert, after a fractional pause, ordered both.

'Congratulations, bonny lad.' The sergeant tipped back his great head and in seconds emerged, beaming, with the pint glass two-thirds empty. He reached for his whisky.

'You were saying . . .' Sergeant Storey turned his gaze on a blank-faced Smith M.

'Me?'

'Something about eight pounds?'

'Eight pounds nine ounces,' said Bert. 'Roger Albert we're calling him.'

'He's a corker,' said Smith M.

* * *

The telephone rang on three separate occasions that evening, back at Dorothy's house. It was only possible, for one reason or another, to answer the last of these calls.

She went out to deal with it. George idly picked up the novel from her bedside table. 'Cassandra is an Oxford don,' he read from the dust-jacket. 'Turmoil of emotions . . . stunning parable of our time . . .' Groaning, he let it drop.

'It's for you,' called Dorothy, waving the phone.
'Benbow,' said George, puzzled.
'Beavis,' said a familiar voice.
'Hello. How did you find me here?'
'This is the number you gave me,' said Mr Beavis, senior. God, thought George, I must be obsessed with this woman.
'It's about your ceiling. I've been thinking . . .'
'I'm sorry,' said George. 'I was miles away. The ceiling?'
'Yes. You were saying it was probably crated in sections. Fairly weighty stuff?'
'That's right,' said George, now alert.
'Well, it suddenly came back to me. We had a bit of a hitch with one consignment – I remember my old man damned nearly blew a fuse. Had to find some heavy lifting gear to get one of the trucks back on the road . . . and that wasn't easy at the time, I can tell you. They'd managed to get bogged down in some sort of farmer's field in the back of beyond. I was putting two and two together. Came up with five.'
'Mr Beavis . . .'
'Yes?'
'Mr Beavis. Do you recall where, exactly, this happened?' George hardly dared to draw breath.
'No. 'Fraid not.'
'Oh.' George closed his eyes.
'Not exactly.'
'Oh?'
'Memory's not what it was back in . . . back in whenever it was.'
'But do you have some rough idea?' asked George.
'Well, very rough. It was some castle or other, somewhere in the Vale of Evesham. I'm sure about that bit because we found a heavy towing truck at a place in Pershore . . .'
'Collingbrook?'
'Sorry. Don't recall the name of the firm. But they'd be in Yellow Pages. Always assuming they're still in business.'
'No, the Collingbrook Estate. That must be it. The Vincent didn't place possessions anywhere else in that area . . .'
'I just hope that's some use,' said Mr Beavis, making his goodbyes. 'Roger dodger. Wilco. Over and out. And all that sort of bollocks. Goodnight.'
'Thank you. Thank you . . .' George dropped the phone on to its rest and turned and swept Dorothy into his arms.

A Good Looking Man

'I would like to tell you,' he said a little later. 'I would like to tell you about the day my father died.'
'Come to bed,' said Dorothy. 'Tell me there.'

* * *

Wally Benbow enjoyed a charmed life in many ways. He may have fallen off ladders and flown over the handlebars of his bicycle – three or four times, actually – and run himself over with his own lawn-mower, but he also had the good fortune to fall in love at first sight with a beautiful and passionate woman. At the time he was a National Service infantryman, aged nineteen; Joan Bates was five years younger and – as he never tired of recalling – she was wearing a pair of dark blue games knickers.

Their paths crossed because Wally, having missed a bus, settled to smoke a cigarette in the corner of a convenient field. It was only when he woke up an hour later, lying in the long grass, that he discovered it was a school sports ground. He found Joan sitting about eight feet away, avoiding her third form's session in the long jump pit.

Wally asked her to meet him after school for a cup of tea and a rock cake. He found her astonishingly mature for her age. She was already forthright in her opinions. They decided within a matter or days that they would, sooner or later, be married. In the event they had to wait six years.

Their wedding took place in Coronation year, 1953. Within thirteen months their first child, a girl, Heather, was born. They would have to wait another fifteen years before their son, George Benbow, arrived in the world to be greeted with all round exclamations of pleasure and surprise.

By that time Wally Benbow was working on his own account as a general builder, employing three men. It was a busy time and he was moderately prosperous. He had one particularly profitable contract: replacing with ready-made, double-glazed frames the windows in two large estates of council houses and flats.

He was a kind and emotional man, easily moved to tears, who wished only to provide well for his wife and children. He liked to say that their happiness was all whatsoever his soul lusted after, according to the blessings. Wally was particularly close to his son, George.

He took the teenaged boy to see his last job. He had been brought in as a sub-contractor to prepare the site for a granite memorial raised in tribute to merchant mariners involved in the Falklands conflict. It was a simple and impressive slab.

The Benbows, senior and junior, were there on the morning that the Queen Mother was due to perform the unveiling ceremony. It was exactly forty-three years, bar six days, since she had made her famous remark about staying beside her husband, the King, through the blitz.

The main contractor, hyperventilating in panic, caught up with Wally and his boy in the car park only half an hour before the event was supposed to begin.

Wally calmed the poor man to the point where he could make himself understood. The official party was kicking up a fuss. A steel stanchion, four inches high, had been left protruding from the concrete surround in front of the memorial. It was feared that the royal foot might come into contact with this obstacle. Disaster threatened on a scale unparalleled in peacetime.

'Right,' said Wally. 'I've got the angle grinder in the back of the motor. Lead the way.'

He was still cutting the steelwork, in a shower of sparks, when the royal car pulled into the approach road. A policeman had to tap Walter's shoulder to point out the impending arrival and what promised to be an undeniably awkward encounter.

There were numerous witnesses to the events which followed. These included: young George Benbow; Queen Elizabeth the Queen Mother; a lady-in-waiting; a chauffeur; a guard of honour found by the Sea Cadets; a nine-year-old girl holding a bouquet of carnations; her mother (also named Elisabeth, but with an s); eleven police officers; one Lord Lieutenant; three St John Ambulance first-aid volunteers; three press photographers; one news agency reporter; a colour writer from the *Daily Express*, which had run a campaign for the memorial to be built in the first place; and a crowd of 1,212 other people – including parties from two primary schools, waving union flags and, for some reason, towels, and a passing group of scientists from the Sea Mammal Research Unit at Cambridge. They all watched in astonishment as Walter Benbow backed away from the royal visitor, as though intending to hide behind the draped monument.

They were astonished mainly because his turn-ups, which had taken the full rush of sparks from the grinder – running too hot for safety – had now started to smoulder. They were already giving off

A Good Looking Man

smoke. The glimmer was fanned by a breeze whipping in at ankle height.

As the Queen Mother, who was wearing a lavender blue hat, a matching silk coat and a lop-sided, uncertain smile, approached the dais, Walter Benbow's best wool-and-polyester-mix trousers burst into flames.

'Oh, my God,' said Dorothy. 'Whatever did you do?'

'I borrowed one of the children's flags. To smother the fire, you see.'

'Why not a towel?'

'This was a patriotic occasion,' said George.

Walter Benbow had, in fact, flapped about, laughing like a storm drain. He believed the Queen Mother had found it fairly funny, too.

It was his last great laugh.

The day had ended in tragedy. Back at home, Wally had climbed on to his workbench to hammer a horseshoe into place on the workshop wall. For good luck, naturally. The nail hit, plumb centre, the main 240-volt electricity supply line – the company's incoming cable, as it is known in the trade.

There was a frighteningly sharp crash and a distinct flash. Half a mile down the line a trip was thrown, casting into darkness more than two hundred properties in the area. Wally was not holding the nail at the time and, therefore, escaped the immediate consequences of his action. He did not suffer any sort of electric shock.

But in his own little self-induced blackout – so far as they could tell, piecing together the evidence afterwards – he must have lost any sense of his whereabouts. Having been left in the dark, he turned and walked towards the door.

He had forgotten that he was standing on the benchtop. It was a fall of only thirty-four inches. It was sufficient to break his neck. Wally was found lying dead on his workshop floor.

* * *

George was jerked awake by the breath of a cat, peering into his face from a distance of about a quarter of an inch. He flailed both arms about in surprise until he remembered where he was.

Kenneth took off vertically like a Harrier jet, all four legs stiffening and his back arched. A bedside lamp fell over during this disturbance, although nobody afterwards could say for sure whether it jumped or it was pushed.

Dorothy looked into George's eyes. 'You and your father must have been very much alike,' she said.

'Well . . .'

'He sounds like a lovely man,' said Dorothy. And then she was fast asleep again.

Chapter Thirty

'I will, obviously, be making a full written report to the committee in due course. But I wanted, more immediately . . .'
Dr Hilary was finding his telephone conversation with the chairman fairly sticky going.

'Yes, sir, I realize that it is unfortunate that certain items had been moved to Maze Hall only a matter of months ago. But . . .'

He held the receiver away from his ear and raised his eyes to heaven. Why did he have to trouble himself with the minutiae when there was planning and thinking to be done on the grand scale? They were at the dawn of an epoch.

'You hardly need me to say, Mr Chairman, that Oliver Mackie took his decisions on the basis of what seemed best at the time. The construction of an air base – for heavy bombers, I believe – at Scotton-All-Saints, close to St Philibert's, created an obvious . . .'

There was a tap at his office door. Bert Tongue entered, backwards. He was wheeling a porter's trolley, loaded with box files.

The director looked down again. 'I think, sir, that we have to regard these items as casualties of war – and I'm afraid we have to prepare ourselves for more losses. When a conflagration is consuming all of Europe, we cannot expect to escape entirely unscathed. The great comfort is that the most valuable of our possessions are, to my personal knowledge, in the safest of hands. I have, of course . . .'

Tongue was unloading his boxes.

'I was just about to say, Chairman, that I have already instituted the most stringent review of fire precautions at all outstations. I was also going to point out that while postage stamps might have a certain – how to put this? – curiosity value, they will probably never attain great monetary worth. They had not figured very prominently in my draft plans for the future development of . . .'

Bert stood loosely to attention, as though awaiting orders.

'Thank you, sir. Thank you. And my very best wishes to your good lady. I will. Yes, of course. Goodbye. Goodbye.'

Dr Hilary slammed down the phone. 'Right, Tongue,' he snapped. 'I'd better draft a note about fire precautions at the other damned houses before we lose something really important.'

Bert coughed discreetly. 'I think you'll find that's already in hand, sir.'

* * *

'You are quite the best thing that's happened to me,' said George Benbow to Dorothy Parker, 'since Elsie the Cow.'

'Thank you very much, Benbow.' There was a slight pause. 'Should I take that as a compliment?'

'Naturally. When I was a kid I went to the Royal Show and entered a competition. You know the sort of thing. One of those promotions they do on the sales stands. Fill in a coupon and win a prize. In this case it was Elsie the Cow.'

'And . . .?'

'I went in for it.'

'Yes?'

'And I knew, with absolute certainty, that I was going to win. I kept plaguing my mother, asking her if Elsie had arrived through the post. She didn't think I had a cat in hell's chance, of course. But I knew she was coming to me. And, sure enough, she did. A lovely red and white soft toy cow.'

'Well, thanks a lot, Benbow. You really know how to please a woman, don't you?'

'I couldn't have been happier. Then or now.'

'Good,' said Dorothy.

'We're going to have to go back there, you know.'

'Where? Hayes Avenue?'

'Well, yes we are. But I actually meant Collingbrook. The castle place. I've got to know what's happened. We've worked hard for that ceiling.'

'They weren't very friendly,' said Dorothy. 'They wanted to make you into chicken feed . . .'

'But I need to find out, once and for . . .'

'But what are you going to do when – or if – you ever find it? Your precious plasterwork was probably smashed up years ago. But if not, what's to be done about it?'

A Good Looking Man

'Obvious, isn't it? I want to put it up in my flat. I thought it would look best in the bathroom.'

'Of course.'

'But I'll tell you, if there's the faintest chance, then I want to see it restored. Technically, it must still belong to the Vincent. It was a bequest . . .'

'George. Why don't you come back to bed?'

'It's funny, but I never heard that sort at talk from Elsie the Cow,' he said, taking Dorothy's hand, baring his incisors and raising her fingers to his lips.

'That's Bela Lugosi. In *Dracula*, isn't it?' said Dorothy. 'You know, you do that incredibly well . . .'

* * *

Dorothy had been making inquiries about Albert Tongue, the foreman assistant at the Vincent from 1939 until 1945, a period of tenure coinciding exactly with the duration of the war in Europe.

She had very quickly discovered from the personnel records that his appointment came to an end on 8 May 1945. What she did not immediately know was that this was a significant date: the day of victory celebrations, when huge crowds spontaneously took to the streets and, with abandon, rejoiced that – in the western hemisphere, at least – there need be no more shedding of blood, sweat and tears. It was a great party. There would, as is the nature of these things, be a long hangover.

To give Mr Churchill his due, he did try to temper the joy with realism. 'I wish I could tell you tonight that all our toils and troubles were over . . .' But, more urgently, it was a day and a night of release.

Bert Tongue might have stayed home and celebrated quietly in the bosom of his family.

That he did not was due entirely to a particularly fine pygmy hippopotamus. It was also, indirectly, the fault of a three-legged elk with apparent suicidal tendencies.

The Keeper of Natural History at the Vincent had been campaigning for years, since well before the outbreak of war. He wanted to replace the clapped-out wapiti. Its threadbare appearance and dicky leg had been letting down the Athill Collection, an otherwise well-regarded group of creatures. The elk was an embarrassment. The keeper detested the idea of welcoming the new era by having to put it back on display in that form.

He had, on one of his regular visits to Messrs Rowland Ward, the taxidermists, fallen head-over-heels for the stuffed pygmy hippo. He had also remembered the Scrivens Bequest Fund, which had proved so helpful before the war and whose assets had accumulated in the intervening years. To his satisfaction, he gained permission to buy the hippopotamus.

It was agreed that Bert Tongue should visit Ward's shop to make arrangements for transporting the specimen and its display cabinet. By chance, the next convenient day all round was Tuesday, 8 May.

'I'll make it a quick call. I don't want to hang around,' Bert told Stella. He planned to take young Roger to feed the ducks at the pond on the heath. His boy, now twenty months old, was the apple of his eye. They couldn't get enough of each other's company, Stella used to say.

So Bert set off in the morning, intending to waste no time with what he described as the giant stuffed dormouse. He had always found these preserved animals faintly ridiculous.

But then he met the crowds surging through Trafalgar Square and into Whitehall. He thought he saw Mr Churchill himself, on his way to the palace. He certainly saw him later on the balcony in Whitehall and heard the crowds singing 'For He's A Jolly Good Fellow'. Bert gave him several V-signs.

One way and another he never got to the taxidermists.

Chapter Thirty-One

By late afternoon Bert Tongue had had a few. He wasn't drunk; he was extremely happy, in harmony with the mood that spread through drab, battered London and intoxicated its people on VE Day. It was suddenly a brighter place.

At the top end of St Martin's Lane he fell in with a bunch of American sailors and some friendly ATS girls. They shared a bottle of Dewars and Bert, for the first time in his life, smoked a Lucky Strike. Then he thought he saw Sergeant Robbie Storey, ploughing through the crowd like the *Titanic* – or, more likely, the iceberg which sank it, he said to himself. At least, he believed he did but a woman standing nearby, wearing a French matelot's hat, flung her arms around his neck and roared: 'Give us a kiss then, Mister – what's your name?'

'Clement Attlee,' said Bert, hooking his fingers under the cups of her brassière and drawing her closer.

He emerged with a smear of vivid red lipstick across the bridge of his nose. The woman made a whooping noise: 'Blimey-O-bloody-Riley! If Mr Dashwood could see me now!'

By then the sergeant had disappeared. Bert was almost certain that his large friend had had a woman on each arm.

'Take that man's name, Sergeant-major, take his name,' Bert shouted at nobody in particular.

Later, he joined the press heading for Piccadilly Circus. Shaftesbury Avenue was clogged with people singing, dancing, linking arms and going nowhere very much, very slowly. It seemed a good idea to strike off and find another route to the hub of the party. He ducked and dived, cutting down side streets; in one doorway he found two couples making love noisily, side by side.

One minute he was in a packed Haymarket, the next he was in a road he did not recognize. 'Hey,' he shouted to a tall man, hurrying by. 'Hey, where am I, mate?'

Andrew Moncur

'You're in St James's Street,' the man replied. 'I'm sorry. You'll have to excuse me.' And he hurried on. Bert reckoned he was the most polite and sober gent he'd met all day.

'Hey! You need a drink,' Bert yelled. The man was rushing to catch up with a bunch of women. Well, it seemed like a good idea. No. There were two middle-aged women and a couple of teenaged girls. Bert decided that this would do. 'Wait for me,' he called, joining in the pursuit.

He caught up with them as they ran up against the crowd surging towards Buckingham Palace. 'What a party! What a night!' said Bert to the taller of the girls, who smiled at him shyly. Then, seeing that they meant to weave their way towards the front of the crowd, he was overwhelmed by a sense of gallantry.

'Make way for the ladies. Make way!' Bert was enjoying himself enormously. The older girl caught his hand and he elbowed and squeezed his way through the cheerful mass. At one point, glancing back, he saw the tall man whom he had first approached in St James's Street. He was obviously struggling to keep up. His face was a picture of utter consternation. Bert roared with laughter. 'Look at old Worryguts,' he said to the girl.

'It's Major Phillips.' She had to shout to make herself heard.

'Your dad, is he?' asked Bert, but she didn't catch his words.

'Come on,' she called to the younger girl. Probably her sister, thought Bert.

'Right, my lovelies. Let's give them a good old roar,' boomed Bert, putting an arm over each girl's shoulder. 'We want the King!' he bellowed. 'We want the Queen!' The girls joined in.

Soon the chant was swelling through the crowd. 'That's the stuff. Let's have a good old sing-song. A night to remember, eh?'

And then there they were, up on the balcony, looking very small. 'There he is! Always looks like a worried corgi. And she's a bit of a dumpling,' said Bert. But nobody heard. The crowd loved it. The cheering and the singing went on and on.

Bert and his new friends had a wonderful time. Suddenly, Major Phillips was leaning over to speak to the girls. The two older women were clucking in the background; one looked rather frivolous, the other didn't.

'I'm afraid we really should be getting back now,' the major shouted over the din. The girls turned to follow him.

'Where are we going now, then?' Bert couldn't believe they were

A Good Looking Man

calling it a day; they must be going on somewhere. 'Here! Hang about,' he yelled. 'Wait for me!'

The little party worked its way across the packed face of the palace railings and turned to follow the high brick perimeter wall. Bert was bobbing along trying to keep up.

Unexpectedly, they turned towards a small gate set in the wall. It could only possibly lead into the grounds of Buckingham Palace. 'Where are you going?' bellowed Bert. 'You been invited in? Wait a tick, I'm coming, too!'

The tall major was standing in his path. 'That won't be necessary, thank you,' he said coldly.

'Aw, come on,' said Bert. 'The party's hardly started.'

'I'm afraid that for the princesses it is already over,' said Major Phillips. And he shut the gate in Bert's surprised face.

Some hours later, when it was already VE Day-plus one, Bert found himself outside Charing Cross station. He didn't particularly wish to be there; it just turned out that way. He had had some vague idea about making for Fleet Street and cadging a lift home.

A woman had approached him in Green Park and he had given her a smacking kiss and a slap on her broad bottom. Then he walked on. Afterwards he realized that this was not necessarily all she had in mind and that he might have accepted her invitation. But it was Stella he wanted. Stella and the boy.

She would never believe him, of course. My night out with you-know-who. She'd just about die.

He only had fourpence in his pocket. He must have had more earlier. He couldn't think where it had gone. His packet of cigarettes had become squashed and bent; there were only two fags left. He lit one and blew out a long column of smoke.

He was suddenly tired. His feet ached. And he was hungry. His stomach rumbled. 'Pardon me,' said Bert.

A cup of tea. He needed a cuppa. The Embankment. There was always a late-night snack bar down there. Now which way was it? Downhill to the river, of course. Nice and easy, downhill, beyond the railway arches. It was pitch black along there. He was very happy.

Albert Tongue had survived not only the horrors of the Great War but also nearly six years of total warfare on the home front. He was killed by a bicycle. By a bike, of all things. And a puddle. A pool of oily water, only a couple of inches deep.

Andrew Moncur

The bike wasn't even in motion. It had been left leaning against the wall. The end of the pedal caught his trouser leg as he brushed against it in the dark. He pitched forward and cracked his head against the corner of a great granite block at the foot of a brick pillar. Bert fell face down in a shallow puddle.

Several people stepped over him in the course of the night. They assumed he had dropped there and was sleeping it off. It had been that sort of a party.

It wasn't until the next morning that anybody realized there was something dreadfully wrong.

Chapter Thirty-Two

'It's the perfect opportunity. It couldn't be better.' George's eagerness was positively infectious.

They had arrived on a largely unplanned expedition. He had thought, vaguely, that he would check the lie of the land and, all being well, confront the owners of the Collingbrook Estate.

This time he would be more forceful; there would be no more unfortunate scenes with dogs and muddy Land Rovers.

George had admitted on the journey that he didn't even know what constituted the estate. He assumed that there was a farm – possibly more than one – and a main house. There was, presumably, a good deal of land. Perhaps a few businesses of a rural nature: some commercial timber growing or, since the farm hand had mentioned it, poultry rearing. Eggs. Maybe they were touchy because they were running a politically sensitive business, like battery chickens. It was possible that they felt at risk from the attentions of animal rights activists.

Dorothy, who had volunteered to drive, parked outside the post office in Halfpenny Wick. They had stopped there, briefly, on their last visit. They knew that the estate's boundary extended to the fringe of the village, just beyond the churchyard and the cricket pitch. It was bounded by a high wall which seemed to run for miles, overhung by dark tangles of woodland and pierced occasionally by a wrough-iron gate or a farm track.

They could not even be sure which of these, precisely, was the one from which George had been seen off by the dog and its even more ill-tempered master.

This time Benbow had been into the small store to make inquiries. He had learned that the main entrance to the estate – the Castle Approach, as the postmistress called it – was down the lane beyond the village school. 'You'll be here for the dancing,' she said, enigmatically. Or had she said prancing? He was wondering about that as he strolled back to the car, opening a packet of peppermints.

There was a small debate inside the Morris Minor. George was for making an immediate frontal assault. Dorothy was counselling caution.

They hardly noticed the coach which pulled up behind their old car. George was busy explaining, by way of an analogy, the Light Division's storming of Ciudad Rodrigo. 'Did you say "the Forlorn Hope"?' asked Dorothy, taking a mint.

There was a smart rap on the roof. The coach driver was bending to Dorothy's window.

'Excuse me, sir,' he said, talking straight across her and addressing himself to George on the far side of the car.

'Hello,' said Dorothy. 'I'm the Invisible Woman. How do you do . . .'

'Excuse me,' said the driver, still ignoring her. 'We're looking for Collingbrook Castle. The women's caper.'

'The what?' Dorothy was speaking almost straight up his bony nose.

'The Women's League of Health and Beauty. The, errh, what do you call it? The divisional display,' he told George. The man showed no sign of recognizing Dorothy's existence.

'It's a little way down here on the right,' she said. 'We're just going there ourselves. And, if you have a moment, you could explain the meaning of a word you use. What is this thing you call a woman?'

'Thanks very much, guv'. I'll follow you . . .' And he was gone.

'Benbow,' said Dorothy. 'Can you see me? Am I here? Or am I just imaging all this?'

George was already composing in his head a letter to the editor of the *Daily Telegraph*: 'Sir, I wish to object in the strongest possible terms to the masculine tendency to treat women as though they are invisible. Yours faithfully, Captain R.S.J.Legge RN (retd). PS: if you are by any chance a woman, kindly disregard this letter . . .'

The Morris engine fired into life.

'It's the perfect opportunity,' said George again, with a strange and alarming brightness coming into his eyes.

* * *

Albert Tongue's funeral at St Mildred's Church, and afterwards at

A Good Looking Man

the Stanley Park Crematorium, was a bitterly sad affair.

Stella insisted that young Roger should be there and he called out gleefully, many times, during the church service. The poor mite didn't understand, everybody said. Worse, held in the arms of his distraught mother on the steps outside, he repeatedly asked for his daddy.

Big Robbie Storey could not hold back his tears. Smith M., seeing this, admitted to himself for the first time that old Bert really was gone. It hardly seemed possible. That the sergeant should weep, he meant.

Everybody wanted to do the proper thing, although Bert had not stepped inside a church since his discharge from the army in 1918. He used to tell a story about the Regimental Sergeant Major, abusing him in the vilest possible terms during a church parade in Aldershot. The RSM had screamed at him – in church – for desecrating the house of God, by neglecting to take his hat off.

Dr Hilary gave a short address. He pointed out that Albert, a name he had never uttered in Bert Tongue's lifetime, had served the Vincent in the key role of foreman assistant effectively from the first day of the European war until the very last.

'I have to say this about Albert, he set an example to the entire staff. He was always respectful and unfailingly courteous. His care for the Vincent's possessions was, well, it was remarkable. You know, Albert's devoted work helped to shape the future of our museum and art gallery. Tragically, he has not been spared to enjoy the fruits of his labours.

'I think I can say without fear of contradiction that with Albert the Vincent's treasures were in a safe hands. I ask you this: where would they now be without all his efforts?

'I am happy to think that we were not only director and foreman – but also friends. Comrades in arms, if you like.'

Mrs Hilary, seated two rows behind the young widow, raised her eyes and examined the church's ancient roof timbers.

Smith M. took Stella home later. Her parents, Mr and Mrs Hopkins, had gone on ahead to make tea. He was exceptionally kind with the boy, who was bursting with energy. Later he gave Stella a little hug and she wept inconsolably on his shoulder.

'Thank you, Michael. You're a good man,' she said as she showed him to the door.

He had hardly liked to mention Bert's remaining stock of ex-Navy submariner-style oiled wool sweaters.

Andrew Moncur

* * *

The estate's drive was surprisingly busy. Three more coaches were crawling ahead in convoy, followed by a line of private cars. There were pedestrians, too. Dorothy passed a number of women, sensibly wrapped up in sheepskin jackets and headscarves, and a couple of girls pushing a child's wheelchair. Further on there was a crocodile of school children. Every one of them seemed to be carrying a shoulder bag in luminous pink or green.

The drive snaked uphill through a stand of trees and then, as it breasted the hill, they caught a glimpse of the red sandstone house. It was a castle of sorts. Victorian gothic revival, George said. They could see a range of farm buildings over to the left. On the other side of the house, covering what must have been its hockey-pitch-sized lawn, was a large marquee.

'I've always thought it would be interesting to get into that business,' George remarked. 'I'd set up a firm called de Sade . . .'

'Why?' asked Stella, then groaned.

A handwritten sign indicated the coach and car park in a paddock. A burly figure was standing at the gate with a familiar-looking black and white dog crouching at his feet. George slumped in his seat and pretended to be absorbed in the road atlas. Stella smiled brightly at the farm-worker and bowled straight ahead into the parking area. Fifty yards away, a boy in a green anorak and a tweed cap was waving to indicate a space at the end of a row of cars.

'Now what, Benbow? Nothing stupid, please.' Dorothy gave him a look of genuine concern.

'You should pop along and take a look at the prancing, or whatever it is . . .'

'And you?'

'I'm just going to stretch my legs a bit. Take a breath of fresh air.'

'Oh, Benbow . . .' She reached across the car and gave him a long, soft kiss.

And then he unbuckled his seat belt and was out of the car, disappearing from sight behind the tail of a parked coach. So, thought Dorothy, that's what a man looks like when he's in hot pursuit of a ceiling.

Chapter Thirty-Three

On the evening of the funeral, Stella Tongue – needing to tell somebody of her special worries – decided to take her father into her confidence. First, she asked for his word that he would keep to himself all that she was about to say. Not even her mother was to be brought into this. He nodded and took her hand.

Bert, she told him, had lived with a secret. Where to begin? During his working life he had put aside one or two things, mainly for the sake of young Roger. 'He loved that boy, Dad. He'd have done anything for him . . . really anything. Bert wanted Roger to enjoy some of the things he never had. You know Bert didn't get much of a childhood. This was the only family he ever knew. What he did wasn't right, maybe. But it was – well, it was understandable . . . He was thinking ahead for his boy even before he knew he was going to have one.'

Stella's father, still unclear about what, precisely, his late son-in-law had done, decided to allow her to get to the point at her own pace.

'When they moved out the stuff from the museums, it was just chaos,' Stella said. 'Nobody, except old Dr Mackie, had a very clear idea about what had gone where – and even he was confused. Then he died, of course. There's been so much death.'

Stella blew her nose and then gathered herself.

'We, that is to say me and Bert, realized that some bits and pieces were going to go missing. Well, the whole country was likely to be invaded anyway – and, if not, we were all going to get bombed to bits or gassed. So we decided that if the valuable stuff was going to get lost, one way or the other, then we might as well see that some of it came in our direction.

'It didn't seem like theft. It still doesn't. Half of it had been lying around in the stores for years anyway. It was probably going to go straight back there after the war. Just collecting dust. And it didn't seem as though we were taking it from anybody. Not anybody with a name or a face. Does that seem terribly wrong to you? Do you think any the worse of poor Bert? I'd hate to think . . .'

Mr Hopkins held her in his arms and patted her back clumsily as she sobbed.

'What was all that about?' his wife asked later. She was sitting up in bed, wearing her curlers and nursing a hot water bottle.

'Only that Bert nicked some stuff from work,' said Mr Hopkins, sitting on the side of the bed and easing off his slippers. 'The trouble is, he never got round to telling our Stella what he'd done with it – or, more to the point, she never asked.'

'What. You mean, he flogged it?'

'No. He told her he was going to keep it out of sight for a while – years, she said – and then he was planning to sell it off. Nice and safe, see. Wait until everybody's forgotten all about it. Bright boy . . .'

'What sort of stuff?' Mrs Hopkins was sitting bolt upright.

'Silver, mainly. Old stuff. And some gems, Stella said. She told me she only knows where he hid one item – and that's on top of her wardrobe. And remember, mother, you don't know anything about this. Understood?'

'Course, you silly old fool. And what's she going to do about it?'

'Well, if she takes my advice, bugger all. I told her that it's best to forget it. It can only cause trouble. She's better off not knowing.'

'Are you ever going to come to bed? It's been a terrible day,' said Mrs Hopkins.

* * *

The tin-roofed barn had a line of upended railway sleepers all along one side, forming a massive wall. George scuttled by in the lee of the building. At the corner he stopped to button his jacket and then, very cautiously, he peered round the edge of the last heavy timber.

'Wahh!' He sprang back, heart racing. Then he poked his head round the corner again.

The calf, whose wet pink pad of a nose had met his own, had by now shied away across the pen. It was rolling its great, blue-black eyes and trying to butt its way into the crowd of beasts milling about at the back of the pen. There was a sweet smell of crushed

A Good Looking Man

straw. Tubular fencing ran across the open end of the tall barn. The bolder calves, curiosity overcoming fear, started to approach George, weaving their heavy heads and alternately lowing and huffing down their nostrils.

'There, there,' he whispered. 'Good cows. Or whatever you are.' He could actually see the whites of their eyes and their wet, rasping tongues.

Ahead lay an open concrete yard which had recently been hosed down. A tractor and trailer were parked on the far side, in front of a range of low workshops or animal sheds. The third side of the square was contained by the front wall of a far older building.

George was sufficiently interested to note that it was a fine medieval barn; stone-built with wooden doors tall enough to admit a double-decker bus – with Liverpool City football team, and the FA Cup, perched upstairs. It must be the oldest building on the estate, he thought; probably monastic; not at all unlike the great barn at Abbotsbury, in Dorset. There wasn't a soul in sight.

He decided to make a start with that big barn. He skittered along the front of the calf pen, causing the animals to start another mini-stampede, and then followed the line of a cement wall. Heaps of old car tyres, piled on the far side, cast eccentric shadows in his path. He reached the angle of the barn wall and then headed towards the massive red-painted doors at its centre. They loomed over him. God, how was he going to open them?

Praise the Lord. A wicket door was set on the right-hand side; its long bolt had been left undone and it was secured only by a hank of baler twine. George's fingers, suddenly clumsy, fought with the knot.

At that moment a door crashed open, across the yard near the tractor. George froze. With appalled fascination he watched a bucket emerge, in mid-air, from the open doorway. It described a perfect arc and then clattered down on the concrete. It was followed, seconds later, by a shovel. It landed with a heavy clang and slid across the yard.

Any time now someone was going to step out into the sunlight after them.

The knot parted and the wicket door, tiny in comparison with its big companions, swung free.

'Too right, I'm bloody fed up. Always the same bloody thing . . .' A girl – George recognized her as the Land Rover driver who hadn't cared much for visitors – stamped out of the low building over to his right. She was wearing blue jeans, black boots and a sleeveless jacket; she looked hot and angry.

He stepped swiftly through the door and pulled it shut behind him, wedging it closed with the end of the length of nylon twine. It was cool and dark inside, with a sense of vast, lofty space. In that second, breathing heavily, he couldn't see a thing. Half-kneeling, George put his eye to the crack.

The girl had picked up her bucket and was marching towards the spade, lying in the centre of the concrete strip. She turned and shouted towards the open doorway: 'And you just sit on your arse, scratching . . .'

As she spoke, another movement caught George's attention. Round the corner of the metal-sheeted barn, by the calf pen, came the heavily-built farm worker he had recognized at the outset. At his heels trotted the sheep dog, with one blue eye, one brown. They seemed to be heading straight for the door where George was cowering.

Simultaneously, he felt a gust of warm, sweet air on the back of his neck. Quite gently, but firmly, he was given a nudge between his shoulder blades. His face bounced up against the door jamb. He knew, for the second time in his life, the creeping sensation which he now recognized: his hair was standing on end.

Turning, very slowly, George found himself crouching face to face with an enormous cow. It was built like an overweight grand piano with a leg at each corner. It had a reddish-brown complexion with a broad blaze of tufty white running down between its eyes to the end of its broad nose. The nose had a ring in it. A steel ring. This cow was a bull.

'Oh, Christ,' he whispered; partly to himself, partly to the small-eyed, deep-chested Hereford, which now lowered its mighty head and snorted terribly. George began to yawn uncontrollably.

Chapter Thirty-Four

The woman at the card table, inside the entrance to the marquee, was in a flap. 'Do you have the correct change?' she asked, before Dorothy had had a chance to take her bearings.

'For what?'

'For admission and a programme. That's £1.20 for both. If you give me a £5 note I shall have to go and put my head in the microwave.'

Dorothy found a 20p coin in her purse. And a £5 note. The woman cast her eyes to heaven. 'You're going to have to do something, Jean. It's a complete disaster . . .'

Another, larger woman, wearing a ginger tweed jacket and sensible shoes, walked briskly across. She took a clear plastic bag from her pocket and tipped a pile of pound coins on to the table top. 'There you are, Rosemary,' she said. 'It's not the end of the world, is it?'

The light inside the tent was diffused; a sort of soft, salady green. It was as though the sunshine had been filtered through a spring onion. The marquee seemed to stretch ahead for half a mile; it was filled with a low murmur, suddenly overwhelmed by an awful screech.

'Testing, testing. One, two, three . . . Mary had a little lamb . . .' Then the microphone and the loudspeakers quietly died. The undercurrent of women's voices rose by half a dozen decibels. It sounded, thought Dorothy, like an slightly subdued children's playground.

Hundreds of seats – orange plastic shells with stick-like metal legs – had been arranged in rows facing the lowest possible stage. A wide area of boarding had been laid only inches off the turf at the far end of the tented hall. Behind, a wall of dusty red curtains stretched the entire width of the marquee.

Dorothy found a seat by the aisle in the back row. When George showed up they might want to disappear smartly. 'A display of movement and dance by the South Midlands Division of the Women's League of Health and Beauty,' she read from the front of the programme. Secretary, Mrs Jean Partridge. Any connection with the Partridges of Swinton, Dorothy wondered?

The canvas hall seemed to be filling rapidly. Women mainly, although here and there Dorothy could pick out an isolated man; invariably he seemed to be craning round, as though looking for support. It's funny, she said to herself, how some men – particularly those of a certain age – look as if they have been dressed by their wives. Home-knitted sweaters, the sort you only expect to see in *Woman's Weekly* or on the front of pattern books. In winter they held out oddly stiff hands, with fingers splayed and rigid inside brown leather gloves with knobbly stitching. It gave the impression that there was a piece of elastic attached to each glove and running up the jacket sleeves.

And their trousers and shoes . . .

'Eeeee-caawhh!'

There was another deafening whistle from the loudspeakers. A broad-beamed woman – Dorothy recognized her as the one with a pocket full of pound coins – had made her way to the stage.

'Ladies and gentlemen . . . Yes, there are some gentlemen here, I'm very pleased to say. Good afternoon and welcome to Collingbrook Castle and to the principal event in the calendar of the South Midlands Division of the Women's League . . .'

Dorothy looked over shoulder towards the entrance. Where was George? She found herself wishing desperately that his ridiculous smile would appear. She could imagine him handing a £20 note to that woman by the door, counting piles of loose change. Please, she said to herself, don't dicker about, Benbow.

'. . . very great pleasure to introduce our divisional chairman – although, as you know, she is very much a lady. She had travelled from Warwickshire to be with us this afternoon. Ladies and gentleman, Mrs Julia Trembath.'

There was a desultory round of applause. At least three hundred women in the audience took the chance for a brief word with their neighbours. The few lonely men turned chicken necks, looking for one another helplessly. A slight, neat woman was walking hesitantly towards the microphone.

God, thought Dorothy, and some grown women still looked as

A Good Looking Man

though they were dressed by their mothers. Including this Mrs Tremble, or whoever she was.

'... what a joy it is to be with you all today, for what I know will be a splendid event. We want...'

Mrs Trembath's mouth continued to open and close but only fragments of her remarks emerged from the loudspeakers. Dorothy watched her lips as the poor woman kept going, shaping words that vanished into the useless microphone. She was darting her eyes to left and right in what looked like rising panic.

'We want to say it's a pleasure to welcome you ladies and, of course, your husbands – it's good to see them – coming to support us today,' she appeared to be saying.

'We want to... pleasure... your husbands,' blurted out the loudspeakers.

A swell of whispers started to rise from the audience. A woman, bent double and moving at a trot, came scuttling across to kneel at the foot of the microphone stand. She started to make frantic adjustments.

'... greatly help our cause.' Mrs Trembath sagged with relief. 'And now, to the display of movement and dance...' Dorothy crossed her long legs and tried to relax.

'There, there, Elsie,' said George, trying to keep his voice at a calm pitch. He was scratching the enormous bull between its white-rimmed, hot little eyes. What was the rule? Were the bulls of dairy breeds more dangerous than the beef ones? Or was it the other way round? And, for Christ's sake, were Herefords dairy or beef? And was it even a Hereford – or some sort of Belgian Chatelaine or whatever? Why did you never pay proper attention to these things when you had the chance? When they talked about being gored by a bull did they mean it knocked you down and stamped all over you? Like the All Blacks? Well, it didn't have horns, did it? Oh, God.

The centre bay of the great barn formed the bull's pen. It was bordered by stout fencing poles, running the full width of the building. George, his eyes becoming used to the dusty gloom, noted the earth floor. It seemed to stretch away to infinity.

An airport control tower on wheels was parked over to the left. A combine harvester, he supposed. Beside it a tangle of other farm machinery was drawn up; George could only begin to guess at its function. One tall red machine looked as though it was something to do with the fire brigade – or a mobile escalator, perhaps. Its upper end was resting against one of the beams supporting another floor which appeared to lie across the last quarter of the barn, casting that end of the building into even deeper shadow.

On the right, there was a huge stack of bales. Beyond it, an ancient-looking caravan was at rest – more or less terminally, George thought. There was more machinery in the far corner, covered by dark tarpaulins. The barn was lit only by a few narrow windows, shaped like arrows slits.

Elsie the bull gave an appalling snort and nudged George again, hard, under his ribs.

At that moment there was a scratch and a whine at the door, immediately behind him. The bull stamped backwards three or four paces, ducked its head and let out a full-blooded, lowing roar.

George found himself composing a small prayer. Behind him, a rabid dog with master, similar, who had promised to feed him to the chickens. Before him, a mad bull, about to be overcome by berserker-style blood lust. Elsie seemed to have been brought to the boil by the presence of a natural enemy: the dog. In the middle – the meat in the sandwich, so to speak – George Benbow, an uninvited guest.

What have I done to deserve this? George was moaning to himself again. Somebody get me out of here. Any second that wicket door was going to open. Any minute the bull was going to put down his head and charge, taking with him George, the barn doors and at least a wing of the mock Gothic castle.

'Come away,' snapped a man's voice, outside in the yard. 'Get away, girl. Bloody bull doesn't need you sniffing around.'

George could actually hear the dog's toenails clicking off across the concrete.

'And what are you moaning about, Tess? No use chucking your tackle around the place. Somebody's got to do these jobs.' The man seemed to be walking away from the barn, presumably towards the girl whose bucket-throwing had given George his first minor heart attack.

Thanks be to God, said George. That just leaves me to worry about a slight goring.

And at that precise moment, Elsie the bull lowered his head and charged.

* * *

A Good Looking Man

The first group of dancers, about forty of them, tripped on to the stage and ran into position. They stood poised in a diamond-shaped formation. Satin knickers and blouses, thought Dorothy. This takes me back.

The music started with a shattering blare. Gracious. Paul Simon. Bridge Over Troubled Thing. The dancers, as one woman, came nimbly on to their toes – and they were off. Arms looped to left and right; legs skipped and kicked; heads bobbed and knees bent in perfect time to the music. New patterns formed and then, very sweetly, broke up. God, are you supposed to be able to bend like that?

Some of them are, well, big women, Dorothy noted. But they're graceful enough. How do they manage to keep smiling so while bouncing about? My word, they're putting their backs into it. And their bottoms. And everything else. When are they going to run out of puff? A few of the women were positively elderly, with no roundness left on their legs but, instead, a certain leathery muscularity. A fair number were in middle life but jolly and bouncy. One or two were quite stunningly beautiful. It wasn't fair to talk about prancing...

The music died in mid-bar. For a ghastly moment the second rank hesitated, wobbled and thought about stopping. But the front line, still smiling bravely, carried on womanfully. By now the separate halves of the team were detectably out of sequence. For the first time it was possible to hear the slap of their bare feet on the boards.

Then the music sprang again from the loudspeakers. The front rank had, to its credit, remained in perfect time. The women did not miss a beat. Here and there, in the back line, their team-mates performed little shuffling steps to catch up.

'Benbow,' said Dorothy, under her breath, 'they're putting on a really good show here – while you're out there, somewhere, frightening the poor farm animals.'

Chapter Thirty-Five

El Higgins, the matador, would have been proud. Instinctively, as the bull put down its enormous head and charged, George stepped to the left. Elsie, already moving at impressive speed, hit the wicket gate with splintering force. George felt, rather than saw, the remains of the door cartwheeling away, torn off its old hinges.

The rectangle of light was instantly filled with the bull's tremendous neck and shoulders. Next, its bulky hindquarters, propelled by those comparatively short, stocky legs. Then the doorway was empty, flooding the centre of the barn with sunlight. Elsie, scenting freedom and revenge, was off at full pelt across the yard.

'God almighty! Watch it! The bugger's loose.' The girl's piercing yell galvanized George, still leaning against the door frame, open-mouthed. He turned and sprinted towards the combine and the other machinery.

Without hesitating for thought, he launched himself at the foot of the red escalator-like machine. It was a big conveyor belt, an elevator, he supposed, climbing at a sharp angle towards the platform above. George, grasping the edges on either side, started powering his way up the ramp. The belt gave beneath his weight. It was like running up the slippery chute of a children's playground slide.

For every two paces he took forward, he was slithering back one. Gripping the red-painted sides, George dragged himself, hand-over-hand, to the top of the ramp. He leapt gratefully on to the upper floor.

There was a square of light ahead. A window or a loading door set in the end wall of the great barn. George tore towards it, hurdling a line of apple boxes scattered in his path. He didn't see the old hay rake until it sprang up and smacked him squarely between the eyes.

Benbow was lying flat on his back. He'd been run over by a bull called Elsie. He was now going to be stomped to pieces. He was too young to die. The bull was pawing the ground. No it wasn't. His own feet were threshing about feebly. He'd run into an angry bean pole. It had got up and hit him, very hard. He must have trodden on it. Lord, that roof was beautifully made. Look at the size of those timbers; the cuts left by the original carpenter's adze, dressing the oak, could still be seen the length of each great beam.

George tottered to his feet. There was a vicious ripping noise and he felt a cool breeze on his thigh. The right leg of his trousers, caught on a wood splinter, was hanging by a thread. Without hesitation, he tore at it and then stepped out of the redundant cloth tube. He felt the rip extending upwards into his groin.

He leant against the wall and peered down through one of the narrow embrasures. The scene in the yard below seemed frozen. Elsie had backed into the space between the parked tractor and the workshop wall. He seemed to be at a loss to know where to rampage next.

The man whose voice George had heard earlier was standing, motionless, with both arms raised, across the open mouth of that fortuitous pen. He had what looked like a stout stick in one outstretched hand and a length of rope in the other. George guessed that he was aiming to loop it through the bull's nose-ring. The girl was peeping round the corner of the workshop door.

The calm was suddenly shattered. The dog, obeying instinct, came flying in around the far end of the tractor and darted at the bull's heels, driving him towards her waiting master.

The unfortunate man yelped and jumped aside. Elsie let rip again. At last, a target for his monumental fury: a black and white running dog.

George watched, aghast, as first the sheepdog and then the furious bull went careering off. Cornering on two legs, they swept around the blind bend by the calves' pen and disappeared towards the front of Collingbrook Castle.

'God almighty!' roared the farm-hand. And then he set off in pursuit.

George drew breath. Could he be charged with manslaughter? The accused Benbow did, with reckless disregard for the safety of a dance troupe, provoke a bull to run amok, your worships . . .

George leapt towards the sunlit square in the barn's end wall. It was a loading door, covered only by thin sacking. He ripped

A Good Looking Man

this aside and looked down. Below was the roof of a long shed, covered with tarred felt. There was a drop of about ten feet.

He glanced around, seeking some sort of rope or pulley. There was none to be seen.

He shuffled towards the edge and, closing his eyes, stepped into space.

Benbow, dropping feet first like a man on the scaffold, landed heavily on the shed roof. Then he passed clean through it, with a firecracker splintering of aged pine planks.

His fall was broken by wire caging, which folded and crumpled under this sudden assault from above. Even in that split second of trauma, George was aware that his other trouser leg had gone. His jacket, catching on the jagged edge of the hole he carved through the roof, whipped up and briefly enveloped him – again helping to slow his rate of descent – before it was ripped off his back. His wallet landed on his head.

There was an explosion of sound all around. A cacophony of frenzied fluttering and squawking.

George Benbow, minus his trousers, had finally come face to face with the chickens he had heard so much about.

The first half had been reasonably enjoyable. The break for a cup of tea at the interval was welcome, not least because it gave Dorothy a chance to stretch her long legs. It was surprising how stiff you could be made to feel by watching other people take violent exercise. And, talking of physical jerks – where, in the name of all that's merciful, was Benbow?

'Have you ever thought of joining us?' asked Rosemary, the harassed doorkeeper, as Dorothy peeked outside the marquee. All was calm out there.

'What? I'm sorry, I was dreaming.'

'Have you ever thought of joining our movement, if that's the right word? The league?'

'Well, no. I can't say . . .'

'You should consider it, you know. Health and beauty. The two go hand in hand.'

Like Bonnie and Clyde. Jekyll and Hyde. Burke and Hare. Benbow and Parker.

Dorothy was almost relieved to take her seat for the second half of the display. It was at least a distraction. He really should have been here by now.

The music boomed again. The performers, in greater numbers now, skipped out once more to form two parallel lines: one at the footlights, the other three paces to the rear.

The chicken shed was lit by a looping string of naked bulbs. George, picking his way clear of the mangled multi-storey cage, came eyeball to eyeball with the hen who occupied its squashed top floor; she was clearly in shock.

'I'm terribly sorry,' he said aloud. He was answered by a thousand tremulous squawks. Two thousand unblinking eyes peered down the avenue of galvanized wire, nakedly alarmed by this flying invader. A genuinely jumpy clutch, thought George. Obviously, I'm a particularly large and threatening raptor; dropping feet first from a great height to stoop on my prey.

There was a terrible stench in the shed. It was – what do you call it? – yes, ammoniacal. It made his eyes smart. George suddenly had a good idea of which task had awaited the girl, Tess, and why she should have been throwing her tools about.

Well, nothing seemed to be broken – apart from a few square feet of roofing and at least one chicken's cramped quarters. George got to his feet. A row of scrawny necks, worn featherless by contact with metal bars, turned as one to follow his movements.

How can we do this to living things, George asked? It's all so carefully kept out of sight and out of mind. We boil them, fry them, poach them, scramble them – but we prefer not to think where the wretched things come from.

Benbow, the fearless animal liberator, slipped the bolt cutters from his belt. Pulling back the black balaclava helmet which covered all but his fanatical eyes, he called down the length of the hut: Right, you chickens! Follow me!

'Let's get the hell out of here,' George muttered. He limped towards the side of the hut. No windows. No natural light. Just rough wooden walls that looked as though they had been cobbled together out of packing cases.

Out of packing cases.

Or crates.

There was still a label stapled to one coarse plank directly at eye level. George reached out and smoothed its curled edges.

'Property of the Vincen . . .' it said in faded black letters. Then there was a tear. The bottom section of the white card was still in place. It bore a number: 'C 2902'.

A Good Looking Man

'Ohmygawd,' whispered George.

About three yards down the shed there was another visible marking: 'Fragile. Handle with care.'

George charged back across the building. The wall on that side was totally obscured by tiers of caging. The chickens gobbled and clucked fearfully as he approached.

With a sudden burst of energy, fuelled by anger, George laid hold of the bottom line of cages and heaved. A section of ten swung towards him and away from the wall. The upper decks teetered dangerously but George, spreadeagling himself, managed to steady them. The chickens shrank as far as they could – which was not far – to the backs of their wire boxes.

He pushed his way into the gap and looked along the line of the exposed wall.

The face of a cherub peered back at him.

Chapter Thirty-Six

The sheepdog, tearing round the side of the castle, was confronted by an unbroken wall of canvas, stretching as far as her panicking eye could see. Behind, a thunder of heavy feet sounding like a frightful, inrushing tide advancing at galloping speed.

She did all that a dog could do in the circumstances. Nose first, she burrowed under the taut white wall of the marquee and pushed her way inside. Then she streaked across the stage, between the two lines of exercising women, throwing themselves into the grand finale. She departed under the far side of the tent in exactly the same way.

Only the back row of performers realized that anything untoward had happened. Again, they faltered. Several lost their step altogether. They were all still smiling.

Forty satin-knickered women in the star-studded front line each raised a muscular right leg and swung their arms and shoulders over to the left.

In the wobbly back division, twenty-two right legs were lifted in unison. Another eighteen left legs rose at more or less the same moment. Arms went this way and that, colliding solidly. Forty pairs of eyes followed the low-flying black and white thunderbolt as it hurtled across the stage. They watched in fascination as it vanished, head first, making for the distant hills of its ancestral Welsh home.

The bull did not take quite such a subtle approach. He simply lowered his head and charged the marquee. He hit the canvas at exactly the point where the dog, on all fours, had scrambled her way in.

His small brain was capable of holding only one thought at a time; now it was filled with red-tinted rage focused on a fleeing, terrified bitch. He wanted to assault and batter that dog. And, yes, to toss it. Nothing else would do.

The walls of Rome would not have deflected him. The unbleached cotton barrier surrounding the South Midlands Division of the Women's League of Health and Beauty did not remotely stand a chance.

The bull erupted into the tent. Its momentum carried it clean on to the middle of the stage.

The music thumped on. So did the entire front rank, real troupers to a woman. They might have been baffled by rending noises and the sudden heavy-footedness of their colleagues in the rear. They were certainly aware of the expressions of stunned horror spreading across the faces of their audience. But they didn't show it.

The forty women in the back line had come to an abrupt, total standstill. They were too surprised even to scream.

All this meant nothing to Elsie. Not the noise. Not the lights. Not the prancing women. Not the other row of dancers, knees and elbows at all angles, frozen into immobility. Not the bank of shocked faces filling the marquee.

His furious little eyes had detected the last portion of a black tail, snaking under the canvas on the far side of the stage. He gave a snorting, triumphant bellow and charged on, roaring through the flimsy wall and off towards the estate's wide open spaces.

The all-star, front-of-stage ladies continued their routine. It took a while before it dawned on the first of them that something had gone terribly wrong. One by one, their gay little smiles came unfixed.

It was almost black with ancient grime; it was speckled with chicken droppings and stray feathers. But it was, unmistakably, a chubby-cheeked, angelic child.

George stretched forward and kissed it.

To left and right he could make out dimly the familiar raised patterns of fleurs-de-lys.

Turning back, George realized that above the finely moulded cherub's face was the outline of the cartouche it, and its three matching fellows, had been designed to support: an oval of elaborate scrollwork. At its centre, so coated in filth and feathers that he had to touch it to know, was a smooth-cheeked bust.

One of the Nine Worthies, he guessed. It was a popular theme among seventeenth-century craftsmen. The Nine: Clio, the muse of history; Euterpe, lyric poetry; Thalia, comedy; Melpomene, tragedy; Terpsichore, choral dance and song; Erato, erotic poetry;

A Good Looking Man

Polymnia, the sublime hymn; Urania, astronomy; Calliope, epic poetry.

He was standing in his torn boxer shorts, in the middle of a chicken shed he had entered by almost certainly illegal means. And he had successfully remembered the whole lot of them.

What's more, he had found his ceiling.

Its long journey from Pudding Norton had ended here. It had survived the upheavals and hazards of roughly three hundred and ninety-four years. It had been rescued from the demolition men. It had been saved from Hitler. Now it was in three sections, laid end to end to form the greater part of one wall of a battery chicken house.

Its splendid strapwork decorations seemed to have escaped serious damage. By feel, George could identify heraldic symbols and, here and there, a flower: roses, he suspected. There were animal figures, too. He could not help wondering whether they included a bull.

A bull. George heaved the tiered cages back into position against the wall. He scuffed the torn remains of his clothing underneath. Then he ran towards the door at the far end of the shed. One thousand fearful cocked heads followed his progress.

The door was secured on the outside. George gave it an enormous kick and it flew open; it had only been held shut by a wooden peg. He took a deep, grateful breath of fresh air and felt the thin sun on his face and legs. Oh, Christ. He was still an unwelcome trespasser, who had caused God knows what mayhem – and he was now charging about in his underpants.

George turned and, running down beside the packing case wall of the hen house, headed for the back of the great barn.

He thrashed through a bank of stinging nettles hiding unimaginable lumps of scrap iron. Squealing silently, he tried to tell himself that it didn't hurt. He didn't believe a word of it. His legs. Poor legs.

Then he was confronted by a muck heap of immense proportions. George ploughed ahead, steadying himself with one hand on the barn wall. His feet made disgusting squelching noises; at one point he felt that his shoe was going to be sucked off. The same gagging stench rose all around him. He was splashed to the thighs with khaki-coloured liquid which, he was pleased to discover, seemed to calm the rage of his stings. That was about all that could be said for it.

George finally reached the end corner of the barn. There was nobody in sight.

Ahead was the tyre mountain. He now saw that the heaps of tyres covered a black plastic-sheeted mound. What was it? Silage? God only knows. He launched himself at the north face, bringing a pile of worn Goodyears bouncing down all around. Quickly he scrabbled his way up and crawled through the maze of tyres. His shoes seemed to be leaving a greenish trail.

He could now see the castle. Beyond, and to one side, stood the big marquee. In a field about half a mile further away, across a small valley, he could make out moving figures and – could that be a Hereford bull? Elsie seemed to be grazing peacefully.

'Hey! Who the bloody hell? You . . . you up there!'

A young man in a tartan shirt, standing in the concrete yard outside the workshop door, was gesturing wildly at George.

'Here, let's be having you . . .'

He started to run towards the wall at the foot of the tyre heap. Then, changing his mind, he sprinted across the open end of the metal-sheeted barn.

Aiming to cut me off, thought George, quite rationally. Then he lost his head and went careering down the far slippery slope of black polythene. Tyres bounded off in all directions.

George hit firm ground and broke into his fastest loping run, heading for the castle and the tent. Dorothy was there. Dorothy and the car keys.

Chapter Thirty-Seven

Only an English audience could have remained so calm. Thunderstruck, maybe, but unwilling to panic merely on the basis of the evidence of their own eyes, thought Dorothy. There were one or two muted shrieks. Some children whimpered; a complete row of orange chairs tipped over backwards as a group of Women's Institute members from Banbury sprang to their feet, as one. There was even some applause. Clearly a few impressionable souls felt that the bull's flying entrance had been choreographed as part of the last big number.

A young man from the *Evesham Journal* was also on his feet. He thought, although he wasn't entirely sure, that he might just have a story on his hands. There was definitely a gaping hole in the marquee wall over there. And another over here. The performers had certainly fled in disorder behind that curtain.

He hadn't imagined it. An enormous mad cow had stampeded right across the stage. Hadn't it? It had been followed by Mr Henry Staunton, who looked like a farm-worker but was, in fact, the owner of the Collingbrook Castle Estate. Then his daughter, Tessa. The young reporter had an idea that there had also been a dog at some point of the performance. He sat down again, still uncertain, as the large gingery woman marched to the centre of the stage, dragging with her the microphone stand.

Only a troupe of British women exercise enthusiasts could have bargained for what happened next.

'Right,' boomed the woman – Dorothy remembered that her name was Jean. 'We're going to do that last routine again. Can't go home remembering that sort of shambles, can we? Hilda. Music, please.'

Dorothy lowered her head into her hands. Somewhere at the back of this Terpsichorean disaster, she knew without a shadow of doubt, was that lunatic Benbow.

* * *

George caught the sound of music – a frisky sort of disco beat – as he thundered around the end wall of the castle. Or was it just the pounding of blood in his ears? He was very nearly finished, taking great sobbing gulps of air. The back of the marquee was only a dozen yards away, across a gravel path.

'Come here. I'm going to bloody . . .' The bullocking young man, his face now the colour of a Victoria plum, tore at George, who was visibly flagging. He misjudged his lunge and lost his footing, sliding harmlessly by on his backside,

Benbow, making one last effort, skittered across the path and dived through the flap at the back of the tent.

He was in some sort of a changing room. Clothes were scattered over plastic chairs. There were bags lying about and discarded shoes here and there. He had no doubt now about the source of the music. On one side there was a line of mirrors. George peered into a glass and recoiled. A scarecrow was staring back at him. His bare legs, emerging from his boxer shorts, were scratched and filthy; his shoes and ankle socks were still ridiculously in place, although soaked and green; his grimy shirt was ripped from shoulder to midriff; his face was blackened and his matted hair seemed to have exploded. A vision of loveliness.

Then, in the mirror, he saw a dark outline against the white wall of the tent. The young man seemed to be thrashing about, looking for the entrance. George could have sobbed in weariness. He didn't have the breath.

He trotted across to the red curtaining and, still looking back, stepped through into the bright lights.

'And then what happened, Kevin?' Pauline Trowmans, the chief reporter of the *Evesham Journal*, was nothing if not a patient woman.

'Then, in the middle of the last number, this man in his undies comes shambling on to the stage . . .'

'A man? In his underwear? Was he wearing satin knickers, Kevin?'

'No,' said the reporter, referring to his notebook. 'He was wearing blue string . . . strapped . . .'

'I think you'll find, Kevin, that's the outline for striped,' said Ms Trowmans, reading the shorthand note upside down.

'Blue striped pants. He was covered in shit and feathers. And he

A Good Looking Man

was right there, in the middle of the women doing their dancing . . . Honest, Pauline, you've never seen nothing like it.'

'And what happened, Kevin?'

'Well, there was this big round of applause. Everyone thought it was the comedy turn or something. You know, after all that exercising and stuff. He was like a walking muck heap.'

'And?'

'Then the women, they kind of stopped again. Hell of a mix-up. Some of them was laughing, and all. And the man – him in the undies – he starts jumping about, joining in the show. After that this other bloke comes on stage, too. That's Jack Stanley, the boss's son . . .'

'Isn't that Jack Staunton, Kevin? You've got to learn to get these names right, you know.' Ms Trowmans was a careful teacher.

'Sorry. Anyway, he's trying to grab hold of this first bloke. Takes a swing at him. Everyone thinks that it's part of the show, too. Only it looks a bit serious. He was using – you know – like language.'

'We won't mention that, Kevin.'

'Then the one covered in shit jumps off the stage and starts running up the hall. There's a woman – tall, fair – standing right at the back, hollering his name. Benson, or something. And Jack, he comes after him. Then, wallop. This other woman tackles Jack right round his ankles. It was Mrs Partridge, the divisional secretary. That's Jean Partridge. She was livid. Her and about three other women, they . . . well, they sat on him. Jack, that is.'

'Yes?'

'And meanwhile the other bloke, him in the striped shorts, and the tall girl . . .'

'Girl, Kevin? Was she under eighteen?'

'Sorry. Woman. Anyway, they done a bunk out of the front door of the tent and disappeared. Got clean away.'

Pauline Trowmans sat back and chewed the end of her pen. 'Right, Kevin,' she said. 'I want you to write this just the way it happened. Think how you might describe it to your own mother. Now, for a start – are you absolutely sure it was a cow?'

Chapter Thirty-Eight

On 14 August 1945, when Britain and its allies started celebrating the surrender of the Japanese, there was little rejoicing in Stella Tongue's household.

The cheerful crowds and the planned street parties could only remind Stella of the day when she lost Bert. Sometimes she wondered whether young Roger remembered him at all – and that made her awfully sad.

It was a kindness, then, that Smith M. should have come to her door to suggest a little outing, away from all the happy crowds. He was only offering a walk on the heath but she was grateful for that.

Little Roger liked him, too. They were going to feed the ducks together.

'Did you hear what happened up here last week? Funny business, except for the poor sod concerned.'

No, said Stella, she had heard nothing. What had taken place on the heath?

'Over that end, beyond the Nissen huts – you know, where the squatters have moved in,' he said.

The homeless, despairing of finding places to live in the aftermath of a destructive war, had started to take the law into their own hands. The huts built to serve the wartime gun sites were soon occupied by dozens of young families.

'This bloke was flying a kite up there. His girlfriend was helping, you know. He had control of it, of course. She was holding the kite, trying to get it up in the air. And what happens?'

Stella said that she had no idea.

'He only steps on an unexploded shell, doesn't he. He gets blown up. The girl doesn't have a scratch. Nor does the kite.'

Stella called little Roger to her side. She held his hand firmly all the way to the pond.

* * *

'So,' said Dorothy, lying on Benbow's tangled bed. 'It's a happy ending. Virtue is rewarded. Dog is rescued. Man gets ceiling. Woman gets terrible shock over state of man's underwear.'

'Miss Parker, I have never been so pleased to see a women's health and beauty class, I can tell you. I was just about finished. And then, when you stood up and shouted my name . . .'

'Why don't you come over here?' She patted the bed beside her long right leg.

'I was so happy to find the ceiling. I felt – well, I felt so lucky. And then I thought I was going to die . . .'

'He looked a bit tough, Benbow, but he was never going to slaughter you.'

'No,' said George. 'I mean, I thought I was going to drop dead from heart failure or something. I had a sudden, vivid picture of something which happened in the seventeenth century when that ceiling was first . . .'

'Come on. Come here, now.'

The image which had arrived, unbidden, in his mind was of a small boy climbing over the newly-leaded roof of Egmere Old Hall, at Pudding Norton, in Norfolk. He was Zebulon Cole, eight-year-old son of the man who levelled most of the medieval hall and conceived and built the great Jacobean house which took its place.

George had seen it all. The boy had climbed on to the roof from a doorway in the upper chamber of the clock tower, which stood in the centre of the south front of the hall. From that vantage point he could see across the still raw terraces where gardeners, aided by numbers of women and children, were laying out geometrical patterns of walks and hedges; beyond the beech trees and the river, the distant tower of St Margaret's church caught the sun. Skylarks were pumping themselves up towards the clouds.

A deep gutter, already speckled with wet leaves, and a stone parapet ran the length of the roof. The boy leaned over this low wall, looking straight down the sheer face of the house into the dry moat far below. It was a dizzy drop. The house front was tall and sheer, like a brick-built cliff. His father, Mr Cole, was somewhere down there, probably in his parlour which would serve as the dining room of the family's new home.

A pigeon flew by at speed, following the line of the building about fifteen feet below the boy's perch on the roof-edge. He craned out to watch the bird as it rounded the west turret. The child's feet slipped away so easily it was as though they had been greased. For a few heartbeats he was perfectly balanced on his stomach, swaying over the terrible drop. Then the horizon rose up sickeningly – and, quite slowly, he somersaulted over the rail and fell.

It was strange that the boy made no sound. All that could be heard was the wind, whipping and cracking at his clothes as he dropped head over heels. By the time he passed the great windows he was falling feet first, his arms stretched high above his head.

'A boy fell off the roof but was saved by his clothing. It all billowed out, like a parachute, and he wafted down and landed on his feet – quite unharmed. They all thought it was a miracle, which it was,' said George, taking her face gently between his hands. 'In exactly the same way, I knew that everything was going to be all right for me. I just had to reach you and let you know what had happened. Then all would be well.'

George lay beside her and took her in his arms.

'Errh, Benbow . . .'

'Yes, my love?'

'Benbow, you still seem to have something – something sticky – in your hair. It's getting all over the pillow . . .'

George didn't seem to care at all.

In the car, where they had quickly decided to abandon Benbow's revolting footwear, George had described his discovery in affectionate detail. The ceiling seemed to be largely intact; fortunately the farmer had at some stage tacked sheets of corrugated iron on the outer face of his unusual shed wall.

The questions of its recovery and its eventual destination now had real meaning.

To Dorothy Parker, whose life revolved around the institution, the required course of action seemed simple: the Vincent Museum and Art Gallery must be informed of the find. It could be relied upon to take the necessary administrative, and possibly legal, steps to recover its property. The ceiling would then be returned to the Vincent and, eventually, restored and put on display – in the manner which, on the basis of George's enthusiastic description, it so richly deserved. There. Perfectly straightforward.

'Don't you think they might be a little reluctant?' George had wrapped himself in the car rug. Driving with the windows wide open might be necessary, in all the circumstances, but it was not too comfortable for a man in only his underpants.

'Why?'

'Well, it raises so many other questions. About how, for instance, could a responsible museum manage to lose a whole ceiling? And the far more embarrassing one: what else did the Vincent manage to mislay during the war?'

Dorothy, as though oblivious, overtook a line of a dozen cars waiting at traffic lights and then, at the last possible moment, cut in at the head of the column. There was enraged tooting from behind. She ignored it.

'I know what I'd do if I were your director,' said George. 'I'd very properly, but very quietly, arrange to recover the ceiling from Collingbrook. I'd bury the whole business in the middle of some boring, obscure report to the committee – and then I'd bring it back to the museum and lose it all over again.'

'What do you mean, Benbow?' Dorothy was refusing to take any notice of the boy racer in his Ford Escort who, seeking vengeance for having been humiliated by a woman driver at the last set of traffic lights, was now screaming up alongside, gesturing violently.

'I'd want, above all, to avoid all the awkward questions and explanations. I would simply bring it home and put it away in that graveyard – you know, up in the storeroom. Up there with the bonking polar bear. What do you call it?'

'The stacks,' said Dorothy. The angry man was now leaning across to the passenger window of his Ford and bellowing abuse. He seemed to be totally unaware of the roundabout ahead.

'So it would never see the light of day? It might as well stay in a chicken shed? Is that what you're saying?' She changed down a gear and slowed for the approaching junction.

The young man in his Escort snatched a hurried glance at the road ahead and – baring his teeth – slammed on his brakes. His car, in a screaming slide, mounted the roundabout and came juddering to a halt in the middle of a rhododendron thicket.

Dorothy motored on, as though nothing had happened. 'What can we do? After all this mucking about we can't let your precious ceiling simply . . . well, fade away.'

'Suppose – just suppose there was a certain amount of publicity,' said George.

'What? Egghead Unscrambles Chicken Shed Mystery, Shock!'

A Good Looking Man

'Well, not exactly. I was considering something a tiny bit more sensible. Maybe a call to the local paper in Evesham, for starters. And, say, the *Architectural Review* . . .'

'I'll say this for you, Benbow – you really think big, don't you?'

George pulled the rug more closely under his filthy chin. His legs were itching abominably.

'And I want to take you to Nottingham,' he said.

'What, now?'

'Next Saturday. For a game of cricket . . .'

'Forgive me, Benbow, but there's something more pressing to worry about first,' said Dorothy.

'Yes?'

'I don't know. A car-wash or a pond, anything would do. A bath, a shower; maybe a fire station. Nothing personal, but, frankly, you could do with being hosed down.'

Chapter Thirty-Nine

Stella Tongue first went to bed with Smith M. on Sunday, 6 July 1947. It was an event deriving more from loneliness than from any great passion. This was also the first real opportunity which had presented itself since they started walking out together – as her mother, Mrs Hopkins, described their relationship – when Stella was still newly widowed.

Young Roger, who had recently celebrated his fourth birthday, was being taken out for the afternoon by his grandparents. Stella was due to see her friend – she could never quite bring herself to call him Michael; instead she adopted the form universally used by his workmates: Smithem. They had intended to go for a walk and then return for tea. Stella had some ironing to do. It was not shaping up to be a very special day.

But, for some reason, there was a slight charge in the atmosphere from the moment that Smithem arrived on the doorstep.

'Nobody home?' he asked, looking around the empty hallway. 'Then you can show me how you look in these.'

He handed Stella a white paper bag. Inside there were two pairs of sheer nylon stockings. He worked in the market and knew people who knew people. Stella called them spivs but he wouldn't have it. 'Traders, my dear. Businessmen.'

'Come on then,' said Stella. Thinking about it afterwards, she was unable to explain to herself why she had taken him by the hand and led him to the stairs.

She made him sit on the end of her bed while she took the bentwood chair. Slowly, she smoothed the stockings over her legs – they were still in good shape, she thought – and fastened them high on her thighs. It had been a long time since a man, any man, had looked at her like that.

'Come here,' said Smithem, his voice strangely thickened.

Then Stella stood up and lifted her flowered dress over her

head. Quickly now, she unclipped her bra and allowed it to drop to the floor. She raised her arms and felt the weight of her thick, red-brown hair.

'No,' she said, as he reached for her. His hands were very strong and very urgent. 'No, I want to keep them on.'

* * *

'Did you write this?' Henry Staunton pushed that week's issue of the *Journal* across the table towards the young reporter.

They were sitting in the kitchen at Collingbrook Castle, a large stone-flagged room which would have been wholly inhospitable but for the Aga stove throbbing warmly under the chimney breast. Mr Staunton was in his stockinged feet but his green and brown patterned hat was still perched on the back of his head.

'I mean, is that all your own work?' He stabbed a blunt finger at the news story stripped across the top of page one.

Young Kevin preened himself. So this was recognition. This was the way it felt to deal with your public, your readers.

'That's me,' he said, leaning forward with a bright grin on his face.

'Then you're a dick,' said Mr Staunton. 'A colossal, prize dick.' He snatched up the newspaper and began reading aloud: 'Song and dance as cow steals show . . .' He gave the reporter a stare of concentrated venom.

'Women ran screaming for safety as a mad cow joined the hoofers at a dance display . . . The crazed animal was chased on to the stage by farm owner Henry Stoaton . . .'

'That's a printer's error,' said Kevin.

'. . . accompanied by his dog, an English setter. Mr Saundon's eighteen-year-old son, Jack, had to be restrained by members of the Women's League of Health and Beauty when fighting flared in the audience . . . The marquee was seriously damaged in the rampage . . . Mad cow disease has caused widespread anxiety over food safety standards . . . Claims for compensation for . . . Later twelve children had to be treated for shock. A St John Ambulance spokesman said: "It was just like the blitz . . ."'

The burly man flung the paper across the room.

'I'm sorry about your name. It wasn't my fault, honest . . . you see, the printers are . . .'

A Good Looking Man

Mr Staunton stood up and loomed across the table. 'Sonny,' he said, very quietly.

'Yes, Mr Staunton?'

'Take a tip from me.'

'Yes?' Kevin looked up at him, all ears.

'Start walking towards that door now before I get my shotgun and give you both barrels up your arse.'

'Errh, Mr Staunton . . .'

'You've got ten seconds.'

'But I've got to talk to you about this ceiling . . .'

'Nine.'

'We've had this letter about a Jaco . . . an old ceiling, nearly four hundred years old . . .'

'Eight.'

'Found in your chicken shed. Left over from the war . . .'

'Seven.'

'From the Vincent Museum. And it's true . . . we spoke to the museum and they know all about it . . .'

'Six.'

'The director said they're sending an expert to look at it . . . They seemed quite surprised we knew about it . . .'

'Five.' Mr Staunton had started to walk towards a gun cupboard in the lobby just inside the kitchen passage.

'Well, you see. I wanted to ask you some questions about the ceiling . . .'

'Four.'

'And we were thinking about sending a photographer . . .'

'Three.'

Kevin was gathering his notebook and his raincoat. 'Well, perhaps I'll give you a ring,' he shouted as he fled through the back door and into the yard.

* * *

Smithem, seeing no cause for delay, made his proposal of marriage to Stella Tongue on the following Wednesday, in the front room of the home she shared with her parents and fatherless son.

Stella, seeing no better prospect for herself and the boy, accepted.

They broke the news immediately to Mr and Mrs Hopkins, her father and mother, who were pleased. They thought it was only fair that Stella should have some happiness and right that young

Andrew Moncur

Roger should have a new dad. Since he clearly liked Mr Smith, who regularly took him to feed the ducks, it was all for the best. 'Our Stella's still a cracker,' said Mr Hopkins.

Stella told her intended husband nothing of Bert Tongue's wartime enterprises. Neither did she explain to him the part she had played in the cover-up. It was best forgotten.

The new administration at the Vincent seemed to share that attitude. They were too busy arranging exhibitions and organizing a wholesale reconstruction of the display areas to trouble too greatly about the casualties of war. The entire wartime experience was seen as being attached in some way to the old regime. Theirs was a bold new world.

Stella had only visited the Vincent once since Bert's funeral. She had barely recognized the place.

She did not intend to call there again.

* * *

The county cricket ground at Trent Bridge is the home of the Nottinghamshire club and of a remarkable collection of historic cricket bats; it has been a venue for test matches since 1899. Garfield Sobers, possibly the finest all-round player of his – or any other – age, belonged there. So did George Parr, an outstanding cricketer in the first half of Victoria's reign, who had a famous tree named in his honour at the Trent Bridge ground. He was a member, in 1859, of the first English cricket team to tour overseas. It went to the United States.

The radio commentary box, overlooking this historic ground, was washed with hazy sunshine on the third day of the fourth test match, England versus Australia. The game was charged with competitive tension, as is usually the case in matches between these two old rivals.

The radio team was engrossed in the morning's play and in a series of gigglish remarks about a woman sitting on the far side of the ground, near the scoreboard, who was wearing a bright yellow baseball cap. Why a woman's choice of headgear should make grown men behave in this way – particularly when the men concerned were wearing cricket club ties and hats with bands in remarkably vile colours – is one of the mysteries of cricket and broadcasting.

A large and grossly over-decorated cake was being admired in

A Good Looking Man

a ribald way by the men sitting at the rear of the box, where it had recently been delivered by a messenger. The producer leaned over and placed the cake on the shelf running in front of the duty broadcasters; he propped a card against it.

'Another bloody cake,' he had scribbled. 'Best say a few words of thanks to a Mrs Crotch – yes, Crotch – who sent it in. Careful how you word it!'

Down below on the cricket square one of England's opening batsmen was still at the crease, supported by the all-rounder batting at number six, a player whose lack of form had given rise to hurtful comment in a number of newspaper reports in the days leading up to this big game.

He was facing the Australian's main attack bowler, now working up to his full pace.

'Woocchh,' the commentator inhaled dramatically, in company with maybe 14,001 other spectators in the ground, as the batsman played at, and missed, a viciously-rising delivery.

'And he didn't get hold of that at all. It goes through to the wicket keeper and there's no run. That's the end of the over. What a dreadful stroke! What did you think of that stroke, Fred?'

'It were terrible. Honest, it were. I don't know what 'ee's playing at. I don't understand it at all. I really don't,' said Fred.

'Yes,' the commentator said. 'I think we can agree that it was an absolutely appalling stroke. It would have looked pretty pathetic to any boy in his First XI at prep school . . .'

'Bollocks,' said a tinny voice.

'Errh. Sorry? Fred? Did you make a, uhmm, remark?'

'Bollocks,' snapped the little voice again. 'Typical of the sort of rubbish you talk on this programme.'

The producer had sprung forward and was now gesturing violently to the commentator, making a cut-throat gesture with the side of his hand. 'Mind your language!' he scribbled on the pad.

'Wankers! Wankers!' said the disembodied voice, audible not only to the radio audience at home but also to listeners tuning-in around the globe to the BBC World Service.

'What did they say?' asked a retired teacher in Wollongong, New South Wales.

'Something to do with Wagga Wagga,' said her husband, without looking up from his newspaper.

'Wankers!' The voice seemed to be growing louder.

'I'm sorry, ladies and gentlemen. We appear to have a slight technical prob . . .' The commentator was looking around wildly. His expert analyst, Fred, sat as though transfixed.

'Why do you always assume that everyone went to a prep school? Why do treat your listeners as though they are perpetual school children? And why do you all behave like schoolboys, too? Why all these stupid nicknames? Aggers? Johnners? Blowers? . . . Wankers!'

'It's the fookin' cake,' yelled Fred. 'That fookin' cake's talking!'

His chair went over backwards as the old cricketer jumped to his feet. A cup of tea was knocked sideways, flooding across the scorebook and the meticulously annotated charts laid out in front of the programme's scorer. His stopwatch fell into the puddle.

'Oh, Jesus Christ al-bloody-mighty,' the scorer bellowed, snatching up the cup and flinging it backhanded towards the commentator, who was now clutching at the neck of his microphone with both hands.

'I'm sorry. There's been a change of bowler. We've missed a couple of balls . . . Errh. What's the score now?' he said, trying manfully to regain control of the broadcast. 'I say, what's the – aaghh!' The cup, unaimed, caught him a painful blow on the bridge of his nose.

'My node!' the cry was made only marginally less piercing by being filtered through a bunched handerkerchief, stemming the trickle of blood.

'Fookin' talkin' cake! Get it out of 'ere,' roared the old cricketer. He had turned surprisingly pale and beads of perspiration had formed above his upper lip. A distinct tic had started around his left eye, making his whole head jerk and lunge spasmodically. 'Somebody shut that thing up! I'm not to be spoken to like that by no fancy cake . . .'

Then, with a last flickering display of the speed and strength which had made him a formidable player forty years earlier, he propelled himself forward and head-butted the cake. There was an explosion of icing sugar, crumbs, candied fruit and decorative chocolate buttons. A microphone toppled out of the open window in front of the commentary position.

The old player sank to his knees. Slowly he capsized, rolling on to his side beneath the desk. Traces of cake clung to the craggier parts of his face as his breathing became steadier and settled into a stentorian rumble.

There was an odd, rolling movement from the very centre of the ring of debris. A cheap, plastic receiver – it looked like part of a child's two-way radio kit – bounced across the desk and fell to the floor.

It came to a halt beside the open mouth of the superannuated sports star, lying on the floor of the radio commentary box in a foetal position.

* * *

'Did you really do that? Go on, tell me honestly.' Dorothy was regarding George Benbow with a wary sort of sideways glance.

'You'll never know, will you,' said George, 'since you never listen to cricket programmes on the radio.'

Chapter Forty

'Your man Tongue, the foreman, didn't survive the war,' said Dorothy. She was holding a struggling Kenneth in her arms.

George wished that they could change places. He would promise not to fight at all.

'What, killed was he? Got bombed?' asked George. Kenneth was now walking in mid-air, his legs thrashing as Dorothy held him at arm's length and examined his furry undercarriage.

'No. He died on the last day of the war. Actually, just after that. When they were celebrating the defeat of Germany. Some sort of accident on VE-day. It seems poignant, doesn't it? Perhaps he was the last casualty of the war in Europe.'

Kenneth was now upside down, his nose pointing directly at Dorothy's feet. A kamikaze cat, thought George. Any moment, he's going to launch himself on his final mission.

'His wife – his widow, I should say – worked at the Vincent as well. She was secretary to the old director, Oliver Mackie. The one who died in . . . when was it? In 1941? Or 1942?'

George was suddenly alert. 'Did she? Heavens, between the two of them they must have just about run the entire show . . .'

He paused and looked at Dorothy thoughtfully. The cat had finally achieved his liberty and was sitting at her feet, cleaning himself vigrously; one back leg was held rigidly in the air above his head. He looked like a member of some high-kicking chorus line.

'And what became of her? Of Mrs Tongue?' George smiled directly into her face.

'I was afraid you were going to ask me that. Benbow . . .'

He reached for her hands. 'Yes?' he said, very gently.

'Benbow. Don't you think you've done enough? Finding that ceiling was a wonderful piece of work. Couldn't you just leave it at that? Sometimes it's better not to stir up too much that's past and forgotten . . .'

'Just tell me what became of Mrs Tongue,' he said softly.
'Why, George?'
'Because I simply need to know. Is she still alive?'
'As far as I know, yes, she is. She was on a small pension, of course. It's all in the records: Stella Tongue and her little boy, who must be – what? In his fifties by now. Then she remarried in 1948 and the link with the Vincent was broken.'
'What about an address? Did you find out where they were living at that time?'
Stella looked at him very steadily. Then she gave him a swift kiss on the lips.
'Yes, I did,' she said. 'I've written it down for you.'

* * *

Stella Tongue became Stella Smith at a brief ceremony on a cold Saturday in March 1948. Little Roger Albert was dressed for the occasion in a borrowed kilt and full highland regalia. Neither side of the family was remotely connected with Scotland; in fact, Mr Smith said that he'd never been to the place. As far as the handful of guests was concerned, this really did not matter at all. The boy looked charming.

So did the bride. She was a very bonny woman, all things considered, Mr Hopkins told his new son-in-law.

The couple took a brief honeymoon in Weymouth, where they strolled on the sands in a perishing wind and took one another's photographs beneath the lighthouse on Portland Bill.

They had decided, on their return, to move in to Stella's house. The boy Roger had never known any other home and he was contented there, surrounded by friends. There was no good reason for upheaval. Her mother and father would remain. There was room for everyone – and they were all good friends. It was to be a happy family home.

In time, said Smithem, there will be more family to come. He was to be disappointed.

Stella's mother died in 1961 at the dawn of an era she would have disapproved of. Mrs Hopkins had had certain old-fashioned values; she knew her place and she believed that others – including dance band singers and dressmakers – should know theirs. It didn't do to get above your station, she often used to say.

Her husband survived her for only eleven weeks. He had aged

A Good Looking Man

overnight, said Stella. Really he became quite pathetic after mum died. It was as though he didn't wish to live. At the very end he confused Smithem with Bert Tongue and spoke to him, in a rambling way, about the battlefields of the First World War.

Mr and Mrs Hopkins were buried in neighbouring plots in the municipal cemetery. It was kept up very well, said Stella.

What she could not guess was that poor Smithem would follow them there within the year. Cancer, said the neighbours, shaking their heads with a grim sort of relish. Stella was widowed for the second time.

She expected that life was now going to be a struggle. She was touched to discover that her second husband had done his best to provide for her and the boy.

They laid him under a simple headstone. Somehow it had seemed fitting to Stella that it should be inscribed only: 15 June 1902 – 4 October 1962; Smith M.

* * *

In the Felton Square gardens, beyond the tennis courts, the small white bird with the orange legs settled again on the scrape it had made in the children's sandpit. Its three pale greenish eggs, with blotchy dark brown freckles, were almost ready to hatch.

The elderly, frail man, standing bent-backed under a cherry tree, slowly lowered his binoculars.

'Bless my soul,' said Mr Pilgrim, one of the few surviving members of the old Home Guard unit which had once played invasion games in this very park. 'God bless my soul.'

Then he set off in a fast, shuffling walk. He could barely wait to reach home and tell his dear wife. Whoever would have thought it possible that a little tern (*Sterna albifrons*) should have made its nest here, right in the heart of town.

Chapter Forty-One

George Benbow and Dorothy Parker approached the front door of 41 Hayes Avenue together. George had wanted to go alone but Dorothy would not hear of it – and, to be honest, he was pleased.

The house was in a poor state of repair. The little front garden looked sad and neglected; a Cambridge blue delphinium had been blown down and it lay as it had fallen, with its heavy head across the path.

George knocked twice. Then, for good measure, he rang the bell. This was, after all, his ancestral home. There was no point in hanging back.

There was a long delay. Finally the door was opened by a plump, elderly woman – George felt that her face was faintly familiar. She was wearing an overcoat and with her free hand she was tucking stray hairs under her woollen hat. She looked from one to the other. Then she tapped George on the chest.

'Ah, it's you,' she said.

'Yes . . .' he said, cautiously.

'Meals-on-wheels. Never forget a face. You'd better go up.'

'We . . .' Dorothy started to say. George gripped her arm.

'She's upstairs in the front room,' said the neighbour, stepping outside and holding the door open for them. 'I'm doing a spot of shopping for her. Bits and pieces.'

George ushered Dorothy inside and, pausing to wave, closed the door. The rose-patterned hall wallpaper was yellowed and peeling. The place probably hadn't been given a lick of paint for over twenty years. A dusty bowl of artificial anemones stood on a table at the foot of the stairs.

George gestured with his head. They climbed the stairs in single file. On the landing he took the lead and approached the bedroom door. He tapped lightly.

'Mrs Smith?' he called. 'Or should I call you Mrs Tongue? May we come in?'

She was sitting in a faded pink armchair beside the bed. Her wrists and ankles emerged, freckled and stick-like, from her red dressing-gown. She still had a fine head of hair, swept up and pinned on top of her head. It was perfectly white. She seemed to be asleep.

George let his eyes follow the edge of the white and blue rug towards the fireplace. The old gas fire was bubbling gently.

The pipe ran off to the right and then ducked through a hole drilled in the floorboard.

'Mrs Tongue . . .' Dorothy walked over and touched her thin arm.

'Is it that time already?' said the old woman. Her eyes had been washed to the same colour as the delphinium.

'Mrs Tongue. I'm from the Vincent Museum and . . .'

'So, you've come,' said the woman. 'I always knew you would.'

'Yes, we've come,' said Dorothy.

'It's no good asking me. Bert never told me, you see.'

'Never told you what, Mrs Tongue?' asked Dorothy.

'Where he'd hidden the stuff. It's taken you long enough to come looking for it. He always said you'd forget it. But I knew you'd come, sooner or later.'

George knelt beside her chair. He smiled at her. 'We're not really bothered about the museum's possessions, Mrs Tongue. They'll probably turn up one day. I have a personal reason for being here . . .'

'Personal?' She looked at him sharply.

'Yes. My father lived in this house as a boy. Immediately before the war . . . the evacuation and all that. He left something here which I've always meant to come back and collect. For his sake, you see.'

'What's your name?'

'Benbow . . .'

'Benbow?' She looked across the room and several decades. 'We were buried alive, you know.'

'No . . .'

'In the Anderson shelter. They had to dig us out. We lost everything. The house was smashed like firewood. So much broken wood . . . and the slates. All those bomb sites. There was nowhere for us to go. But Bert – my Bert – he found us this place and we all moved in. There was a widow, poor woman.'

A Good Looking Man

'Yes...'

'We sent on her post.' She looked at George again. 'Was that your mother? That lived here before us?'

'Grandmother. My father grew up here...'

'Your grandmother? Mrs Benbow?'

'He left a box of toys – Dinky cars – right here. In this room, I mean. Under that floorboard.' George bent and rapped the board with his knuckle. 'I want, with your permission, to take a quick look under there. What do you say?'

Mrs Tongue glanced up at Dorothy, then back to George. 'All right. Can't hurt.'

'Shall I get you a cup of tea?' Dorothy touched the old woman's arm again.

'Please. No sugar. There's milk in the fridge downstairs.' She watched Dorothy leave the room.

George was kneeling beside the fireplace. He drew his screwdriver from his jacket pocket and slid the blade between the boards. He was aware of Mrs Tongue – she obviously still thought of herself by that name – standing up slowly, meandering a little towards the wardrobe and, finally, moving to his side.

The floorboard lifted easily. George could instantly see a dust-coated white box lying between the joists. He reached for it very carefully. His grail, he thought, smiling to himself.

He laid in on the floor and, very gently, lifted the cardboard lid.

Inside was a bright-shining little snarl-up, bumber to bumper, of miniature cars.

There was something else.

Lying on top of the toys was a square of white card; at its centre, a smudge of dull purple.

George turned it carefully. The head was facing to the left. It was balding and bearded. At the top were the letters I.R.; at the foot, the word Official. The sixpenny Inland Revenue Edward VII stamp.

He was not to know this, but the stamp was issued in March 1904 for use by revenue officers mailing letters in the provinces. It was withdrawn exactly two months later. Only a handful – perhaps a dozen – remained in existence. The last unused specimen to change hands had fetched £10,000 back in 1972. To put a value on the perfect example now in George's hands, you could multiply that figure by at least a factor of five. It was the rarest of all United Kingdom postage stamps.

There was a lengthy pause. George did not think that he had drawn breath for about three minutes.

'Somehow, I don't think this was my father's,' he said, raising the card. Then he looked up.

He was staring into the twin barrels of what he guessed to be a 12-bore shotgun.

George noticed that there were slight imperfections around the gun's muzzle; possibly rust, nibbling away. It probably wouldn't make a great deal of difference. There was still a dull blue shine on the metal.

Mrs Tongue's hands did not waver at all. The gun was absolutely steady. And it was pointing just above his eyes, roughly at the centre of his forehead.

'As I said, I knew you'd come.'

'Yes,' said George.

'And I said I didn't know where any of the stuff was. Only this. It was the first thing Bert brought home.'

'I don't . . .'

'He just put it up on my wardrobe.'

'I see . . .' George looked from the twin black unfathomable eyes of the gun and into her pale face.

'He only did it for the boy, you know. He loved that boy.'

'Mrs Tongue,' said George. Then he cleared his throat and tried again. 'Mrs Tongue . . .'

'He was a good man. Do you know, he never seemed frightened. Not of anybody.'

'No, but . . .'

'I think he wanted to have this in case we ever needed to take care of ourselves . . .'

'Mrs Tongue,' said George. 'That isn't a gun at all . . .'

'What?'

'It isn't a gun, you know. The label says it's a police rattle, of carved wood, carried by Henry Minnis, probably about 1810.'

And then Stella Tongue lowered the shotgun. She dropped back into the seat and ducked her chin. Her whole body seemed to be shaken by a strange breathless sobbing rising from her frail chest.

When Dorothy returned with the tea tray she found George on his knees beside the chair, gently rocking Mrs Tongue in his arms.

The old lady was shaking with laughter.